TRAILBLAZER

MICHELLE DIENER

ECLIPSE

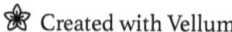

THE VERDANT STRING SERIES

The seven planets of the Verdant String, the green, fecund sources of life spanning five solar systems, comprise the Verdant String Coalition.

This is the setting for a new science fiction romance series from award-winning science fiction romance novelist Michelle Diener.

While the people of the Verdant String know they have a common ancestor, a group of explorers who colonised the planets at the same time thousands of years ago, the mysteries of who they were, and where they came from, persist.

Each book in the series can be read as a standalone.

Books in the Verdant String series:

Interference & Insurgency Box Set

Breakaway

Breakeven

Trailblazer

CHAPTER 1

TALLY CAME awake standing in the dark.

She flinched, but she was getting better at coping with finding herself far from where she went to sleep. It happened almost every night, and while the terror of not knowing how she got here, or where on the abandoned spaceship she was had not abated, her acceptance of the fact that this was her life now helped her keep calm.

Calmer.

That is what her life had narrowed to. A series of fine distinctions.

If the pattern of the last ten days ran true, she had woken here for a reason--just like every other time this had happened to her. And that reason was there was something nearby that would be useful to her.

She had gained blankets and even a heating unit in previous forays. Been shown bedrooms she'd been too afraid to sleep in, and given cups, bowls, and even a pillow. She didn't know if she'd ever been to a place twice--whether she'd returned to the places she'd been led to in the beginning, when panic and fear had caused her to run.

Slowly, she crouched down and carefully extended her hands, batting gently at the air and the ground in front of her. She almost knocked whatever it was over, but she was able to grab it before it toppled.

She picked it up, and tried to guess what it was by feel, frustrated by the true lack of any light in this part of the ship.

It wasn't a familiar shape, and she sank down, cross-legged, and put it in front of her.

A sensation came over her, as if something was trying to take control of her hands, and she fought it, but she was tired, and she was weak. Her food had run out two days ago, and she was rationing her water.

If she could see--impossible in the pitch darkness--she would have watched her hands manipulating the device she was holding with horror. As it was, she simply had to endure the feel of her hands behaving as if they didn't belong to her.

A light blossomed, suddenly and with a warm glow that wasn't too harsh on her eyes, although after so long in the darkness, she blinked away the lights dancing in front of her vision.

She had control of her hands back, and she lifted the item, saw it was a lantern of some kind, and when she looked at the controls, realized that her hands had been hijacked in order to switch it on.

She set it down on the floor and looked at her right palm for the first time since this nightmare began with the benefit of a good, strong light, not the low-intensity lights of the old engine room she'd made into her base.

Her skin looked normal.

She bent to look more closely, rubbed it with the fingers of her other hand, but she couldn't see or feel anything wrong.

Fear of what was becoming of her, what she may be turning into, choked her, and she rubbed her hand on her bent knee, and felt the familiar sensation of being forcibly calmed. Of something like medication being injected into her system.

"No! No, I'm fine, I will calm myself."

The sensation halted, and she breathed deeply.

It listened to her. At least it listened to her.

Sometimes.

Unless it thought her safety or comfort would be better off if it didn't. Then it did what it wanted to do.

So far, she had to grudgingly admit, it hadn't been wrong.

And so far, everything it did was to protect her. Help her. Make this terrible situation better.

She didn't understand it, but she was grateful that it was an ally, even if its methods and the seemingly all-powerful control it had over her frightened her sick.

She had lived with it from the second day she'd been onboard this floating ghost ship, and while she didn't feel the constant panic she had at the start, sometimes, like now, it blindsided her, and her mind jumped to thoughts of parasites, or symbionts or even some kind of mind trick. She'd even considered that she was maybe lying in a coma somewhere, and none of this was real.

Maybe she'd been hit along with Rew, and was lying, dying, somewhere next to his decomposing body.

The breath she sucked in was ragged, and she leaned forward, tried to get a grip.

The floor beneath her hands was cool and very real. The light helped to convince her she was alive and well and in her right mind, even if she was temporarily sharing it with something . . . else.

Rew was still dead, though. She'd found herself checking on his body a few times, much to her shame, when the creaks and groans in the ship had made her too jumpy.

She hadn't been able to shake the thought that if she was

being manipulated after she went to sleep, what was to say Rew wasn't lurching around, a reanimated corpse.

She had always had a very active imagination.

She shuddered, pulled herself together. Rew had been exactly where she'd left him, every single time.

And since the Caruso had stopped towing the ship, the creaks and groans had ceased. She'd woken one morning to the silence, and had braced for the Caruso to board and come looking for her. She'd almost hoped they would, because by then, she'd been alone with Rew and whatever was interfering with her mind for five days, and she would have given anything to see another face. Even a Caruson.

But they never came, and she had eventually had to assume they'd released the ship and left it floating in space.

She didn't know if that would make it harder for her team to find her or not.

The look on Bertie's face as they'd come under fire from the Caruso, as the emergency doors had closed Bertie off inside the small cruiser, was imprinted on Tally's brain.

Bertie wouldn't leave her out here. She knew Tally was alive.

She would push for them to look for Tally, even though the Caruso had clamped the strange, floating ghost ship and raced away. Why they'd done that and then abandoned it was just one more mystery on top of a pile of them when it came to this ship.

If the ghost ship was still broadcasting its distress signal, maybe the team would be able to find her again.

If they didn't do it soon, it would be too late.

Her own rations, and Rew's, were long gone. Food and water were fundamentally more important than a light.

Whatever was helping her would have led her to more if it had been available.

There had been a lot of food on this ship at one time, though. That was clear from the cold store she'd found one night, waking up in front of it to discover, with horror, that she'd been dragging Rew's body with her on the thin blanket they all carried in their packs. It was the third night she'd been onboard, and Rew had started to decompose.

She had been so worried about what to do with his body. Had wanted to preserve it for the sake of his family.

And whoever was now pulling her strings had delivered a solution.

That was the night she'd stopped letting her fear incapacitate her. She'd put him inside the cold room, closed the heavy door, and then wandered for hours to find her way back to her little nest in the engine room.

It had taken her a few days to find her way back to the cold store, but now she knew the way as well as she did any route on the ship, using her screen as her light source.

The screen was dead now. Had died three days back, even with her careful usage, and the lack of any light had worried her more than even the food situation.

Which is why whatever was helping her had found her a light tonight, she suddenly realized.

The more she thought or worried about something, the more likely it was that it would lead her to a solution.

"My wish is your command, huh?" She tried to make the comment a light one. Wasn't sure she quite carried it off.

Her voice sounded thin and insubstantial, and she cleared her throat.

She stood, lifting the light up, and saw a corridor stretching in either direction, giving her a perspective she hadn't had before. Up 'til now she'd moved about this ship in small increments, learning it more by feel and by a circumference of light that didn't extend much beyond her own feet.

In the last few days, she had done it in total darkness.

She took a deep breath and realized she felt better than she had in a while, despite the gnawing in her belly. It was good to see where she was going.

She began moving forward, light raised, and after about a minute of walking, the walls on either side of her dropped away, and she stood at one end of a walkway with railings on either side.

Cautiously, she stepped onto it and raised the light even higher, looking over the railing to see what was below.

Dead gardens, she realized. Beds of what had once been plants, possibly edible plants, and a few trees that were now nothing more than twisted, rotting trunks.

The space was massive, and it was also the first real sign that this had been an explorer ship, looking for new life.

It had occurred to her more than once that this ship was very much to her own proportions. That everything she'd found was built for hands like hers.

Could this be a lost Verdant String ship, from before the eight planets of the Verdant String had found each other? From those first centuries of space exploration?

Or even--her mind reeled at the implications--from another Verdant String planet, one they had yet to find?

Whatever it was, it was a major historical find.

She reached the halfway point across the walkway, and looked over the other side. It was more of the same, although there was also tanks that looked as if they'd once held liquid, now long dried up.

She shivered, her sense of isolation and insignificance seemed amplified in this massive space, and she moved a little faster as she headed for the other side of the walkway.

A door blocked her way. She stepped close to it, but it didn't open automatically. She looked around for a button or handle, but there was nothing except a screen attached to one side.

She hesitated, then touched it, and it flickered on, an outline of a hand showing in pale gray.

A hand exactly the shape of her own.

Cautiously, she pressed her palm against it, and with a gasp that startled her, the door slid to one side.

She stepped into the room, and knew immediately it was the bridge, the center of the ship.

She lifted the light, but there was nothing in here, just chairs and machines.

There was one light, throbbing a dull red rather than glowing, and she walked up to it. She couldn't understand the label written above it, but she accepted what she was going to do.

She pressed the button.

CHAPTER 2

THREE DAYS LATER, she had come to the conclusion that the button had no effect whatsoever.

She had moved her little nest onto the bridge, and she'd stopped wandering the ship.

Her water was gone, she hadn't eaten in five days, and she knew she would die soon unless help came.

She hadn't woken up standing in some strange corner of the ship since the time she'd found the light and the bridge, and she guessed there was nothing more to find.

Whatever had helped her to this point had run out of useful gifts to lead her to.

She heard a clang, so faint it was almost an echo, and struggled to sit up from where she was lying, head cocked. It came a second time, equally faint, and she drew her legs up and hugged them close.

It could be space rocks, hitting them, but it could also be a inter-ship vessel locking on.

She didn't have the energy to go look. But if she did have visitors, they'd come to her.

Even if it was the Caruso coming back, she'd probably be better off. She'd be a useful bargaining chip with the Verdant String, at the very least.

She hadn't realized she'd dozed off until the sound of banging on the bridge door jerked her awake.

She stood, grimly cataloguing how unsteady she was on her feet, and she walked to the door.

The banging came again, and she stood in front of the door and wondered why they didn't simply put their hands to the screen plate and open it.

The voices on the other side were indistinct, but there was something familiar enough about the tone and pitch that had her heart skipping in excitement.

She touched the plate on her side of the door and it slid open.

Bertie's tight, worried face was the first thing she saw.

"So something was helping you." Dr. Vetna watched her with calm, intelligent eyes.

Tally felt her throat tighten, and wished she'd never said anything about it. "That's what it felt like."

"You never saw anything, though?" Commander Hopl was leaning against the counter in the med bay, and he was less calm, his thin, lanky frame seemed unable to stay still.

She shook her head. "I was mostly in the dark, though."

"Your eyes have adjusted very well to full light, I'm pleased to say," Dr. Vetna said, looking small and round next to Hopl. "Sometimes they can take a while, but you've bounced back incredibly well. Given your lack of food and water in the last five days of your time aboard, I'm also impressed with your vitals. You're one of the healthiest individuals I've ever seen."

Tally sent a nervous, sidelong look at her. "And the blood tests .
. .?"

"Nothing concerning. Obviously you had very low blood sugar,
were clearly dehydrated, but it took you very little time to bounce
back to normal levels."

There had been nothing in her blood.

She slumped back on the raised bed, and closed her eyes.
Nothing in her blood.

She had worried . . .

And then she went still.

When she worried, whatever it was that had wormed its way
into her made a plan to appease that worry.

Nothing in her blood meant nothing, other than whatever it
was was able to hide itself from Dr. Vetna.

"What is it? What have you remembered?" Commander Hopl's
tone forced her eyes open again.

"Nothing." She cleared her throat. "There was a bead. It felt
like a metal bead. Or a ball bearing." She paused, unsure if she
should say this.

Would it make things better, or worse?

Hopl lost interest immediately. Vetna kept her steady gaze on
Tally's face.

"What about the bead?"

"It felt like it sank into my palm when I picked it up."

"Could you have dropped it?" Vetna asked gently.

Tally paused, then nodded. "I was disoriented. Dragging Rew's
body around with me, so I didn't lose him. It was before I found
the engine room, which had some ambient light."

"Which palm?"

She held out her right palm, and Vetna took her hand,
studied it.

"I looked myself, when I found the light. I know it looks fine."

Vetna squeezed her hand. "You've been through more than just physical trauma, Tally. Alone in the dark for almost two weeks with nothing but Rew's body, some of that time being towed by the Caruso. I'm amazed you're able to keep up a coherent conversation." She shot the commander a pointed look.

Hopl cleared his throat. "So let's get this clear; the VSCS *Uma* was doing a standard run from base to our outer boundary and you intercepted a signal."

Tally gathered he wanted a response, even though they'd gone over this twice already, so she nodded.

"You encountered a ghost ship, with no discernible life forms, and you and four others, under the command of Lieutenant Bertrand, approached in a small inter-ship vessel."

Again, he looked at her, and she gave him the nod he required. "And then what?"

"We couldn't get a lock on the ghost ship's access port, so Rew and myself suited up and went out on the line, to see why not."

"And what did you conclude?"

She drew in a breath. "We had assumed it would be a standard ship access port, but it was completely alien to us. There was no compatibility with our own locking mechanisms. We relayed the information to the team, and Lt. Bertrand decided we'd clamp on beside the lock and go in manually."

"Did that make sense to you?" Hopl asked.

Tally jerked her head up. "Yes. It was the only option I could see."

He grunted, settled back against the counter. "Continue."

She paused, her gaze on him. Was he trying to find a scapegoat for this? Trying to burn Bertie?

Hopl made a sound of impatience, and she tightened her lips.

"Rew and I got to work on opening the port while everyone else suited up, and just as we'd spun the lock mechanism and were about to lift it up, a Caruso small fighter crested the side of the ghost ship and opened fire."

She remembered the sudden laz fire, the brightness making her flinch away. Then the panicked look on Bertie's face from the door of the inter-ship vessel as it snapped closed just in time, as the laz fire danced over it seconds later.

It was all intertwined with the cry Rew gave over the comms, her feeling of desperation as he fell, of her refusal to let him go, terrified he'd drift off into space, never to be found, as she heaved the port access open and pulled him in with her.

And then the solid thunk of the Caruso attaching a line to the ship, and the creaks and groans as they shot away, far faster than the Raxian vessel, or even an explorer like the VSCS *Uma* could go.

"Was Officer Rew dead when you got him into the ship?" Dr. Vetna asked.

Tally nodded. "I hoped he was just injured. That he'd gone silent because he was unconscious, but he was dead. The laz fire caught him directly in the torso." She looked over at Hopl. "What's going to happen now? The Caruso attacked us. Killed a Raxian officer."

Hopl's face, already hard to read, shuttered completely. "That's not something I'm at liberty to discuss at the moment." He narrowed his eyes. "You haven't finished the debrief. The techs want to know how you worked out how to unclamp the ghost ship from the Caruso. Did you find a manual?"

Tally stared at him. "I don't know what you're talking about."

"Your fingerprints and tracks are clearly all over an area at the back of the ship where the Caruso attached their clamp. Looks like you detached that part of the ship. A whole section is gone. Given the speed they were going, suddenly losing the ghost ship weight would have turned the clamp cable into a whip. The techs assure me it would have damaged the Caruso warship. Chances are they either couldn't find you again by the time they'd dealt with the damage, or were so damaged they had to limp home, rather than go back for you."

"I . . . don't remember that." She felt like a fool as she said it. She remembered the morning she'd woken up to the silence of the ship, the realization the Caruso were no longer towing her. How tired she'd been that day. Well, sounded like she'd been up all night.

Hopl watched her, face tight.

Did he think she was lying? Or crazy?

"You don't remember any of it?" Vetna's voice was irritatingly gentle.

Tally tried to mitigate the damage. "Vaguely. It's all so jumbled up." She rubbed her forehead.

"You're telling me you just guessed how to shear off part of the ship?"

Tally lifted her gaze to Hopl's. "No. I'm saying I probably tried multiple things. Pushed every button I could, turned every lever. I didn't think I had much to lose."

Hopl's gaze cut to Vetna, but the doctor didn't say anything.

She wet her lips. "Can you tell me when I'll be reinstated?"

The doctor *had* just said she had bounced back well.

Hopl scowled at her. "Not immediately. Someone goes through what you have, it's best to take a rest."

Dr. Vetna clucked her tongue at the commander in rebuke. "I'd hardly consider the Veltos Trail a rest, Dirk. It's mentally and physically challenging, but it is a break from the norm, and I think that's what Tally needs right now."

The Veltos Trail?

Tally stared at the doctor in astonishment. "That's for soldiers who've been wounded in the line of duty."

Dr. Vetna nodded in agreement, her face serene.

"But I haven't . . ."

She trailed off. Mental wounds. That's what Vetna had been alluding to.

She should never have mentioned the bead. But no, they'd already decided, before she'd told them about the bead. This was about her stopping the Caruso from towing the ghost ship. And then not mentioning it.

The fact that she was telling them the truth when she said she couldn't remember was even more damning, in Hopl's eyes. She was either lying or crazy.

And now she was going to pay for it.

CHAPTER 3

"SO YOU'RE in charge of the food?" Frangi shifted on her chair, discreetly moving her leg with her hands. Then, as if remembering she didn't need to do it that way, she very deliberately lifted it and rested her ankle on her knee.

Tally sank down into her own chair, and lifted her feet to rest on the seat opposite. She'd met Frangi as they waited for security to clear them from the Situ spaceport onto the military runner taking them to Veltos.

The soldier guarding the entrance had ignored them as he took his time looking through their forms, and the impatience and annoyance on Frangi's face had been such an accurate reflection of Tally's own feelings, they'd immediately begun talking together like old friends.

"I'm in charge of the food," she confirmed. "My doctor thought it would be a positive thing for me to be in control of, given my last experience."

Frangi inclined her head. "You ran out of supplies?"

Tally gave a nod.

Frangi's lips curved. "I'm in charge of medical supplies for the same reason. Do you think they coordinate?"

Tally smiled back. "Maybe. What happened with your medical supplies?"

Frangi tapped her leg. "Got my leg ripped off, and it took so long to reach me, with no working med kit, they couldn't attach my old leg back. This one took two months to create, and needs to be constantly monitored to make sure it's still working and healthy."

"Why are they sending you on the Trail when you obviously need monitoring?" Tally was outraged on her behalf.

"I put my hand up for it. Completing the Veltos Trail will put me fully back on the roster. Right now, my CO is playing it super safe, out of guilt. And I want to be a full member of the team again." There was something in her eyes, a look of desperation that Tally understood only too well.

"So you're medical, I'm food. What's left?"

"Power, equipment and comms, I'd guess." Frangi slumped in her own chair, put her feet on the chair next to Tally. "There's usually six in a group. Five soldiers and a guide."

Tally turned as the door opened and a man and a woman stepped inside. She pulled herself up, and dropped her feet so they could get through.

That strange sense she got these days when she met someone new, a sort of elevated flight or fight, a hyper concentration on their faces and their body language, washed over her, and she fought it. She was always fighting it.

She nodded at them. "I'm Tally," she said, and gave the Raxian greeting of hands lifted, right fingers curled under left, and a slight bow.

"I'm Soo." The woman gave a Bodivas greeting in response.

"Lenny." The man with her was also from Bodivas.

"I'm Frangi." Frangi had taken longer to drop her feet, but Tally thought it was more due to reluctance to admit newcomers to their little group than because she was having difficulty doing it with her new leg. She gave the Kalastoni greeting.

The sound of the engines firing as Soo and Lenny took a seat had Tally frowning. "I thought there was always a group of five?"

"Seems like the last person is coming from Arkhor. He'll meet us on Veltos." Lenny settled into his chair.

"Arkhor?" Frangi asked, and Soo spread her hands, as if to say, what are you going to do?

"Do you think they were injured in what happened at Cepi?" Lenny asked. "Wouldn't mind hearing about that."

"No Arkhorans were injured in the Cepi incident." Frangi's words were cold.

"Ah, right. You're Kalastoni. Did you see Cepi being destroyed first hand?" Lenny seemed not to notice the chill.

"Yes. I was on one of the warships overseeing the destruction."

"Is that why you're here?" Lenny's gaze moved over her, as if looking for why she might be here.

Tally was interested, too, although she could see Frangi was reluctant to answer.

"I'm here because since we destroyed Cepi some of the weirdos who were sucked into the Calling, the cult that was created as cover to delay Cepi's destruction, have been trying to steal pieces of the ruins that are floating in space. One of them shot my leg off." Frangi spoke through gritted teeth.

"But I thought the Calling had been exposed as a bogus organization." Soo leaned forward, as interested as the rest of them.

"It was, but obviously some of the members the insurgents duped into joining were genuine believers. They think the whole thing is a huge conspiracy and cover-up. They won't go away." Frangi massaged her thigh.

"Full regen?" Lenny asked.

She nodded tightly.

"Me, too." He lifted his arm. "I'm in engineering, but a smuggler ship came at us while I was making an outside repair, took a shot at us before they pinched to the black, and I lost my arm."

Frangi relaxed a little. "Giving you any trouble?"

He made a so-so motion with his hand and they exchanged a knowing look.

"And you?" Soo asked, and Tally gritted her teeth.

It occurred to her she could lie. But no. There were comms about her. About what had happened. If they found out, more like *when* they found out, it would not look very team-oriented of her that she'd hidden her reason for being here. And maybe she would be reassessed.

"My team and I were the ones who found that ghost ship."

There was silence.

"That was you?" Frangi's voice was soft. "Stuck alone with your teammate's body on a ghost ship for two weeks?"

She nodded, the movement tight.

"And you were being towed by the Caruso some of the time, right?" Lenny shifted his body in her direction.

"For a few days."

"Whose ship is it?" Soo had moved to the edge of her seat. "That's the big mystery."

"I don't know." Tally lifted her shoulders. "But whoever they are, the former occupants were the same size and shape as us."

"That's what I heard." Frangi nodded. "They're saying it could be an ancient Verdant String planet ship. From before the planets found each other."

Tally slouched further in her seat. "Could be."

"It's a real find." Lenny was watching her with interest.

Tally made a neutral sound.

"So why'd the Caruso stop towing you?" Soo asked. "That seems to be a point of a great deal of speculation."

Tally suddenly felt a lot more friendly toward Commander Hopl. "I've been asked not to talk about it."

Everyone's eyes lit up with speculation.

"What about you, Soo?" Tally asked. "Why're you here?"

Soo gave her a look that said she knew this was a deflection. "I was bitten by a grass spider on Garmen."

Tally blinked at her. "You were on Garmen? I thought that clean-up was being done by the Arkhorans." The breakaway planet of Garmen had recently been brought back into the fold as a vassal, and Arkhor, as the closest Verdant String planet, was in charge of the mess.

"They're running things." Soo shrugged. "But I was part of a Bodivas team sent under the Verdant String Cooperation Initiative."

Ah. The VSCI. The bane of almost every commander's life. A plan to more fully integrate the seven remaining military forces of the Verdant String.

The idea was to get to know one another. To forge connections. Especially when a war with the Caruso was becoming more than just a distant possibility.

"So, what's a grass spider?" Frangi asked. "Sounds small and harmless."

"Yeah." Soo shot her a dark look. "That's what it *sounds* like. What it *looks* like is a monster about the size of my palm, with hairy green bristles sticking out of it so it resembles a clump of grass." She shuddered. "Did I mention it's the most poisonous spider on Garmen?"

"Where'd it bite you?" Tally asked.

Lenny started laughing.

Soo looked over at him, finger pointed, eyes narrowed. "Lenny, you can kiss my--"

She cut off her sentence, and from the way Frangi hooted, she got the joke at the same time Tally did.

Even Soo joined in with the laughter.

Eventually.

CHAPTER 4

BEN STOOD outside to watch the military runner come in.

The flare of the engine was visible because dusk had already fallen and the sky was the indigo blue that shouldn't be unique to Veltos, but somehow was. There was just something special about the color here.

"Nervous?" Irwin stepped out to join him and looked up, following the runner as it fell toward them.

Ben glanced at him, wondering if the guide actively worked to be this annoying, or whether it was just a gift.

"Should I be?" He kept his tone mild.

Irwin glanced at him, shrugged. "Most people are a little nervous to meet their fellow Trail walkers. It's a two week journey, and there's no getting away from anyone who's difficult."

And certainly no getting away from them if they were the guide.

Ben crossed his arms and watched the runner touch down lightly on the hoverpad a thou away. It was close enough that he could hear the hum of the engine and the silence when it cut off.

"So you never said which warship dropped you off." Irwin had turned to watch the runner, too.

"No, I didn't." Ben kept his answer short.

Irwin gave a snort. "Super secret, huh?"

Ben said nothing.

"Do you Arkhorans actively try to irritate the living shit out of the rest of us, or is it just how you're made?"

Irwin's comment was so similar to what Ben had thought about the guide, he couldn't help the laugh that burst from him.

"Let's leave it at 'super secret'."

"So you're what? Arkhoran Special Forces?"

Ben looked at him, eyes glittering.

Irwin raised his hands. "Whoa. The dead-eyed look. Listen, I'm leading you all through difficult terrain. If you're Special Forces, that's better for me, I have someone who can more than keep up. I just like to know my group's strengths and weaknesses. It's not like you're in enemy territory."

But Irwin was lying. Ben could see it.

The trail guide didn't think having a Special Forces officer was better for him. He didn't like it at all. His fists had clenched, the knuckles showing white.

It was almost as if he was furious.

And as for the other . . . this might not be enemy territory yet. But someone was trying to change that.

That was why Ben was here.

"Should we go help with the supplies?" Ben just made out the doors of the runner opening.

"There's an automaton there that will load them onto a hover," Irwin said, and turned back to the building. "I'll go check that the accommodation is in order for everyone."

He disappeared through the door of what was essentially a semi-permanent supply station, domed and single-story, with three rooms full of beds, a dusty lounge and a ridiculously large kitchen.

Ben didn't like it.

Massive trees populated large swathes of Veltos and some had been cleared to make room for the supply station, but those around the clearing had spread their branches and several had grown above the building. Leaves and twigs seem to fall incessantly onto the domed roof. He'd spent the night waking to the skitter and slide of small objects above him that sounded just like someone trying to move stealthily through the bush.

He'd had no trouble looking like a jumpy soldier sent here to overcome some trauma this morning.

Irwin was still suspicious of him, though.

It hadn't helped that Ben had come early. He guessed Irwin had counted on an extra day to himself, and Ben's arrival had put a spoke in that wheel.

His CO had stressed that they couldn't run into the runner bringing the other four members of his group from the Situ way station. It wouldn't do to land by hover, and be unable to explain where his own battle cruiser was.

They'd know immediately from ship scans that there was no warship in near-space. And that's because Ben and his team had been on Veltos, quietly looking around, for more than a month already.

There had been murmurs from the ethics committee about involving outside parties who didn't know what was going on, but they couldn't seed the whole Veltos Trail team with covert operatives--there was a waiting list, and they'd had to fight to get Ben on as it was.

"It's just surveillance, there won't be any action," his CO had said to the administrators who had quibbled about endangering others not in the know. "And besides, they're all soldiers, aren't they? They're not exactly helpless."

No, they weren't helpless, Ben thought as he saw them coming toward him on an open hover, a second hover following behind them with the supplies. But they thought this was a safe place to be, a place for personal challenges, not outside danger.

And if he and his team were right, that wasn't an accurate assessment of the situation at all.

CHAPTER 5

BEN HAD ASKED for the files of everyone who'd be on the trail with him, and while he knew Lenny Fraouk and Soo Willis were both from Bodivas and knew each other from previous assignments, they hadn't worked together recently. Frangi Torvil and Tally Riva had never met each other or the others, but you wouldn't think that, looking at them.

It must have been a friendly trip out from Situ, because they behaved like a unit when they arrived, jumping down and helping each other with bags and joking amongst themselves.

Ben's lips quirked up. If he'd been a genuine Trailer, why, his feelings would have been hurt at how left out he felt.

Irwin waded into the camaraderie, trying to assert his leadership with the subtlety of a wrecking ball, and failing.

Ben felt eyes on him, turned his head, and found Tally Riva watching him. Her face was tight, the humor and teasing he'd seen from her only minutes before gone.

There was something fragile about her, and yet, he knew she must be incredibly resilient and tough. She'd survived on her own, with almost no food or water, alone on a dark ghost ship, and had somehow managed to work out how to shear off part of it to save herself from the Caruso. He'd seen the full file, and he had read between the lines that her commanding officer was both impressed and worried about what she'd managed to do.

There was a footnote from a Dr. Vetna which mentioned hallucinations, and Ben guessed being in the pitch dark for two weeks on an unknown ship with the body of your teammate nearby might send anyone a little mad.

Her involvement was the only thing that had given him pause. He'd looked up at his CO after reading her file, and Reskit had grunted, his lips twisted in acknowledgment.

"Can't be helped. She was fast-tracked, because the sooner she's more herself, the sooner they'll get more out of her. And it doesn't hurt to have her out of reach for two weeks. Her CO doesn't want her talking to anyone if he can help it."

"The Trail isn't some magic solution, though. There's no guarantee she'll recover." Ben couldn't understand the reasoning behind it at all.

Reskit had shrugged. "It's the best way to bring her out of herself, the experts say. Give her something to do that isn't life or death, and give her more control over her environment than she had before."

He was just here for reconnaissance, there should be no life or death about it, Ben reminded himself as he looked into her blue eyes, almost too big in her face. They were in sharp contrast to the warm brown of her skin, and her golden brown hair, which was pulled back into a knot at her nape.

Nevertheless, guilt and a surge of protectiveness at what they'd dropped her into washed over him as he took in her almost too-sharp cheekbones and the slenderness of her body.

He moved toward her, hand outstretched for the standard Arkhoran greeting, and then stopped in surprise as she stepped toward him, her own hand outstretched, and grabbed his hand before he could hook his thumb around hers and curl his fingers around the back of her hand, and instead gave his hand a firm shake.

They both paused awkwardly, and he realized she was as surprised as he was at what she'd done.

"My apologies," he said, as he watched her cheeks flush. "I'm so used to the Arkhoran greeting, I didn't think."

"No, I'm sorry." She looked stricken. "I wasn't paying attention, myself."

What was left unsaid was the handshake she'd given him was not the Raxian greeting, either. He didn't know where it came from.

It looked like she didn't either.

"I'm Ben Guthrie."

"Tally Riva." She curled her left fingers over her right in the standard Raxian greeting this time. "We didn't know if you'd already be here."

"I was dropped off last night," he said, then turned as Lenny shouted to Tally to come help with the supplies.

He walked with her, letting her introduce him to the others, and he began helping unload while Irwin spoke to the hover pilot who'd brought them and the supplies over from the hoverpad.

Ben kept the two men in his peripheral vision, feeling a faint tingle of suspicion at the way they huddled together, but then Irwin clapped the pilot on the back and stepped away, and Ben saw the flicker of annoyance on the pilot's face, and the tingle dissipated. It was just Irwin being Irwin.

"Have you all worked together before?" Ben asked Lenny as he and the big Bodivan carried a heavy box to the front of the supply station. He knew they hadn't, but it was a reasonable question for someone who hadn't seen their files to ask.

Lenny shook his head. "You could say we had a bonding

moment on the way over, when we spoke about why we were sent on the Trail."

"I'm sorry I missed it." He didn't know if that sentence was a lie or not. It was better if he didn't get too close to his fellow Trailers. He wasn't being honest with them, after all, but it wouldn't hurt to be part of a good team, especially if things went sideways.

"We'll give you your chance to bare your soul." Lenny's mouth twitched.

They set the box down, and turned to see the three women carrying the last of the supplies, and the hover disappearing into the falling dark.

"That's the last contact we'll have with the runner until we reach the exit point at Rainerville." Irwin grinned at them and rubbed his hands together. "We're on our own."

"Well, not really," Soo said, setting down her box. "I'm in charge of comms, and we can actually contact them any time we want to."

Irwin frowned at her. "It's true that we can, but we don't. Not unless there's trouble."

"Sure," Soo agreed easily, and Ben thought she was very carefully not looking at Tally. "But we can if we want to. For any reason."

"There's never been a reason. Not on my trips." Irwin strode through them and into the station. "Let's get this stuff moved inside and sort it into piles."

"Where's the supply hover that'll be coming with us?" Frangi called after him.

Irwin didn't answer her.

She waited a moment and then made a face.

"I saw it around the side. I'll get it." Ben started walking that way, and Lenny fell into step with him.

"That guy always an asshole?" he asked as they unhooked the supply hover and began towing it around.

"So far." Ben sent him a quick grin. "But I've only been here a day. Maybe he improves."

"Pity we got him. I know someone who's done the Trail, they liked their guide."

Ben shrugged. "It seems to be luck of the draw."

He knew that for a fact. His CO had tried to see if they could influence who led the trip, find the most experienced guide, but there was a roster, and all kinds of questions would be asked if they tried to mess with it. In the end, it hadn't been worth raising any suspicions.

And Irwin might not be the most experienced, but he was experienced enough. This would be his third year working the Trail.

As long as the guide didn't get in his way, he'd put up with him. Probably.

CHAPTER 6

TALLY WAS awake when the sun rose, gently lighting the semi-opaque domed roof over the room she, Frangi and Soo had commandeered for themselves.

She'd jerked awake over and over again in the night, the sound of leaves and small twigs falling from the overhanging trees above to skitter and slide over the roof was too close to the strange sounds her imagination had conjured up on the ghost ship.

They had unpacked the supplies last night, each taking charge of their assigned part, and stacked the supply hover that would follow behind them on the trail.

She'd packed a feast for their last night, and then worked backwards, smiling at what she'd managed to requisition.

It seemed no one was going to tell her 'no' when it came to food on this trip, and she'd pushed it as far as she thought she could go.

She grinned as she imagined the faces of everyone starting at lunch today, when they got to their first stop.

Irwin was responsible for breakfast this morning, but after that, she would take charge.

Her thoughts jumped from the surly, overbearing Irwin to the quiet, dangerous Ben, and her grin faded.

Her newly heightened senses had shot into overdrive when she'd met him yesterday.

While she fought the prickle of reaction that swept through her when she first saw him, she acknowledged she'd have known, even before her little helpers took up residence, what he was.

A warrior.

Her cheeks flushed again at the memory of him extending his hand. She'd been so busy fighting herself, so busy trying to feel normal again, she'd reacted automatically--taken his hand without thinking. And her little helpers had run things for a second or two.

Whatever that greeting had been, it was nothing she was familiar with.

She shivered and tried to push the thought away. She was tired.

Tired of fighting herself, of being fearful of what was inside her.

And yet, she wasn't willing to give up. Or speak more frankly with Dr. Vetna or anyone else to see if they could find out what it was.

She knew she was being illogical, and wondered if her reluctance to speak was her own doing, or something that was coming from whatever had gotten inside her. It was in its best interests to stay hidden, after all.

She sighed, and sat up as Frangi stirred.

Soo groaned, lifted the covers over her blue black hair, and tried to burrow deeper into her pillow.

"Is the comms equipment unpacked?" Frangi stood and walked over to Soo's bed. There was a jerky, almost nervous energy about her.

Soo made what sounded like a grunt of confirmation.

"Could I use it?"

Soo pulled the covers down a little, so one hazel eye was showing. "You could. Why would you?"

"Because a special . . . friend gave me his call signature for written comms and I want to let him know I'm here safely and that I'll be in touch in two weeks."

There it was again, that slightly nervous edge to Frangi's voice.

"What's the call signature?" Soo pushed up on her elbows.

Frangi squirmed. "I'm not sure I'm allowed to say. Or that he was allowed to give it to me."

Soo rolled her eyes. "Okay, go ahead. But depending where he is, it'll most likely be on relay. He might get it after we've finished the Trail."

"That's better than nothing." Frangi lifted her shoulders.

"You serious about him?" Tally asked her.

Frangi sent her a sudden, blinding smile, but there was a hint of vulnerability there, as well.

"Yes. Yes, I am."

"And he's Kalastoni?" Soo asked.

"He is." She edged toward the door. "He's in comms, like you, so he'll be watching for the message."

"Where's he stationed?" Soo was obviously trying to work out the call signature.

"He's on a deep space repair job. I'm not sure of the ship's name." She was at the door now, clearly eager to be off.

"You'll need the start-up code," Soo said, voice still a little croaky, and called out a list of numbers.

Frangi mouthed them silently, gave a nod and disappeared.

"You also have a lover somewhere?" Soo asked.

Tally shook her head. "You?"

"Sort of. We were getting there, until a spider bit me on the backside."

"Bodivan?" Tally asked on a laugh.

"No." Soo grinned, wriggled her eyebrows. "She's Arkhoran." She paused, and seemed to go inward, her expression pensive.

Tally knew Soo wasn't just here because she'd been bitten in the line of duty. There was more to the story, and she was using the fact the bite had been on her behind to avoid talking about it.

She must have been involved in some official action on Garmen. They wouldn't have given her a coveted place on the Trail for anything less.

A chime sounded from somewhere inside the building, and Tally scooped up some clothes to head to the bathroom. "Looks like we're about to start the Trail."

Soo gave another groan and pulled the blanket over her head.

THE SWEAT and heat felt good.

Tally had run on indoor trainers since she'd left Dr. Vetna's med bay, staying shipside until she landed on Veltos last night.

Pushing through the thick, green foliage of Veltos was a pleasure in comparison.

She knew high-level maneuverings must have happened to have gotten her on the Veltos Trail so quickly after her recovery, jumping her ahead in the queue, and she had resented it at the time.

This was just a path through a forest.

She understood the significance of it, how the very heroism of what happened on this trail helped keep spirits up during the Faldine War, but she hadn't bought into the legend--impressive though it was. The journey undertaken by a small group of soldiers from a variety of Verdant String planets, who'd been shot down on Veltos during the war and had walked for weeks to the enemy base deep in the forest, and then had singlehandedly destroyed it, preventing a sneak attack that might have changed the course of the war.

They were heroes, and within the ranks of the Verdant String Coalition military it had become a privilege to walk in their footsteps, earned by being injured while on duty. Slowly, over time, it had morphed from merely an honor to a rite of passage, a way to help heal the mental scars of trauma.

The Faldine War had only been over for a few years, and already, this trail was immortalized.

But now she was actually here, Tally felt the prickle of portent, could understand the sense those who'd gone before her had felt of being part of something bigger.

The trail snaked through the trees, easier now than it would have been when Commander Rainer had first come through with her team of survivors from the wreck of the VSCS *Dortmond*. The way was not officially maintained, but Irwin explained that each group that walked the trail was expected to pull up growth on the path when they saw it, and cut back branches that had started to grow across and block the path.

He carried the tools to do so in his own pack, either doing it himself or handing it to one of them to take care of, keeping the pace easy.

They had settled into an order, Irwin at the front, just behind the supply hover, with Lenny right behind him, then Soo, Frangi, herself, and finally Ben at the back.

They were strung out, not right on top of each other, and she liked it that way. It almost gave a sense of walking on her own, although she could see Frangi's tight, compact build just up ahead of her, and could hear Ben's easy, unhurried steps behind her.

She frowned at that.

The sound of the birds and animals, the rustle of the branches, had made hearing him difficult earlier, but she could hear him clearly now.

A ripple ran through her, the tingle and prickle of adrenalin that seemed to be ever present since she'd picked up that metal bead on the ghost ship.

She turned to look over her shoulder at Ben as she fought the sensation, when suddenly the quiet was broken by a rumble. It started faintly, as if from far away, and then the ground beneath her feet bucked and rippled. She was thrown to the ground, her eyes trying to make sense of what they were seeing, and then Ben was beside her, his gaze up at the sky, rather than on the ground.

She was just wondering why when, with a crack, one of the trees up ahead fell slowly, twisting as it went down.

"You all right?" Ben raised his voice over the rumble that was still going on and on, and she nodded. She pushed herself to her feet, finding her balance as the ground continued to shake.

The rest of the group was crouched down in the middle of the path. They'd backed away when the tree had come down, and were in a tight circle around the supply hover, all looking up as other trees came down in the forest around them, some catching on other trees, and balancing at precarious angles.

The rumble suddenly cut off. The vibrations coming from the ground persisted for a moment longer, and then everything was still except for the groaning of broken trees leaning against their neighbors, and the snap of their branches as gravity pulled them toward the ground.

"Careful," Ben called out as the others started to straighten up. "There could be aftershocks."

As he spoke, the ground shuddered again, and then stilled. Then shuddered one more time.

Almost straight after it faded, the birds started calling each other again, and Tally could hear the rustle of tiny bodies running across dried leaves.

The aftershocks had shaken more than one fallen tree loose

from its position, and the crash and snap of wood sounded from around them.

"I didn't realize there was any seismic activity predicted on Veltos while we were here." Tally looked around her, saw at least twenty trees were down on both sides of the path. There may be more blocking the way up ahead, but it looked like only one had fallen across their route in the immediate area.

"I didn't either." Ben was looking at a small screen strapped to his wrist, his expression grim. "That was a major tectonic shift, by the standard measure." He seemed a little agitated. "Veltos is known to get them regularly, but a big one like this wasn't predicted for another two months."

"There isn't anyone else on Veltos, though, except the small contingent at Rainerville, is there?" She hoped not. While the damage had been significant here, at least there were no buildings, no large population of people.

Frangi had left the huddle around the supply hover and walked over to them. "Don't they monitor the tremors on Veltos--" She cut off as there was a massive crack from the way they'd just come and another tree came down, blocking the route back to the supply station.

Tally watched it crash to the ground, throwing up dead leaves and dirt.

Frangi reached her, and they stood shoulder to shoulder, both mute at the destruction.

Only the top of the tree lay across the path, blocking it, but Tally could see it had been sheared off a third of the way up its massive trunk.

"You turned to look at me just before the earthquake hit." Ben joined them both, his own shoulder brushing the other side of her as they all looked at the tree.

She nodded. "All the birds and animals suddenly went quiet, and I could hear you walking behind me, where I couldn't before."

She could see him process that information, but before he could respond, Irwin hailed them, and they turned and walked toward the rest of the group.

The supply hover seemed undamaged and so did everyone else.

"There are probably more trees across the path up ahead, so we'll need to pick up the pace." Irwin's gaze flicked over them, and Tally guessed he was checking for injuries. "Given the damage sustained to the path as a whole, I think we can forego any maintenance from now on. That should help speed things up a bit."

He started to say something else, but Tally had stopped listening to him.

That sense, that tingle, was back, raising the hair on her arms and the back of her neck. She tried to fight it down, even as she looked carefully around her.

There was another tremor beneath her feet, and she crouched down, put her hand to the ground.

"Another one?"

She looked up to find Ben watching her.

"I'm . . . not sure." It felt different, somehow.

Ben lifted his arm, his gaze on his wrist unit, turning as if to get a reading, and then she saw the soldier's mask come down over his face.

"A stampede. Probably a herd of kuyer." He ran forward, grabbed her hand. "Everyone, get off the ground. Get off the ground!"

He pulled her toward the tree that had come down behind them, and then his hands came around her waist as he tossed her up.

She grabbed a handhold, scrambling upward, and then Frangi was beside her.

She paused, looking back, and saw Irwin, Lenny and Soo had

been closer to the other felled tree, and had chosen that as their destination.

Irwin had climbed onto the supply hover and had risen up easily, leaving Lenny and Soo to run for the trunk and pull themselves up.

She could hear a strange hooting in the distance.

"Get higher." Ben was suddenly on her other side, his voice low and urgent, and she followed him up.

The kuyer sprang into view just as she heaved herself to the top and turned to sit down. They leapt into the air as if they were on springs, calling with a throaty hoot that rose to a cacophony, forcing Tally to put her hands over her ears.

It seemed like there were hundreds of them, and a few of the strange, long-eared, thin-legged creatures were knocked into the tree as they passed, making it shudder, but the trunk was so massive, Tally felt safe enough up on her perch.

Then, almost as soon as they'd burst upon them, the kuyer were gone, their hoots fading into the distance, with nothing to show they'd been there but the trampled undergrowth.

"Must have been spooked by the quake." Frangi's gaze followed the last stragglers as they disappeared into the thick green of the forest.

Ben gave a grunt of agreement. He was standing on the tree trunk, looking down at his wrist unit. "The area is clear." He looked up, caught Tally's gaze. "You sensed them coming."

She forced down the shiver that threatened to grip her. He looked straight into her eyes, probing for her secrets, and she wasn't prepared to admit them, even to herself. "There were so many of them, the ground was vibrating." She raised her shoulders.

"It was," Frangi agreed. "The whole thing was amazing. I've never seen anything like it." There was a touch of awe in her voice.

Ben's face tightened, his lips going a little thinner, both things she didn't think she would have noticed before the ghost ship. It was as if her vision was better, not worse, after days in the dark. She seemed able to focus in on the most minute facial expression, and when she forced herself to look away, to look toward the others, and the path beyond, she had the strong feeling things were crisper than they would have been for her before.

"Irwin certainly made sure he was all right," she said, her words soft as she watched the guide lower the supply hover back down.

Frangi didn't hear her, she was already scrambling down the side of the trunk, but Ben stood beside her, and he gave a wry chuckle.

"You noticed that, did you?"

They shared a brief, amused look, and Tally relaxed.

He wasn't going to chase her about sensing the kuyer. Why would he? Whatever it was he noticed, it was hardly important.

But she'd have to watch herself. Try to put an even firmer rein on her reactions.

Because if she carried on this way, she was going to give herself away.

That she didn't know what it was she would expose about herself just made it that much more vital she keep it hidden.

CHAPTER 7

BEN LEANED FORWARD and took another kebab from the plate by the fire he and Soo had built.

Lenny and Irwin had put up the individual tents they'd sleep in for their first night out on the trail, and they'd set them out in a circle around the fire.

It was cozy, he conceded.

And the food was amazing.

"We don't get this out on an op. Or ever." Ben flicked a look at Tally before biting into the succulent chunk of meat on the kebab stick.

She smiled. "We don't get it on the VSCS *Uma*, either. And I always thought the food onboard was pretty good."

"How did you manage it?" Lenny leaned over and grabbed another one.

"No one seemed inclined to deny any of my provisions requests." A smile played on Tally's lips as she leaned forward, hands out to the fire as if they were cold.

The temperature *had* dropped with the sunset, but to Ben, it still felt warm. He'd been out on Veltos's open plains until yester-day, and the nights could be bitter.

Tally rubbed her hands together, her fingers long, slim and delicate. The flames illuminated her face, showing the hollows beneath her cheekbones and making her look fragile.

Except she wasn't, he reminded himself.

She'd dealt with the earthquake and the kuyer stampede today as well as anyone. Better, because she seemed to sense both before they happened.

"Why do you think they gave you everything you asked for?" Irwin asked. "I've guided a lot of Trail teams, and I've never heard of that before."

"She was the one trapped on that ghost ship," Lenny told him. "She went without food for a long time."

"I didn't know that." Irwin's voice suddenly changed in tone, softening, although the sound of it still grated on Ben's nerves. "What was it like?"

"I was in the dark a lot of the time. The most interesting part was the big space they had for growing plants."

There was a moment of shocked silence.

"Plants?" Frangi asked.

"Well, obviously none were alive anymore. But there were a few dead trees left. The other, smaller plants were probably nothing but dust. Even the tanks that looked like they had water or some liquid in them were long dried up."

"So, it was a true explorer?" Ben had read the file, but somehow he hadn't taken in the meaning of a propagation area until now.

"Looked that way to me. I didn't go down and look up close, I saw it from a walkway that ran across the top of it, but I'm sure the scientists that are in there now will have some interesting things to say when they've had a chance to look at it properly."

"What about you, Ben?" Soo watched him from the opposite

side of the fire. She was already digging in to the dessert Tally had brought out. "What landed you on the Trail?"

He'd expected this question. Had planned out a story to tell them, but found himself uneasy about telling it, now it had come time.

The people here had earned their place. He was an imposter.

His silence stretched out.

"You're Special Forces?" Tally asked, and he turned his head, nodded. "You don't have to say anything." She reached out a hand and touched his knee, just a fleeting, gentle brush of those delicate fingers.

There was a moment of uncomfortable silence, and Ben felt the bite of guilt deepen.

He had seen some crazy shit in Special Forces, but nothing like Tally had endured. He should be comforting *her*.

Soo's spoon scraped the last of her dessert from the bowl. "If he doesn't have to talk about his experience, then I don't have to talk about mine."

"Oh, Soo, you're so right, you don't have to. I already know all the details." Lenny's grin was wide.

Ben saw Soo narrow her eyes, but there was amusement on her face, and he realized she'd said what she said to smooth over the moment, and take the attention off of him.

He wondered how much guilt he could stand. But at least he hadn't lied to them.

"What are the details?" Oblivious to the byplay, Irwin looked between them.

But clearly Lenny wasn't giving anything away to Irwin, because he shook his head and touched a finger to his lips. "I can keep a secret. Especially for a fellow Bodivan."

"What's that?" Tally stood suddenly, pointing up to the sky, and they all tipped their heads back, saw lights chasing each other high overhead.

"Is that a . . . warship?" Frangi also stood, head thrown back.

Ben tried to make sense of it. It did look like a warship, chasing a smaller vessel--

A flash of laz fire lit the sky, reflecting off the small, thin clouds and turning them momentarily orange.

It had come from the warship, but the smaller vessel either had a good shield, or it had gotten out of the way in time, because it seemed to carry on, unharmed. The warship fired again, and suddenly a light bloomed on the back of the small ship, and it started plummeting toward the ground.

"Shit." Irwin's whispered expletive seemed to capture the thoughts of them all.

"That looks like our runner." Tally's gaze was on the small ship as it got lower.

Ben could faintly hear its engines as it disappeared behind the tall trees. "You sure?"

He hadn't come on the runner, but that made sense. It would be in a holding pattern around Veltos until pick-up in two weeks, or there was an emergency extraction required.

"She's right." Irwin looked in the direction it had gone, even though it was out of sight.

Before Ben could respond, there was a far-off boom and the sky lit up.

"It's crashed." Soo winced. "How far away do you think it went down?"

"We'll be able to see better when we get to the cliffs," Irwin said. He tipped his head back to watch the sky again. "Did anyone see where the warship went?"

"It disappeared after it hit the runner." Tally glanced at Ben. "Do you know what warship that was?"

He looked over at her. "Do you?"

She shrugged. "I can't say for sure, but it reminded me of the

Caruson warship that attacked me and my team when we found the ghost ship. This one wasn't as big, but it's a similar shape."

Ben nodded. "That's what I think, too."

"That's crazy." Irwin's voice was sharp. "Why would the Caruson attack a Verdant String ship over a Verdant String vassal planet? That would be asking for war." His voice rose in pitch.

"They just attacked Garmen and Lassa a few months ago. That put us pretty much on the edge of war," Ben reminded him.

"And then they killed my friend, and tried to tow me and that ghost ship away," Tally said, and Ben could hear the fury at her friend's death in her voice.

"I don't think they're all that worried about going to war, by the looks of things," Soo agreed.

"But why would they do this?" Lenny sat back down. "Sure, maybe they like the thought of conflict--from what I understand, that's kind of the culture on Caruso anyway--but what do they gain shooting down a runner?"

"I don't know." Ben turned to his tent, started packing it up. "But if anyone on that runner is alive, I intend to find out."

CHAPTER 8

THEY ALL ENDED UP GOING.

There would be no sleep for them, anyway, and Tally guessed Irwin couldn't bear to think of Ben taking the glory of getting to the runner by himself.

He was still visibly outraged at the Caruson attack, almost strangely so.

She had to remind herself that he wasn't in the military himself, he was a civilian contractor, and perhaps he had no idea that adversaries did strange things all the time.

"The cliffs are just up ahead," he said, and disappeared between two big bushes.

They were walking mostly in the dark, the moon was out and gave just enough light to see. The military issue lamps that Lenny, as equipment manager, had given them, had proved a failure, not because they didn't light the way, but because of the insects they attracted.

They all wore standard military gear, and that included the small devices imbedded in their cuffs and collars that sent out disruptive sound waves to repel most insects, but the big, hard-bodied fliers that began to appear as soon as the lights came on were obviously less affected. They couldn't resist the light even though the sound waves repelled them. It seemed to confuse them even more, and they hit into each other, and the team, in a frenzied clacking of wings.

Since they'd put the lights away, their progress had been much better.

They followed Irwin, stepping carefully, and Tally found herself on the rim of a wide cliff.

The moonlight illuminated the forest below the cliff, and the vista opened up.

The ground below fell away in rolling hills and valleys, thick with massive trees as far as the eye could see.

Limnos, the one planet easily visible to the naked eye from Veltos, sat fat and low on the horizon, the moon above it.

But, inevitably, the eye was drawn to the fire, burning bright against the darkness in the forest below.

The crash site.

"Does it look like it's near the Trail?" Tally asked.

Irwin nodded. "Luckily, it's not far." He looked over at Soo. "You want to try the comms again?"

She nodded, but Tally knew no one expected anything.

Soo had already tried before they set out, but if the Caruso had taken out the runner, why would they have left the comms satellite untouched?

Of course, if the runner had gotten out a warning before the satellite went, someone would be on the way. And even if they hadn't, the satellite going down would prompt someone to come looking.

Maybe not fast enough, though, Tally admitted to herself.

Soo took the comms transmission from the supply hover, crouching beside it as she pulled up the controls hologram. Her fingers danced and then she waited, tapping her ear piece in a pattern Tally guessed was from long habit.

She looked up at them, all crowded around her.

"Nothing."

No one would have held much hope anyway, but Tally could sense everyone stepped away with a heavier tread.

"How many hours will it take to get to the crash site, do you think?" Ben was looking at his wrist unit again.

"Another eight hours, at least." Irwin pointed to the side of the cliff. "There's a permanent ladder attached to the cliff face that will take us about an hour to get down. Not quite the original dangerous rope descent of Commander Rainer and her team, but hard enough. Everyone has to put everything they're carrying on the supply hover, and I mean everything. If something falls out of a pocket, it could seriously hurt the people climbing below."

"So an hour for the cliff, and you think seven to the runner?"

Irwin nodded. "If it was on the path, I'd say maybe five hours from the bottom of the cliff, but we'll be making our way off the path at some point, and that's going to slow us down."

"So, it's doable without stopping anywhere on the way to sleep." Lenny was looking at the burning column of smoke and flame, and his body language said he was ready to go.

No one, looking at that inferno, would assume they'd find survivors, but they could all hope.

Tally, more than anyone, knew that there was always a chance. Her team would have come back for her and Rew's bodies anyway, but they hadn't stopped sending out an array of probes in the direction the Caruso had dragged her, and as soon as they'd picked up the distress signal from the ghost ship again, Bertie had made sure they'd raced to get her as fast as they could. She couldn't do any less for whoever may have survived the runner's crash.

It seemed the others felt the same.

"We'll have to see how everyone's feeling," Irwin said, non-committal, and Tally decided while he may be annoying, he was trying to balance the wellbeing of them all with the crisis burning on the horizon.

She respected him for it, even though she knew none of them would take the opportunity to sleep until they'd reached the crash site.

"Well, let's go." Soo had packed up her comm set.

"Any of you climbers?" Irwin asked.

Tally shook her head. Frangi, Soo and Lenny did the same.

"I am. You go first," Ben said, looking at the guide. "I'll go last. That way, anyone has trouble, one of us can help."

Irwin nodded, and Tally's little tingly sense told her he was a little too pleased by the suggestion.

She couldn't understand why it would matter, though.

Irwin got the supply hover programmed and it sank down the side of the cliff, then he swung down and disappeared.

Soo looked down after him. "He's really moving." She swung over herself. "See you at the bottom."

At Ben's suggestion they gave each person a five minute lead.

They kept to the order they'd fallen into during the day, so Tally was left alone with Ben after Frangi disappeared over the side.

"Am I right that it seems there's more smoke now, less fire?" Tally asked.

"Yes. Whatever was flammable seems to have almost burned out."

"It's a good thing the forest didn't catch fire."

Ben's mouth quirked. "Fortunately, everything is wet. It was raining for almost two weeks straight before we started yesterday."

"You checked the weather before you got here?" She hadn't even thought of that.

He flicked her a glance. "I always check the weather." There was amusement in his voice.

"I'm so seldom in a place that has weather." That explained it. He must be planet-side a lot.

"Lots of ship's hours?" he asked lightly.

"Too many." She couldn't think when last she had walked on solid ground. She hadn't liked the special treatment she'd received to put her on the Trail ahead of others, but she was suddenly, deeply grateful that she was here.

It felt good to have the soft breeze on her face. Although this particular breeze brought with it the stink of burning ship.

He reached out a hand and cupped her shoulder. "I just wanted to say something about earlier. Nothing I've been through is worse than you had to endure on that ship. I have no right to your sympathy."

She raised her face to his, startled. "It's not a contest."

"No, but you intervened for me--"

She shook her head sharply. "You don't have an obligation to share your pain. However much or little there is of it."

He watched her in the silver moonlight, his face shadowed and hard to read. Eventually, he nodded. "I just wanted to make that clear." He glanced at his wrist unit. "You better get going."

She realized she hadn't been keeping track of the time, and swung down onto the first rung of the chain ladder.

"Tally." He crouched beside her, his face just above hers.

"Yes?"

His position put him almost completely in shadow.

"Be safe. See you down below. And shout if you get into trouble."

She nodded, her hands gripping the ladder tightly, her heart suddenly accelerating in her chest.

She thought for a moment he was going to lean forward and kiss her--that's what her little symbiotic friends were telling her.

As she started down, she wondered if they were finally wrong.

CHAPTER 9

BEN ROSE UP, fists clenched, and stared blindly out over the landscape below while he waited his five minutes.

What the hell had gotten into him?

For a moment there, crouched beside Tally, he had almost leaned forward that tiny, negligible distance and brushed his lips over hers.

This was serious business. He had a satellite to find, crashed just off the Trail path, and now a downed space runner, as well.

There was no way getting involved with Tally Riva would be wise in any way.

And yet...

She drew him like a magnet. There was a wariness about her, and yet she clearly enjoyed the company of her companions, and her sense of empathy ran deep.

He felt another twinge of guilt at her response to him when he hesitated to speak about why he was here, and again when he tried to make it right with her.

He didn't want to deceive her, and the fierceness of the feeling should worry him. He had deceived people before in the name of a mission, and he had never had a moment's pause about it.

The smoke from the burning runner suddenly blew straight into his face as the wind changed direction, and he coughed, then dropped down to a crouch and swung himself over the side of the cliff.

Time to get on mission. Tally Riva deserved someone who could focus on her, who wouldn't disappear in a few weeks.

And he was not that man.

HE CLIMBED DOWN QUICKLY, eager to get moving, and had almost caught up with Tally by the bottom.

They climbed down in silence, although he caught the drift of conversation between her and Frangi a few times.

Less than a minute after she stepped off the ladder, he dropped beside her and frowned when he realized someone was missing.

"Where's Irwin?" He expected the guide to be with everyone else.

"No idea." Soo's voice was more than a little cool. "When I got down, he was gone, and so was my comms equipment."

"What?" Ben flicked on his wrist unit. It could register heat signatures within a small radius on its own. When he was linked to the warship which usually transported him and his team, its reach was a lot further, but he would take what he could get.

Something moved on the edge of the unit's limit, and he turned to face that direction.

"Irwin?"

"I'm here." Irwin's voice was faint, and slightly out of breath, and then Ben didn't need his unit, because they could all hear the guide moving through the bush.

"He was gone by the time you got down?" he asked Soo.

She nodded. "I didn't know what to do. I decided to wait for Lenny, and then the two of us realized it was crazy to go searching for him when we didn't know which direction he'd gone in, so we decided to wait until everyone got down before we made a decision."

Tally made a sound under her breath but when he glanced at her, she was looking in the same direction as everyone else, waiting for Irwin to appear, a thoughtful expression on her face.

"Sorry, didn't mean to scare you." Irwin was carrying the comms equipment on one shoulder. He drew up short. "Everything all right?"

"No." Ben held out his hands, and Irwin hesitated a moment before he handed the equipment over. "You were supposed to be watching at the bottom in case anyone needed help." He set the equipment back on the supply hover.

Irwin shrugged. "Soo was clearly much more experienced than she said. I tried the comms again while I was waiting for her and I got a faint signal. I saw she wasn't struggling and I thought I'd see if I could get a better signal at a different spot."

"And could you?" Soo crouched beside the comms unit and fiddled with it. "I'm not getting anything now."

Irwin shrugged. "I couldn't get anything either."

"But you did, you say?" Ben crouched beside Soo.

"Very faint. Couldn't catch anything. But there was something there, so I didn't think it would hurt to try from a different spot."

"You should have waited for the rest of us first." Lenny's deep voice was a quiet rumble.

"You're big girls and boys, I knew I didn't need to baby you."

"It's not about looking after us." Tally was watching him with that thoughtful look. "It's about everyone's safety. If you had fallen or hurt yourself, we would have had to look for you. And we already have one emergency on our hands."

"She's right." Frangi slid her hands into the pockets of her pants. "I would have thought you'd have known that better than anyone, Irwin."

Irwin lifted his hands. "Sorry. I thought time was of the essence. I decided if I could try to get a signal while I was waiting, it would save us wasting time when everyone got here. Even though that's exactly what we're doing right now."

They were all silent a moment, and then Ben felt the tug of urgency. There was no sense harping on about it any longer, and Irwin had a point.

"Then let's go." He stood. "You going to lead the way?"

Irwin gave a nod. "We'll take the path at least half of the way. Things will get a little harder after that."

He programed the hover, then turned and walked off.

Everyone fell into their usual order, but before Tally could follow Frangi, Ben touched her shoulder.

"What's wrong?"

He couldn't work out the expression she had on her face when she watched Irwin, and it bothered him. She glanced at him, and he could have sworn for a moment she looked both guilty and afraid.

"What is it?" His grip on her tightened.

She closed her eyes, took a deep breath and shook her head. "Nothing. Really, it's nothing."

He dropped his hand and let her turn and start down the trail.

But he couldn't shake that it wasn't nothing. Something was worrying her, and he wanted to find out what.

TALLY'S SENSES said that Irwin was lying.

She remembered how pleased he was to be going down the

ladder first, and she wondered as she walked if he had planned to grab the comms unit and sneak off to use it from the beginning.

Except, why?

What could he hope to gain?

They were alone until the Verdant String sent someone to find out why their satellite was suddenly down, and that could be weeks. Until then, the only group left to communicate with was the Caruson warship that had shot the runner down.

She wondered what the Caruso would do about the Trailers. Would they care they had witnesses to their attack, or did they plan to be gone long before help arrived?

She stopped at a particularly big tree that lay across the trail, another victim of the earthquake from the day before, and waited for Ben to come up beside her. "Do you think the Caruso will come looking for us because we witnessed what they did?"

"Maybe." He waited for her to climb over the trunk, pulled himself up beside her, and they jumped down on the other side together. "If they know we're here."

"Surely they do. It's why the runner was here, and the Trail is well-known."

Ben gave a nod. "But finding us will take a lot of time. Time I'm not sure they've got to spend. There's nowhere obvious to land. They have to know someone's going to wonder what happened to the runner, especially if they got off a warning call. The Verdant String will send someone to investigate. And even if the Caruso hope the VSC will assume they can't contact the runner because the comms satellite's not responding, that will only speed up the VSC response, not slow it down."

"I don't know why they'd invite this kind of trouble."

They were walking side by side in the darkness, the path was wide enough to accommodate them both, and she liked it, despite the topic of conversation. Exhaustion dragged at her, but his presence gave her a little zing, a boost of awareness that she was too tired to examine closely.

"They must think they have a good reason. You're right, they wouldn't take this kind of risk lightly."

He suddenly went silent, his hand forming a fist, an order for her to stop. He glanced at his wrist unit and then subtly relaxed.

She felt a quick wave of fear tingle through her.

She hadn't noticed what he had, that everyone was waiting for them up ahead.

Nausea rose up in her and she fought it back. Whatever had taken up residence inside her was overreacting. Was compensating for not realizing what lay ahead.

Almost immediately her night vision improved, her hearing sharpened.

It had been dulled--no, normal--while she'd been walking. She'd been in control, but the spike of fear she'd felt when Ben had signaled her to stop had her senses heightening again.

Her stomach dipped in dismay.

She wanted to rake her nails over her skin, to dig whatever was in her out.

"You all right?"

She drew in a sharp breath, forced herself to take more note of what she was doing, how she was behaving.

She'd been rubbing her arms in agitation, she realized.

Ben was watching her, and she didn't mistake the worry in his eyes.

"Fine." Her voice wavered a little, and she cleared her throat. "Just having a bit more difficulty with the dark than I thought." The lie tripped off her tongue, even as it shamed her to use her trauma as an excuse.

Although, she comforted herself, her trauma had led to this sense of panic. It wasn't a complete falsehood.

"This is where we leave the path." Irwin pointed to a narrow break in the undergrowth.

Soo looked up at the clear night sky. "Let's try the comms one last time because once we go in there," she pointed into the thick undergrowth, "it'll be much harder."

Irwin made an impatient movement. "Waste of time."

Soo shrugged and crouched beside the comm unit. "It will only take a few minutes." She fiddled for a bit, but then closed it back up and stepped back in disgust. "Nothing."

"It's always worth trying, but it's not like we didn't expect it," Lenny comforted her, and she gave a sigh and a nod.

Irwin huffed. "Going off the path, we'll need to walk closer together. Always keep the person in front of you in sight. The big predators on Veltos are out on the plains, but there are small mammals here with teeth, and while we've got a full medkit, a bite won't be pleasant." Irwin sent the supply hover ahead and then pushed a branch aside and stepped off the trail.

They followed him in silence, and when Tally looked up, she could just see the black column of smoke above the treetops.

They were heading right for it, she only hoped there was something--someone--left to find.

CHAPTER 10

THE FOREST WAS alive around them.

Not that Tally hadn't noticed it on the trail, but off the path, where the massive ferns that grew beneath the trees brushed constantly against her, and the ground was spongy with dead leaves and damp earth, it was far more obvious.

She had to fight against her heightened senses as well as try to navigate the dense undergrowth.

The fright she'd gotten when Ben had made her stop had over-stimulated whatever it was inside her that tried to keep her safe.

Every drip of water from the leaves, every rustle on the ground, caused her heart to accelerate and her skin to prickle.

She stumbled more than she would have normally, starting at insignificant sounds.

When a branch caught at her jacket, she jerked away, stubbing her toe hard on an exposed root.

The pain brought tears to her eyes, and she hopped a few steps before fetching up against one of the massive tree trunks and leaning back against it, bracing her hands on her knees.

"Enough. That is just enough." She said it out loud, and

winced, because Ben was already beside her, crouching down, and Frangi had turned at her cry of pain.

"What is it?" Frangi put a hand on her shoulder.

"Nothing." She squeezed her eyes closed. "I just stubbed my toe. Nothing to worry about."

"Did you sprain it?" Frangi crouched on the other side to Ben.

Gingerly, Tally wriggled her toe in her boot. She could already feel her body responding, she could almost feel the little . . . things . . . racing to her toe, repairing the damage.

It still hurt, though. She sucked in a breath. "I don't think so. Just gave it a really hard rap."

And whose fault is that? She thought to her invaders. *Whose fault is that?*

"Your face is pale." Ben was watching her with concern, and she wondered what she'd looked like to him before she'd stubbed her toe, flinching and shying from every little noise.

"I'm just tired, and unused to being planet-side." She cringed that he must think her nervous and weak, but really, that wasn't far from the truth.

She wasn't the same person she had been the day she'd stepped onto the ghost ship with Rew. That calm, collected woman was gone.

Tally missed her.

She drew in a deep breath, blew it out. She *was* tired. Tired of being afraid of her own body, tired to the bone of carrying the secret of it, and yet, there was no way she'd admit to being the carrier of some kind of alien thing.

They'd most likely think her mad.

Even a thorough blood test had come up with nothing.

As far as the Raxian military were concerned, she was just a little mentally scarred from her time on the ghost ship.

She straightened. "I'm already feeling better, thanks. Sorry I'm slowing you down." And she did feel better. Her toe almost didn't hurt at all, now.

But she was hungry.

She pulled out three of the bars she'd stuck in a pocket before they left the bottom of the cliff, and offered them to Ben and Frangi.

They each took one.

"You sure you're all right?" Ben watched her with careful eyes.

She smiled brightly. "All good."

"You coming?" Lenny called from further up the path.

"Yes," Frangi yelled back, and they started walking again.

Tally took stock as she followed Frangi, chewing on her bar. She felt closer to normal, now. Her resident aliens had pulled back. She suspected her hearing was a little better than usual, but she wasn't in the constant state of fright or flight that she'd been in earlier.

She'd clawed back some control. Or they'd ceded it.

She glanced behind her, caught the severe line of Ben's mouth and quickly turned back.

Whatever he thought of her, it could be nothing close to the truth. And she would make sure it stayed that way.

Dawn was a few hours away by the time they reached the crash site.

Ben upped his pace as they started working through the splintered trunks and ripped up undergrowth caused by the runner's landing. He passed Tally and the others, moving until he was in line with Irwin.

"You're acting like we should expect trouble." Irwin gave him a sidelong glance.

Ben shrugged, pulled ahead of Irwin as well.

He was trained to expect trouble, but he didn't think there would be any up ahead. He just felt the need to get there first, to survey the scene.

He slid down a short slope, which looked untouched, as if the runner had ramped over it, and then, there was the ship.

It still smoldered sullenly, the black smoke almost impossible to see in the darkness, but the smell was overpowering.

Ben lifted the hood of his jacket, activated the air filter protocol, and the thin light strips embedded around the edges of the hood's fabric activated, lighting up his face and creating a barrier to filter the surrounding air.

When he looked back, he saw everyone else had done the same.

He turned on the light Lenny had given him, uncaring now of attracting insects, but perhaps they weren't as populous down here, or the smoke kept them away, because none appeared.

He swept the light around, doing a visual inspection while he kept an eye on his wrist unit. It was hard to pick up individual body heat, though, with the fire that continued to burn.

The night lit up as everyone else took out their lights, and there was silence as they walked the perimeter of the crash, looking for bodies or survivors.

There was nothing.

"If there are any survivors, they're in the ship." Lenny looked up at the runner's door, which was high off the ground.

Ben heard the sound of something being sprayed, and saw Tally had taken a fire extinguisher from the supply hover and was dousing the fire.

The glow of flames cut off.

Irwin rose up on the supply hover as soon as she was done and jumped through the jagged edges of the hole at the back and disappeared.

Ben waited for him to reappear, and when he didn't, he

jumped onto the runner, grabbing handholds and pulling himself onto the roof.

He worked his way to the back, and dropped down into the gaping hole.

"Irwin didn't send the hover back down so we could follow." There was clear anger in Soo's voice. "Can you do that before you go in?"

Ben hesitated. He wasn't sure if it was safe for everyone to be in the ship.

"Tally, Lenny and I actually knew the crew," Soo said shortly, and with a sigh, he reached out and sent the hover back to the ground before he turned back into the darkness of the interior.

He pulled his light out again and winced at the sight of a crew member lying dead, caught against the bulkhead.

Up ahead, Irwin's light moved around, and Ben moved toward it. He saw two more bodies before he reached the bridge.

Everyone who could must have come in here when they were hit. He counted four remaining crew.

Everyone was dead.

"The door was damaged." Irwin crouched beside it, illuminating the massive rip in the bottom of the door. "They had a catastrophic hull breach."

"They were already planet-side, we wouldn't have seen them getting shot otherwise, but they were still high up enough they needed a pressurized environment." Ben saw where the shrapnel from the original hit had torn through the runner, opening it up to the too-thin air of the atmosphere. "They must have hoped they could get down to a lower altitude in time, but they didn't make it."

It had been a very long shot, and it hadn't worked out.

Soo picked her way from the back and joined them, looking at the bodies strapped into their chairs. "Hull breach," she said. Her voice was steady, but her eyes glimmered with moisture in the light he held, and her lips were pressed tightly together.

Ben nodded. "They'd have been dead before they crashed."

She turned around and walked back out, and he could hear her speaking quietly to the others, a small catch in her voice.

"What now?" Irwin asked.

"Get some rest. Try the comms again. Then make a decision on where to go next." Ben looked down at the dead. "We'll have to bag up the bodies." There would be stasis body bags onboard. Hopefully they weren't damaged. But first he should scan the interior, get an accurate picture of how they found the crew.

He told Irwin what he was going to do, and the guide reluctantly conceded it was necessary and left to get out of the way.

Ben walked to the back with him, and then set his wrist unit to full scan and record mode.

He moved slowly through the length of the runner, his gaze taking in everything.

They had been taken by surprise, that was clear enough.

There was a mug lying on the floor, a table with a design screen on it, the program still activated, and another personal screen smashed and lying near the wall.

They'd been relaxing, waiting for the Trailers to reach the extraction point, and the Caruso had swooped in.

Had they sent out an emergency signal?

Ben forced himself to wait until the scan was completed before he checked the control panels on the bridge.

It looked as though they had, but whether that was before or after the Caruso had taken out the comms satellite was unknowable.

Either way, the Arkhoran Special Forces ship VSCS *Galaha* was waiting for his own comm by latest five days from today, and when they didn't get it, they'd come looking.

In the meanwhile, he had his own job to do. He would need to engineer a situation where he could leave the group for awhile.

Either that, or stick to the original plan, and slip out of their camp after dark.

"You need help?" Lenny loomed in the doorway.

Ben nodded. They found the stasis bags and took care of storing the bodies.

"Leave them here? Inside?" Lenny asked.

Ben shrugged. "Better than outside."

Lenny gave a grunt of agreement, looked down at the body at his feet. "We need to get the fuckers who did this."

"That would mean going to war, because the Caruso aren't going to hand whoever was in that warship over." Ben bent, and Lenny helped him lift the body and lay it alongside the others.

"Isn't that where we've been going since what happened on Garmen and Lassa?" Lenny asked.

"Maybe." And maybe what he was looking for on Veltos would be what broke the fragile remains of peace.

He'd have to wait until he found the downed satellite he was looking for to find out.

CHAPTER 11

THEY SAT around the camp fire for a second time.

It was early for a meal, but they hadn't slept in a full day, and everyone was showing signs of exhaustion.

Tally had never planned to impress and astound with the food she'd arranged. It had been partly a control issue, and partly a game with requisitions, but now she was glad she'd been able to serve up a spectacular dinner for their second night. A pall of sadness hovered over them all and the meal took everyone's minds off the bodies lying a short distance from where they were set up.

She kept to herself the fact that it was just going to get better. It had been great fun submitting her requests and wondering when the requisitioning staff were going to put their foot down.

Perhaps they'd had as much fun as her, and had been told to pander to her, because they hadn't so much as flinched.

She'd gotten everything she'd asked for.

"I thought last night's meal was a 'celebrate the first night on the Trail' thing. I didn't think it'd get better." Lenny had already finished, and was leaning back, hand on his stomach as he patted it in satisfaction.

She grinned. "Maybe it will, maybe it won't."

"Don't know how it *could* get better." Ben leaned into the container she'd set by the fire and pulled out his dessert. He spooned up some of the spicy fruit with a sigh of happiness. "This a Raxian dish?"

She blushed a little, because when she'd been choosing the food, she'd been unwilling to take a chance on unfamiliar dishes from the other Verdant String planets. She realized now perhaps not everyone would be a fan of Raxian food. "Yes. Everything is Raxian. I hope you're all up for a Raxian culinary adventure."

"So far, you've got me convinced." Soo groaned as she set her half-finished bowl down, and at Lenny's look, passed it over to him.

"What's next for us?" Tally looked up at the sky. It was clear, the stars bright in a way they never were in the light-polluted cities of Raxia. They seemed like fat, sparkling gems hanging above her.

"We head toward Rainerville. Not at the nice, comfortable pace recommended for the Trail, but at the speed Commander Rainer and her team would have done." Soo said it as if there was no question.

"And if the Caruso are there?" Frangi asked. "I mean, why would they shoot out the comms satellite and the runner if they weren't up to something on Veltos?"

"Might not be at Rainerville, though," Irwin said. "There's plenty of places they could be on the planet."

"Why did the Faldine rebels set up the base that's now the Trail's end where they did?" Tally asked. "What was it about that spot that it made sense to them to choose it?"

She sensed Ben's gaze on her, and when she turned her head, sure enough, he was looking her way.

"They chose it because it's on the far edge of the forest. That means there's plenty of open space on the plains for ships to land directly to the east, and there's a river that curves past the site, as well."

"But that was when the Faldine rebels thought they had the planet to themselves." Frangi waved a hand. "When they chose to ignore what was right, and establish an outpost even though they knew their presence would interfere with Veltos's biodiversity. It's not the same situation for the Caruso. The VSC has people at Rainerville now. The Caruso would have to deal with whoever is there."

"The VSC science officers at the old base will have difficulty defending themselves from armed attack, especially with no access to communications," Soo pointed out.

"And they have buildings and plumbing. Not to mention water from the river, which is actually rare on Veltos. There's a lot of rain in the forest, but the plains are pretty dry." Ben leaned forward, elbows on knees. "But even if the Caruso have done the logical thing and taken the base, we still have to go there and check it out. We'll have to approach cautiously, but we need to know what they're up to if they are there."

"They're there," Soo said. "Bet you."

Ben looked over at her and shook his head. "No bet."

"How long until someone from the VSC ambles over to see what's happened to their satellite?" Frangi asked. "Longer than it will take for a pick-up to be sent to fetch us in two weeks?"

Soo lifted a shoulder. "It depends if someone's watching this area or not. If they've seen the Caruso around before, they'll send someone faster."

"What're you thinking, Frangi?" Tally asked the question softly. Ever since they'd started talking about what to do next, her new friend had been clasping and unclasping her hands, battling with herself.

"I . . ." Frangi twisted her hands together. "I'm not sure if I'm allowed to say--"

"If you think there's any possibility it will help us out of this situation, say it." Tally reached out and took Frangi's hands in hers, and she breathed in one, deep breath and then let it out on a sigh and a nod.

"I have a . . . friend . . . and he seemed to react when I told him I had made it onto the Trail team. I had the strong impression he started to say I'd be close to where he was, although I know close in space is a relative term. He thought better of it, changed the sentence halfway through, but I could have sworn that's what he was going to say."

"What ship's he on?" Lenny asked.

She shook her head. "He didn't tell me."

The way she said it, Tally understood that Frangi had been hurt by that.

"He said he was helping with a deep space repair job, and that the VSC doesn't like to say when any of its warships need extensive repairs, because that'd obviously make the ship a target."

That made sense to Tally, but she could see Frangi hadn't really bought the excuse.

"You didn't believe him?" she asked.

From the quick look Frangi sent her, she got her answer.

Frangi hadn't believed him.

And it was tearing her apart.

"Why would he lie?" she asked. Then cursed herself at the sight of Frangi's pinched face.

"What's his name?" Ben asked, watching Frangi with that look he had, as if they were all far in the distance, rather than right beside him.

"You wouldn't know him," Frangi shook her head. "He's Kalastoni."

"I was involved in the mop-up in the aftermath of what happened on Cepi," Ben said. "I might."

"Oh." Frangi looked flustered. "Linn Fraser."

"I think I do. In comms?"

"Yes." Frangi smiled at him, a brilliant smile. "He'll be amazed we were on the Trail together."

Ben nodded, but Tally somehow got the impression Ben didn't think he *would* be amazed. Which made no sense.

"Why did you bring this up, though?" Irwin spoke for the first time, and Tally realized he'd been unusually silent.

"Oh." Frangi gripped her hands again. "Linn didn't tell me his location, or the ship, but he gave me his call signature. And if he really is close by, then we don't need a comms satellite, do we? We can contact him direct."

"You have his call signature?" Ben went even more blank-faced, and every hair on the back of Tally's neck stood up.

He was never so dangerous as he was now.

Oblivious, Frangi nodded. "He made me swear I wouldn't record it down anywhere. I had to keep it in my head."

"You memorized it?" Ben's voice seemed a little less stark now.

She nodded again. "It's long, but fortunately I've got an excellent memory. I sent him a message already, when we arrived at the supply station."

"Did you get a message back?" Irwin asked.

"No." Frangi's lips thinned. "We didn't have time to wait for a return message. I did give him our call signature, though."

"No message has come through from him." Soo spoke slowly, but unlike Irwin, there was no derision in her voice. "But we've got time, and nothing to lose. Let's try him again."

Frangi nodded.

"Tell him his friend Ben Guthrie says hello." Ben tried to make the request sound casual, but Tally saw his hands fist and then release.

"We're sending out an emergency request for assistance, not a friendly catch-up," Soo said, eyes narrowed.

"I'm a special forces captain," Ben's voice was quiet. "If his superiors are inclined to ignore a message from Linn's friend, they may think twice if they know I'm in the mix."

There was surprised silence.

"No problem," Soo said, giving a decisive nod and then stepping back so Frangi could enter the signature and write a message.

"This is stupid," Irwin said. "What are the chances they'd be close enough?"

"So what?" Lenny challenged him. "Not like we have a whole lot of other options. At least Frangi's way, we have a small chance."

"Very small." Frangi stepped back so Soo could close it all down. "*If* he was going to say he was close by, that could mean anything."

"It's most definitely worth a try," Tally told her. "Thank you for thinking of it."

She glanced over at Ben again as Frangi sat down, but his face was still unreadable.

She didn't know if he was pleased with Frangi's actions, or angry. And it bothered her that she couldn't tell.

IT WAS GOING to be too hard to take the team off the Trail to find the satellite without some uncomfortable questions.

Ben acknowledged that to himself as everyone said goodnight and settled into their tents.

They were all smart, well-trained and competent military personnel, and there was no way a communications expert like Soo wouldn't understand what she was looking at if she saw the satellite.

Which meant he had to go find it tonight.

The vibration of his alarm woke him after a solid four hours of sleep and he rolled silently to his feet, slipped into his boots and jacket, and stepped out of his tent.

The night was full of noise.

They were deep in the forest here, and the wind in the trees, the call of night birds, and the occasional death cry of their prey filled the air.

They had turned in early, so even with four hours of much needed sleep it was now just after midnight.

If his calculations were correct, that should get him to the downed satellite and back before anyone woke up. If his calculations weren't correct, he'd have to come up with a plausible story.

He oriented himself with his wrist unit and set out, enjoying the cool night air and the silver cast of the moonlight.

He was an hour into his mission when a cry of panic and terror stopped him in his tracks.

He turned, because it had definitely come from behind him, and ran back toward it.

He nearly knocked Tally over as he raced through the darkness.

She was kneeling beneath a tree, and it looked as if she'd tripped over a rock.

She looked at him blindly for a moment, and then everything in her seemed to crumple.

"Ben." She said his name with such relief, such trust, he fell to his knees beside her. "Where are we?"

He blinked. Then drew her shaking body against his own and held her close, running a soothing hand up and down her back.

"I thought this was over," she whispered. "I'm sorry if I woke everyone."

"Tally." He drew back from her, but he could see no guile on her face, read no hint of a lie. "We're an hour from the camp."

Her expression changed, closing down. "You followed me? Wouldn't I wake up?"

He rubbed a frustrated hand through his short, dark hair. "Tally, you followed me."

CHAPTER 12

TALLY WALKED BEHIND BEN, throat tight with nausea. She wasn't sure whether it was embarrassment or exhaustion, but probably a combination of the two.

She had followed *him.*

Or rather, her creepy parasites had used her to follow him.

He was so clearly thrown by the thought that he, a special forces captain, hadn't heard her until she fell and woke up, she couldn't doubt the truth of it. She had no idea where they were, and nothing was familiar to her, but Ben obviously knew where he was going, forcing a path through the forest.

"Why did you sneak off?" She kept her voice low, addressing the question to his broad back.

"I'm not answering any questions until you tell me how you could follow me and not know you were doing it." He didn't turn around.

"It's not something I can explain." She bit her bottom lip and felt her stomach lurch.

"Try." His tone wasn't cruel, or even angry, but it was implacable.

"Something got inside me on that ghost ship." Her throat felt raw just saying it.

"What kind of something?" He stopped and turned to face her, face scowling.

"I don't know." She held out her palm. "It got in through here. I picked up a smooth metal ball and it just melted into my skin."

He took her hand, looked at it closely, even though the moon was much lower on the horizon now.

"There's nothing to see. Even the doctor on my ship had a look."

"You sure you didn't imagine it? You were under a lot of stress."

Anger--more like rage--flared up in her. "Yes, I'm sure."

"Okay." His gaze flicked to hers, calm and steady. He still held her hand, and his thumb gently rubbed across the skin of her palm, back and forth. "So what does whatever got into you do?"

She drew in a deep breath, let it out. "Mainly it protects me."

His eyebrows lifted in surprise. "Protects you how?"

"I think it can take over my brain and my body easier when I'm asleep, and it used to walk me all over the ghost ship. It disconnected the ship from the Caruso tow line. It led me to useful things. I'd wake up standing over something like a blanket or a light." She gently tugged her hand free, liking the feel of him too much. "I think it also kept me alive longer, used the water and food in the most efficient way in my body. I don't think I'd have been alive when my team arrived without it."

Just saying the words out loud was a relief.

"But?" Ben's eyes gleamed as he moved his head to the side.

"But it takes control, and that frightens me. It tries to listen to me, but if it thinks something is for my own good, it goes ahead, even against my wishes."

"And tonight? What do you think was happening tonight?"

She had already pondered that while they'd walked in silence. Ben had told her in clipped tones that she'd have to come with him, as he wasn't leaving her on her own, and he had to do what he needed to do and get back to camp before anyone realized they were gone.

"I don't know. It must have heard you leave, and decided to follow. I can't explain it."

He did't look entirely convinced.

Then he rubbed his fingers through his hair again, and glanced at his wrist unit. "I think we're nearly there, so be as quiet as you can."

"Where is 'there'?"

He hesitated, then lifted both hands to cup her shoulders. "I have a confession to make. I'm not a genuine Trailer."

She stared at him.

He shook his head and grimaced. "Don't look at me like that. I'm a captain in Arkhoran Special Forces and we've been keeping watch on Veltos ever since we saw some suspicious Caruson activity in the area. We set a small satellite into the atmosphere a few months ago to monitor the planet, and after two weeks it went offline. We worked out where it would have landed if it was shot down the moment it went offline, but we needed to verify. We didn't want to make a big show of looking for it, because we disguised it to look like a weather satellite, and an official search would alert the Caruso that it was something more. If they're watching."

Tally heard the tacked-on quality to the last sentence. Ben definitely thought they were watching.

"So you needed a way to come looking for it that wouldn't raise any suspicions." Now she understood his discomfort over refusing to say what injury or incident had led him to be nominated for the Trail. She liked that he hadn't lied to them, even though he would have been justified in doing so to keep his cover.

He nodded, blew out a breath.

"And you think it's near here? That's were we're going?"

He nodded again. "And if I'm right, then taking a look at it will prove whether the Caruso are here or not, and whether they shot it down, or whether it came down due to technical failure."

She raised her brows. "The Caruso *are* here. We all saw them shoot down the runner."

"Yes, but if they shot down the satellite, they've been here for months. That'll tell us a lot. Because they've been invisible. We haven't caught so much as a sniff of them."

"Have you been looking that hard?" she asked.

"I've been living on Veltos for the last month, sneaking around to the most likely locations, hunting them."

She tipped her head back to look him in the eye. "That's why you knew what the weather had been doing."

He didn't smile, as she thought he would. "Yes, you picked up on that slip. What gave me away?"

She felt the hunted, nervous feeling of the last month rise up, and then realized she'd told him the truth already, she didn't have to cover up what she'd become. "My ability to read faces and gestures has become extremely good since the metal bead sank into me."

"Again, a protective measure," he mused quietly. "Reading people, to see if they're trustworthy or not, is a survival skill."

She raised a shoulder. She'd figured that out already. "Sometimes it makes me hyper-sensitive though. I think it's still learning how to interact with me. That time we walked through the forest-- after we got off the path--it had me focusing in on too much. I couldn't take the sensory bombardment."

He was still holding her, his big hands cupping her shoulders, and he squeezed her gently. "You haven't told anyone about this before, have you?"

"I tried." She closed her eyes. "I told my commander and the doctor I thought the bead sank into me, but I didn't say how different I felt. It sounded too crazy. And they found nothing in my blood tests. I didn't want a psych eval, and I couldn't see myself getting out of one if I told them the truth." She opened her eyes and sighed. "As it was, they got me onto the Trail ahead of others on the list. They already believed me to be fragile. And I . . . didn't want to give them more ammunition."

He surprised her by pulling her close, and she remembered that's what he'd done when she'd come back to herself, on hands and knees on the forest floor, waking up to realize she didn't know where she was. Again.

She sank into his warmth, his body solid against hers.

She slid her arms around his waist and let her head rest against his chest, and they stood there quietly for a minute before she forced herself to step back.

"So, I guess you want to get to the satellite and then get back to camp as fast as possible." She had to clear her throat to talk.

He nodded, his gaze hooded. "And if I've worked out where the satellite fell, I'm guessing the Caruson might have, as well. Especially if they're the ones who shot it down."

She went still. "You think they might have someone watching it?"

He shrugged. "It would be a real waste of time and a couple of guards, but it's possible. Or they may have set up a perimeter alarm, to see if anyone comes looking for it."

"In the forest?" Tally asked. "Surely that would be crazy?"

"They could use a high-level camera on a tree, measuring for movement around a certain height level to rule out any animals."

She nodded, and when he turned and started walking, she tried to be as silent as she could.

She wasn't as good at it when she was the one running her brain and feet, rather than her free-riders.

They'd managed to outwit a special forces officer.

She almost sensed their smugness.

Or maybe it was her projecting. She didn't know what was real anymore.

It was exhausting.

One thing that was real was the big, muscular man in front of her. He was very real.

She kept her eyes on him, and decided that was good enough for now.

CHAPTER 13

BEN COULD HEAR TALLY behind him.

She was almost completely silent. He was impressed because he knew she hadn't had any planet-side training. But it was in marked contrast to before, when he hadn't heard her at all, even though she'd followed him for an hour.

If anything could convince him there was something taking control of her, it was the difference between Tally before she'd woken up on the path, and Tally afterward.

That, and the very real fear he'd seen on her face as she'd looked up at him.

There was no way anyone could put something like that on.

So that meant she was telling the truth, and she had cause not to trust her own body.

He couldn't imagine what that would be like.

He moved carefully through the bush, and even in the dark he saw the burnt vegetation immediately. Small green shoots were already pushing their way through, nature renewing itself, but if the satellite had come in hot, it would have definitely burned some of the foliage.

He slowed down and Tally pulled up short against his back. She kept quiet, and he thanked the stars she was a colleague, a member of the VSC forces, and not a civilian.

He pointed to the charred remains, and felt her nod against his shoulder.

He eased forward, his wrist unit scanning for any sign of a Caruson guard, his eyes going up, looking for signs of a camera in the trees.

He found one small source of heat a little way up ahead, and began working carefully toward it.

He pointed up to where he was going, and then left Tally on the ground as he pulled himself up into the tree and began to climb.

When he got close to it, it suddenly dropped out of the tree, and gave a soft hoot as it coasted away on the breeze.

When he got back to the ground, Tally was grinning.

"All right." He grinned back. "Better to check it wasn't a camera than assume it was the local wildlife."

He moved forward again, but didn't bother being as careful now. Time wasn't on their side.

The satellite was lying in a small, blackened area, a twisted heap of metal. He shone a light over it, and then crouched low, trying to work out if one of the deep scores in the metal could be a laz fire hit.

"You think that's the proof?" Tally leaned over his shoulder, her eyes on the same deep groove in the satellite's metal casing.

"Maybe." He blew out a breath. "It's so damaged, it's hard to say, but my guess is, yes."

"Which you already suspected."

He nodded. And then rose up to do a full scan of the satellite with his wrist unit. He'd send it to his team when he finally got comms back.

"Time to go." They'd been gone two hours, which meant they'd get back long before the sun rose, and might even get a little more sleep. He turned to face her. "You'll keep this to yourself?"

She pursed her lips. "I'm in no position to blab other people's secrets. Not that I would anyway." She took a step back and then hesitated. "Lenny, Frangi and Soo are trustworthy, though. I think they'd be a help more than a hindrance."

He gave a slow nod. "And Irwin?"

She hesitated again. "No."

"And you think that because . . .?"

She shrugged. "The little creatures in my head have made me think that."

He couldn't help the laugh that burst out of him. "You always talk about them in the plural, not as one single thing, even though it was one bead you picked up."

She pondered that. "It's just a feeling. It seems to me that they are spread out all through me sometimes." She rubbed her forearm.

"And what do they think of me?"

Her look was guarded. "They . . . I . . ."

He let the silence stretch out between them.

"We both like you." Her voice was soft.

"But they followed me." He felt ridiculous saying it, but Tally believed something had taken control of her, and he believed Tally.

She lifted her shoulder. "Maybe they were worried about you."

He stared at her, mute for a moment, and then, unsure what the hell he was doing, he leaned forward and kissed her, his hands sliding up her shoulders to hook around her neck.

She stilled, startled, and then she softened, leaning in to him for a moment before she pulled back. She looked up at him, bemused.

He was pretty bemused himself.

"Well, tell them thank you." He brushed a last kiss on her forehead and then turned and started back.

THEY'D REACHED the camp in silence, and she'd gone straight to her tent.

Ben was right in his prediction that they were able to get a few hours of extra sleep, although she wasn't worried she'd missed four hours. She seemed to need less sleep these days.

The little creatures probably made sure to maximize all her systems.

When the sun rose enough to flood the camp with light, and the birds in the trees around them started up a racket, she crawled out of her tent and started breakfast, frowning because some of the food seemed to be missing.

"What's that look?" Soo rubbed her face as she emerged from her tent.

"Someone's taken some of the food." She quashed the flare of panic. There was plenty. She hadn't stinted. She had over-ordered. They would be fine.

"Maybe it got stored somewhere else." Soo sniffed in appreciation as Tally set down a jug full of hot jah. She poured herself and Tally a cup, and then sat heavily on one of the stools set around the fire pit, and started the fire up again.

Tally approved. It wasn't cold, but she liked to hear the crackle of it, and to watch the flames. It was a treat reserved for planet-side escapades.

The smell of the thin, fried strips of derna meat and cooking eggs drew everyone but Irwin out of their tents.

Tally hesitated before she served herself. "Anyone seen Irwin?"

Everyone shook their head so she sat down with the plate she had intended for him. "I wonder if he's the one who took some of my supplies."

"There are supplies missing?" Ben looked up from his meal.

He hadn't specifically spoken to her this morning, but he had brushed a hand of greeting down her back when she'd handed him his breakfast, and topped up her mug of jah before he'd taken a seat.

"More than I initially thought. A good two days' worth."

Ben frowned, his gaze going to Irwin's tent.

Lenny stood, walked over to the tent and opened it without preamble. "He's not here."

"Maybe he decided to scout ahead?" Frangi didn't look as if she believed it.

No one wanted to respond. They all finished their meal and cleaned up, and then while Lenny and Ben began taking down the tents, Tally took a full inventory of their remaining supplies, while Frangi and Soo decided to transmit the message to Frangi's friend Linn again.

"Someone's taken part of the comms unit." Soo's shout was edged with disbelief.

Lenny and Ben dropped the tent they'd just bagged up and jogged over.

"I'd say, given Irwin is missing, there's no doubt who did it." Tally straightened from her crouch. "He's taken about three days worth of food, as well."

"What the hell?" Soo breathed out. "What's he up to?"

"What's missing?" Ben asked, bending over the unit.

"The transmitter." Soo's hands were fisted on her hips. "He knew what he was doing, too. He didn't damage it, it's just missing a vital part."

"Can you make another one in the replicator?" Frangi asked.

Soo made a face but began to search the supply hover. Tally wasn't surprised when she lifted the replicator, which looked to be standard VSC issue, and showed them all the power pack was gone. Irwin wouldn't have bothered to take the original part in the first place, if he hadn't also taken away the means to replace it.

Replicators were standard equipment, he wouldn't have overlooked something like that.

He'd also taken the spare backpack, which included a tent.

Easier than him putting down his own tent in the night.

Most of the supplies had been taken off the hover, and Frangi lifted the last few crates off it so it was empty. "I'm going up on this thing. See if I can see him." She programed it, and it lifted up, with her standing in the middle.

"How high does it go?" Lenny was looking at it dubiously.

"Maybe tree height," Ben shrugged. "It's not a bad idea."

The hover ended up stopping just above the tops of the trees around them.

"Anything?" Soo called.

"No."

Tally watched as Frangi slowly turned a complete circle, eyes shielded from the morning sun.

And then, out of nowhere, laz fire brightened the sky even further, and Frangi let out a scream of pain.

CHAPTER 14

FRANGI FELL, her body hanging precariously off the edge of the hover.

"Bring it down," Ben roared at her, and ran toward the nearest tree, hauling himself to the lowest branch and then climbing as fast as he could.

When he risked a moment to check on her, Frangi was still lying, limp, on the hover. It remained motionless at the top of the trees, but at least she hadn't fallen off.

"Frangi." Tally's shout seemed to cut through to her friend, because she shook her head. "Frangi, bring it down."

Frangi pulled herself more fully onto the hover and it began to sink, to Ben's relief.

Another flash of laz fire lit the morning sky, but the angle was wrong and it overshot.

Frangi gave a moan of fear as it sizzled over her. Ben was glad they'd tried again, though. It gave him a better idea of where they were shooting from.

He reached the highest branch he could that would support his weight, and slid on the glasses that had a zoom mode, flicking his gaze between the lenses and looking at his wrist unit.

Four attackers.

They'd shot at Frangi while they were still a distance away.

Perhaps they thought she'd seen them, but it was still a stupid move. It had given them away.

He began to work back down the trunk, his descent faster than his climb.

Soo and Lenny were standing guard, each facing outward toward the forest, while Tally crouched beside Frangi on the hover.

When he dropped to the ground, they turned to look at him, and he gave a silent signal, letting them know which way the threat was coming from, how many there were, and how long he thought it would take them to get here.

He estimated they had five minutes.

Five minutes wasn't bad, as far as forewarnings went.

Soo and Lenny nodded, sliding around to face the right direction, but they had no weapons and he realized it was just a need to do something that compelled them.

"Pack the hover up, I'll help move Frangi to one end of it," he said, voice low, and after a moment's hesitation, they started to do it.

Tally must have heard him, because she stood, her hands going under Frangi's armpits, and Ben grabbed her hips.

They lifted her to one end of the hover, and then Tally ran to the only tent they still hadn't put down, and came back out with a pillow and a sleeping bag, which she arranged around Frangi to make her more comfortable.

"It's her leg." Tally glanced at him, and he tried not to wince when he saw the mangled mess of it.

"Good thing it's the fake one." Frangi's voice was so faint it was almost impossible to hear.

"You're right." Tally bent close to her ear. "They can grow you a new one, and they already have all the specifications."

"True." Tears glittered on her eyelashes. "Pity . . . the nerve endings took so well, though. It hurts." She drew in a labored breath. "You should leave me and run."

Tally gripped her shoulder. "Say that again, and I'll kick your ass."

The hover was almost fully packed, Soo and Lenny had thrown themselves into the job, and they both stepped back, their gazes going to him for further instructions. Lenny had found the big hammer used for the tents, and he held it like a cudgel.

Ben glanced at his wrist unit and saw someone coming in much faster than walking or even running pace. He leapt to his feet, mouth open to shout a warning, as a small hover came shooting into the clearing.

There was a single Caruson riding it, a massive laz in his hand. Ben stood on the wrong side of the hover, his hand just closing around the laz he had hidden in his jacket. He'd never felt so impotent.

Tally had started to spin around and rise from her crouch a second before the hover appeared, and she turned the movement and her elevated height on the hover into some kind of springboard. He was hauling himself up onto the hover beside Frangi when she threw herself into a forward somersault.

Her arm curved, hooked the Caruson around the neck as she flew over him, and pulled him off his vehicle.

Ben didn't waste time trying to work out how she'd done it, he followed her lead, pushing off the edge of the supply hover and landing beside the Caruson, who was flat on his back.

He threw his laz at Tally and grabbed the Caruson's weapon. As he shot him in the face, there was a screech of metal and then a thump as the small hover smashed into a nearby tree.

"Lenny, Soo. Take Frangi and the supplies deeper into the trees." Ben was already running across the clearing, in the direction the Caruson had come.

Lenny didn't argue. He was already on the other side of the hover to Soo, jogging deeper into the bush. "Come after us as soon as you can."

"You want to go with them?" Ben glanced across at Tally, who had drawn level with him. He wanted her to say yes.

She shook her head, such a fierce look on her face, it seemed to him she was raging an internal battle with herself.

Maybe she was.

HER LITTLE HELPERS had taken control, and she nearly hadn't let them.

Tally knew the person she'd been wouldn't have executed a somersault like that, wouldn't have known how, but she'd made a split second decision and stopped fighting, and because of that she'd helped to stop the first Caruson soldier.

There was no way she was letting Ben take on the others by himself.

She followed him amongst the trees and then stopped as he slid into the shadow of a massive tree trunk.

"Seems like that was the only hover they had." He was looking at his wrist unit. "There are only three left and they're coming at walking pace."

She could tell his disrespect for their decision to send the soldier ahead. His lip curled, even as he whispered the information.

"You think they have heat sensors?" She pointed to his wrist unit.

He shrugged, but she could see the edge of violence in him, in the way he stood.

Then he seemed to come to a decision. He pointed upward, and when she nodded, he made his hands into a step for her. "Aim for their faces. They'll have an anti-laz layer under their clothes." He boosted her up the side of the tree.

It seemed to her she managed to jump higher than she thought she could. She caught a branch, pulled herself up.

It was wide enough for her to crouch easily, and she shuffled to where the branch met the trunk and lifted the small laz Ben had given her.

The Caruson came marching through the tree below, confident, making no effort to hide.

Ben had told her there should be three of them, but she could only see two.

She waited, tense, knowing Ben was going to attack, and suddenly he was firing the big weapon he'd taken from the Caruson in a wide arc.

They were not expecting it.

Tally wondered if they thought their colleague had already subdued everyone, because they reacted with shock and surprise.

One went down, and she took aim and fired at the one closest to her, narrowly missing him as he jinked to the left and rolled, coming up on his feet with his big laz raised.

Ben had run to the right, and now he opened up again from the cover of another massive tree trunk.

As the Caruson turned to follow Ben, Tally shot again, but while the soldier she hit flinched, his hand going to his shoulder, he didn't even cry out.

The Caruson were big, and their skin was thick, but Ben was right, these soldiers were also wearing anti-laz layers. Her little laz wasn't making a dent.

The Caruson she'd hit turned and looked up, his gaze connecting with hers, and with a snarl, he turned to face her.

As he brought up his weapon, she felt the tingle through her body, knew what was happening, and for the second time that day, she gave in.

She rose into a half-crouch and leapt as the branch beneath her disintegrated.

She fired off the laz as she flew through the air, and the soldier who'd shot at her fell.

She landed on the ground beside him, and a wave of nausea rose in her at the sight of his eye.

She'd done that.

"Tally, take cover."

Ben's angry shout galvanized her, and she dived low and rolled, finding cover behind a tree.

There was another burst of laz fire, and then silence.

"Tally?"

She let herself fall back against the hard bark of the trunk behind her and let out a breath.

"Tally!"

"Here." She had to clear her throat. "I'm fine."

She pushed herself to her feet, and tried not to stagger as she stepped out into the open. Ben was standing in the middle of the carnage, looking more than a little wild.

"You all right?" Her gaze raked over him.

There was blood on his cheek and she must have made a sound, because he lifted his fingers to his face and looked at the blood.

"Just some splinters from the return fire."

As she walked toward him, he checked his wrist unit, and she saw him relax.

"Gone?"

"One got away."

He held still as she took his face in her hands and carefully pulled out a large sliver of wood from the skin over his cheekbone.

"There's more, but I'll need drawing gel, or tweezers." She looked in the direction of the clearing. "Let's go find the others before that soldier comes back with more friends."

CHAPTER 15

"FRANGI CAN'T GO ALL the way to Rainerville." Soo's voice was matter of fact as they huddled around in a small circle, eating a quick meal. "Especially not if we can't use the Trail. She's in a bad way. I saw Caruson laz wounds on Garmen, but I'll never get used to how nasty they are."

"We definitely won't be able to use the Trail." Ben shook his head, his gaze landing on Frangi, lying unconscious on the hover beside them.

Tally was relieved the medication Soo had given her friend had kicked in and sent her into a deep sleep. She winced every time she caught sight of Frangi's leg, but Soo and Lenny had done their best to deal with it and she agreed with Soo's assessment.

"The supply station is two or three days away, Rainerville is about a week away, depending how fast we can travel. You have to go back. And anyway, we can't play hide and seek with the Caruson through the forest with the supply hover."

Soo tapped her lips with a slim finger. "There may be a spare part for the comms unit at the supply station, too."

Ben's eyebrows lifted.

"I thought I saw some equipment in that big communal room." Soo shrugged. "Not sure, but maybe."

"So what's the plan?" Lenny took a slug of water and set the bottle down.

Tally looked over at Ben, and held his gaze for a long beat.

He gave a short nod. "Time to come clean."

Soo's gaze lifted, surprised, but Lenny just got more comfortable, and looked like he'd been expecting it.

When Ben had finished telling his story, Soo blew out a breath. "So what was this attack on us about?"

"They're eliminating the witnesses, which means they don't want anyone to know they were here." Ben glanced up at the bright blue sky. "Which means whatever they're doing is temporary, or secret."

Tally set the plate of food she'd been eating aside. "And Irwin either led them to us, or went out and found them, and told them where we were."

Soo gaped at her and Tally shrugged.

"Why else did he clear out just before we were attacked?"

"He's either been in bed with them all along, and is helping them," Lenny agreed, his voice a low rumble, "or this is a huge coincidence."

Tally snorted, and Lenny lifted his drink bottle in salute.

"I need to see what they're doing at Rainerville." Ben stretched out his legs. "We need to know what they're up to there."

Tally knew he would say that.

"So we have to split up?" Soo gave a sigh. "Not the best solution, but I don't think we have any choice."

Tally touched her arm. "Soo, you obviously have to go back to the supply station, in case there is a chance you can get the comms unit working again."

Soo nodded. She looked over at Lenny, waiting for him to say which way he'd go.

He flashed her a quick grin. "I can't let Soo go by herself, not with Frangi in the state she is." The look he turned on Tally and Ben was almost apologetic.

Tally smiled at him. "I'm glad you're going with her."

Ben turned to her. "You sure you want to come with me?"

She nodded. "I'm not letting you go alone. And Lenny and Soo will be able to handle Frangi. They don't need my help."

"The Caruso may come sniffing around the supply station." Ben's warning was serious.

Soo gave a shrug. "If they do, they do. We'll think of something."

Ben cleared his throat, and Tally thought he hesitated for a moment before looking them in the eye. "One more thing. Frangi wasn't wrong in thinking something was off with Linn Fraser's response. He *is* nearby. He's not repairing a warship down for repairs, that's the cover story all the crew use. He's one of the crew on the Arkhoran Special Forces ship that's in this system, looking for Caruson activity. They dropped me and my team off on Veltos, and they might well be in range. Soo, don't bother with pretending you're contacting Linn. Signal to Commander Reskit. He's my superior officer. Straight out say what's going on."

Soo grinned. "Well, that's some good news, anyway. Rather have a Special Forces warship than one down for maintenance problems coming for me."

"Do you know anything about Irwin?" Tally hitched her pack higher on her shoulders, and kept right behind Ben, her voice low.

"He's one of two guides that work the Trail. They are two

months on, two months off." He glanced back. "This was his second month."

"So he had time to encounter the Caruso, and make a deal with them." She thought about it. "How did they know he'd be amenable to that?"

"Good question." He glanced back at her again, his gaze hard. "There was an accident. The other guide fell down some stairs on Situ, and ended up in the med bay. He couldn't remember what happened, and there was no reason to suspect foul play, but he was lucky to be alive. We wondered about it, but no one had the chance to interview him, and it was Irwin's scheduled time on the Trail anyway, so . . ." He faced forward, and his shoulders lifted in a shrug.

"If it was Irwin's scheduled shift anyway, then why . . .?" She chewed on her lip. "Unless they didn't know how long it would take, so they injured the other guide so Irwin could just offer to stay on?"

"Maybe."

"Why do you think they're here?"

"That's the question--" Ben stopped, lifting his hand in the signal for silence.

Tally slowly drew the small laz out of the side pocket in her pants and widened her stance.

There was the sound of crashing, and then she relaxed as she saw the tension leave Ben's frame.

"It's a herd of kuyer." He moved forward again, and she saw there was a sharp dip in the ground, and in the shallow valley below, she caught the flick of ears and the scrape of hide against rough bark.

Then, as if they were automatons, controlled by the same hand, the kuyer all went still and looked north.

One let out a hoot and then a sudden sizzle of laz fire cut through the hazy afternoon light.

The kuyer ran, jumping and sprinting, barging into trees as they all tried to head west through the forest.

Tally dropped down, lying flat on her stomach, and she could see Ben was crouched, leaning up against a tree, the massive Caruson laz he had taken steady in his hands.

When the sound and chaos cleared, she pulled herself forward just a little so she could look down the gentle slope. The forest was empty of kuyer, except for the three left dead on the ground.

Two Caruson walked through the trees below, the sunlight flickering over them as they walked toward their kill.

Her breath froze in her throat. She didn't think they could see her or Ben, but if they had heat sensors, they wouldn't need to see them.

Ben obviously thought that, too, because she saw him lift his laz a little higher, getting ready to shoot.

But the Caruson didn't glance their way. They joked in their harsh, choppy language, and found a thick branch to tie all three kuyer to, then walked away, their kill swinging by their legs.

As soon as they disappeared from sight, she shoved up onto her hands and knees, and Ben was suddenly beside her, crouching down to her level.

"If they're killing kuyer, they've set up a camp. I'm going to check it out."

She blinked, because that sounded like--

"I'm going to leave my pack with you, and you're going to stay hidden until I get back."

She frowned. "Why?"

"Because I'm trained to do this kind of reconnaissance, and it will be harder for them to spot one person, rather than two. I won't be long, if I can help it. I need to go now, in case I lose them. Find a good spot to set up camp near here."

He slid his pack beside her, and then he was gone.

She rose up into a crouch herself, and thought she just caught sight of his head for a moment, but then, there was nothing.

Well, crap.

She rose up carefully, and tried to work out how she felt.

She wasn't trained for planet-side ops, that was true, and most likely it was better for him to go alone. And he didn't have a lot of time to discuss it because the Caruso were moving away at a fast clip.

But she didn't like being left behind to babysit his pack, either. Ugh.

And what burned even more sharply was she felt like her little stowaways were in agreement with Ben.

She turned a slow circle, looking for a better place to hide their things and hunker out of sight.

Some of the fountain bushes they'd pushed through yesterday had turned out to have a lot of room between the trunk and the cascade of branches that fell like a fountain from the center trunk.

She grunted with effort as she picked Ben's pack up, and then started walking until she found one. Its branches were thick with foliage, and she put both packs down and pushed some of the branches aside, to step into the cool dappled green and gold of the interior space.

It encircled the trunk, with the branches curving over her like a domed ceiling. They were wide enough apart overhead that the sunlight was able to squeeze through, but the leaves were so thick and green, they formed a solid wall that fell all the way to the forest floor.

She stepped back out, and pulled in the packs, resting them up against the trunk.

She leaned up against them, and closed her eyes for a bit, letting the forest settle back around her, until the birds and the small rodents began going about their business again.

But she felt edgy--worried about Ben, nervous about how the

others were getting on. Eventually, she pulled one of the packs between her legs and started repacking it.

They hadn't had time to do more than throw things in, so she might as well sort them out.

Because waiting and doing nothing sucked.

CHAPTER 16

TALLY WAS DOZING on her sleeping mat, half aware of the growing shadows and the lifting strength of the breeze as the day drew to a close, when she heard the footsteps.

She only just stopped herself from calling out, swallowing the shout and putting a hand over her own mouth.

It might not be Ben.

The tread was heavy, and the person was big, but it didn't sound like the lumbering stride of the Caruso.

She carefully eased herself up into a crouch and tried to work out which way they were going.

They seemed to be coming toward her fountain bush, and then they passed her by, but the movement was sneaky, moving quickly and then stopping, then moving again.

Ben would call softly out to her, wouldn't he? Or he'd have found her, because he had the heat sensor on his wrist unit.

So, if it wasn't Ben, who was it?

She lay on the ground and crawled forward through the curtain of leaves, just poking out enough of her head to see what she could.

She froze.

Irwin was right in front of her, his back to her as he looked north.

She eased back, mind spinning.

He was with the Caruso. She didn't doubt that for a moment. So was he looking for her? Had they caught Ben, and they thought they could lure her out using Irwin?

Her stomach dropped and her hand closed over the small laz Ben had left with her.

Either Ben was in trouble, or, if he was coming back to find her, he could run right into Irwin; think Irwin was her on his heat sensor and not have his guard up.

She crawled carefully forward again, and just caught the flash of Irwin moving again, heading north.

The wind kicked up another notch, and she used the sound to wriggle free of her hiding place and start to follow him.

It was relatively easy to track him as he moved down the gentle slope, because she was always above him, but when she reached the valley floor, where the trees seemed to be a little closer together, and she lost the advantage of height, she began to panic when she lost sight of him.

Her panic triggered the prickle through her blood of the unwelcome guests inside her, but right now, unwelcome was too strong a word, because she needed to follow Irwin, and she didn't know what she was doing on her own.

She blew out a breath and relaxed her body, and clearly thought the words: "Go ahead."

She didn't experience any sudden sharpening of her eyesight or her hearing, and confused, she pushed away from the tree she was leaning against, and concentrated.

She heard the frightened shriek of a bird to her left. Her heart beat a little faster and she went in that direction. She caught sight of Irwin almost immediately, his quick, furtive movements drawing her eye.

The way he was creeping helped her. It slowed him down, made him easier to find.

Her worry that he was looking for her, or trying to draw her out, had all but evaporated. His focus seemed to be on moving forward as silently and carefully as he could.

He seemed to know where he was going, which made her wonder why he was sneaking. If he knew where the Caruson camp was, why didn't he simply walk to it openly?

Unless he was trying to keep out of sight in case she and the rest of the Trail team were around.

That made sense to her, and she kept well back, calmer and more sure of her ability to work out which way he'd go.

She made no sound as she followed him, something she only realized after the second time a twig snapped under Irwin's boot.

She sent a silent thank you to her invaders, as she realized they were helping her place her feet with exquisite care.

She heard the sound of conversation before Irwin seemed to.

It stopped her in her tracks, and she eased behind a tree, but Irwin carried on a little way, until she was convinced he wasn't worried about it. But then he froze, cocked his head as if he were listening, and slid behind a tree himself.

It jolted her.

Earlier, she'd waited for a heightened sense of hearing, but maybe . . . maybe she already had it.

She just hadn't noticed.

When Irwin moved again, it was even more cautiously.

He approached the sound of a camp incrementally, and when a low, humming buzz rose up, he froze and then began to move a little faster.

Tally looked up, too nervous to break cover when she didn't

know what was making the sound. It seemed to be getting louder, and she guessed it was a hover of some kind.

She felt a lurch of fear for Ben. If he was caught in the open, he'd be exposed.

She'd pushed him from her thoughts while she'd been following Irwin, her concentration on staying hidden, but where was he?

The sun was sinking in the sky, and while darkness came more quickly among the trees, he had been gone a long time.

She hoped, with a sick, cold lurch of her stomach, that he wasn't wandering around where he'd left her, worried out of his mind.

Although she'd rather that than find him a prisoner, or dead, in the Caruson camp.

Irwin had fetched up against a tree, and as the buzzing noise increased, he climbed it, pulling himself up amongst the branches, where he disappeared from sight.

She gritted her teeth in frustration.

There was no way she could get closer. Either Irwin would spot her, or whatever was flying their way would.

Maybe she'd have to climb, too.

She looked up and worked out if it was a viable option.

Her blood sang with relish at the challenge, and she tried to remember if this is how she'd been before the ghost ship.

She hadn't been planet-side enough to know for sure.

She'd enjoyed challenging herself, but had she seen things in terms of obstacles to overcome?

She forced the thought away, blew out a breath and tried to switch off her thoughts and simply let her hands and feet find what they could.

She half-closed her eyes, working by feel, and was startled when she found herself already at the first big branch.

She scrambled up a few more, and then tried to see Irwin and the camp.

Irwin was still invisible, but she knew the tree he was in, and she thought she could detect an unnatural shiver of the leaves every now and then.

She couldn't see the whole camp, but she could see a slice of it.

While she'd been climbing, the buzzing had gotten louder, and then cut off. It started up again, and she caught sight of a large drone rising up above the treeline, an empty sling beneath it. It banked and flew off to the north east.

Looked like the Caruso had just had a delivery of supplies.

She wondered if that had been pre-planned, because the Caruson surely didn't have their own satellite in the atmosphere. Unless the warship that had shot down the runner was circling Veltos and they were using it for comms.

She caught sight of a Caruson soldier moving around, but he disappeared, and then the sounds of conversation drift over on the breeze. She could smell the aroma of meat cooking over an open fire, and guessed they were roasting the kuyer they'd shot.

The sun had almost completely set, and the sky was ablaze with color. The Caruson were obviously done for the day.

She shuffled on her branch, looking for a better view of the camp. If Ben was a prisoner there, she couldn't see any sign of him.

Eventually, Irwin dropped out of the tree, landing in a crouch and then moving off in the deep shadows.

She waited for the sound of him to fade, and then swung down herself, moving carefully away from the camp.

Should she try to follow Irwin?

Ben was probably looking for her by now, but it was surely worth trying to see where Irwin was going.

She was aware of how much time had passed since he'd

climbed down and disappeared. Picking up his trail would be difficult.

She tried anyway, heading in the direction she'd seen him go, and wondering what he was up to.

Things were a little more complicated than she'd thought on that front. He was obviously not as tightly aligned with the Caruso as it first appeared.

When she reached the gentle slope up to her camp, she had already admitted defeat. She had no idea which way Irwin had gone, and perhaps her heart wasn't in it, anyway.

She wanted to see if Ben was waiting for her.

She was crouched up against a tree, watching the low hill in front of her for any sign of movement before she risked breaking cover, when the back of her neck prickled with nerves, and she checked over her shoulder.

There was someone close by.

Every part of her sang in a symphony of anticipation and nerves. The invaders in her blood making her skin hyper-sensitive and heightening her every sense.

She caught the faintest sound of fabric on bark, someone moving around the trunk toward her, and whatever had taken up residence inside her took control.

She dropped to a crouch and swung out a leg. A soft curse alerted something deep in her brain, so when Ben fell, grabbing her as he went down and rolling to pin her under him, she let him do it.

They stared at each other in the near darkness.

She said nothing, and while she could see he had things to say, he kept his mouth in a thin, tight line as well.

She was so pleased to see him, though, she lifted up a little and kissed him.

It shocked him into stillness, and leeched some of the mad out of him.

"Quick question," she whispered. "Do you want to go back to the camp I set up, or do you want to try to follow Irwin?" She nibbled on her lower lip. "In fairness, I think he's long gone by now, so we might not pick up his trail."

His expression told her he was thrown by her question.

"Which way did he go?"

"West."

He though about it, seemingly content to be crushing her into the leaves of the forest floor.

She didn't mind it, either.

"It's almost dark. Let's regroup and we can make some decisions."

She nodded, and he lifted off her, pulled her up after him when she raised her hand.

For a moment she was flush up against his body and his arms came around her in a single, tight squeeze, then he stepped back, his arms dropping to his sides.

She turned and took the lead up the hill, unable to keep a smile from her lips.

CHAPTER 17

BEN DUCKED through the curtain of leaves after Tally, and found himself cocooned in a space that was high enough for him to stand without bending.

It was absolutely dark, and he flicked on his light for long enough to see the sleeping mats set up side by side, the sleeping bags laid out.

Tally glanced at him, then went down on her knees and crawled to the bags, quickly pulling out a selection of instant food, and once she was settled, sitting cross-legged, with two plates in her hand, he switched off the light and crawled next to her.

"You were gone a long time." She said it quietly.

"I made a trail for them to follow. I could see they were searching for us, and I didn't want them to decide to work their way back toward the supply station."

"No." Her tone was stark. "Soo and Lenny can only go so fast with the hover. We need to lead them away."

He accepted that, but he didn't like the thought of Tally being with him while he did it. They'd be putting themselves in the Caruson's sights if they deliberately gave them a trail to follow.

"Did you see the drone?" she asked after a while.

He swallowed the last of what was a really delicious mousse down the wrong way. She had to have been right next to the Caruson camp to have seen the drone. He hadn't realized that.

"How did you see it?" He said it around a cough.

"I was waiting for you here, and I heard someone walking past."

He went cold. "Irwin?"

"Yes. I didn't know what he was doing. He seemed to be moving so cautiously. I'm not sure if he was scared of bumping into us, or the Caruson. He knew where their camp was, though, and he snuck up to it, watched them for about half an hour and then left."

"He was watching them?" Ben hadn't been expecting that.

"I'm sure he's not on our side, but it looks like he's wary of the Caruson, as well."

Ben thought about it. There were plenty of reasons for Irwin's behavior, none of which made him someone to trust, but it was interesting that he was keeping his distance from the Caruson and checking up on them.

"What's the plan?" Tally slid down on her mat, and he could just make out her pillowing her hands behind her head.

"We need to get some sleep, then when it gets light enough, we need to extend the false trail I started yesterday, then disappear into the forest and head to Rainerville."

"They're going to be looking for us."

He tidied up his plate and then lay down beside her. "Yes."

"And Irwin is definitely not working for our side?"

He shook his head. "No. I researched him before I arrived at the supply station. There is no way he's part of some VSC surveillance I somehow wasn't told about." He thought about the detailed file he'd read on the trail guide. "I can only assume he was gotten to on Situ."

"What could they possibly be offering him?"

Ben couldn't imagine. "Now that the breakaways are back in the Verdant String fold, wealth can't be the reason. But he is originally from Faldine, although his parents moved away before the war started. The only thing I can think of is he resents the Verdant String because of the war."

Tally was quiet, and the sound of her breathing soothed him.

He wrapped his arm around her shoulders and drew her close, and she turned into him with a murmur of contentment, and rested a hand on his chest.

"So, what was that move you pulled when I tried to get next to you without making any noise?" He'd seen her a moment before she'd crouched behind the tree, and he'd had to suppress the shock and fear he'd had at her being so close to the Caruso camp. He'd had the clear sense she was either hiding from someone or following them. He hadn't wanted to do anything to give away her position, but when he'd tried to slide in next to her, she'd taken him by surprise.

"That wasn't me." The words were spoken without inflection, and he could feel she was tense now, no longer warm and pliant against him.

"Your little helpers?" he asked.

"Helpers?" She thought about it for a beat. "I suppose they are, in a way. If you'd been someone else, that move might have saved me."

"Tell me what it's like." He couldn't understand how something could take full control of her. It didn't seem possible.

"It feels like tingles in my blood." She paused. "I find myself reacting without conscious thought, as if I was taking a breath, or sneezing. It has some way to override my brain and take the controls."

He felt a surge of protectiveness.

"But always in your favor?"

She hesitated. "Yes. Always in my favor. They're more symbiotic than parasitical. Their wellbeing is tied to my own."

"I'm glad about that." Ben rubbed his thumb over the curve of her shoulder.

She huffed out a breath. "I'd rather they not be there at all. The hardest part is sometimes I can't remember what I was like before the ghost ship. I'm fighting myself so much, I feel like I blunder from situation to situation, never really in control."

He didn't know how to respond to that, so he simply rubbed her arm with his hand, and after a while, he felt her relax into sleep.

As he felt the tug of sleep himself, he set a silent alarm on his wrist unit to alert him if a big enough heat signature was detected. They would have warning if someone snuck up on them, which meant he didn't need to be hyper vigilant. If he wanted to he could lean over, wake her with a kiss, and explore the attraction that had flared between them from the moment they met.

He held himself back, though.

He'd already decided he was not the man she needed. She'd be whisked off of Veltos the moment help arrived, whereas he'd be cleaning up this mess for months.

The thought of her being taken off was both reassuring and depressing. He wanted her safe. He'd have to get her out of this alive, first, though.

And he intended to do so. No matter who got in his way.

HE CAME AWAKE FULLY, even though Tally made almost no sound as she rose up and stepped over him.

He sat up, and she looked back, but it was too dark for him to see any expression on her face.

After a momentary pause, she simply stepped through the

curtain of foliage and disappeared, and he surged to his feet and followed her.

They were both barefoot.

Now he was outside, he could see better in the moonlight, and she was walking delicately, picking her way across the forest floor in a way that said she was avoiding sharp objects.

"Tally."

His whisper received no response, and he felt a chill wash through him as he came to the conclusion that Tally wasn't in control right now.

But what would have woken her little invaders?

She stopped between two trees, her head cocked to one side, and at last he heard what must have roused her.

The sound of a hover in the distance.

She jumped, catching onto the lowest branch of the tree she stood under, and swinging up with an ease that staggered him. She disappeared and he jogged to where she had been standing and jumped himself.

He pulled himself up with considerably less grace, and began to climb.

She was lighter than he was, and when he couldn't go any higher, he looked up and saw her two branches above him, standing with one hand resting on the trunk, looking out toward the Caruson camp.

He said nothing, afraid asking her a question might jerk her back to herself while she was balancing on a slender branch.

The sound of the hover seemed to pass very close to them and then moved off into the distance. When it cut off altogether, Tally waited another moment or two before she jumped down onto the branch below her, and then swung down to his.

She made a hand signal to him that he'd never seen before, but which he thought meant talk at the bottom, and he followed her back down.

"What did you see?" he asked, as soon as he'd dropped to the ground.

She was sitting at the foot of the tree, leaning back against the trunk and he saw her shoulders tense.

He sat down beside her, close enough for their shoulders to rub.

"What did I do?" she asked, and there was so much pain in her voice he lifted her up and set her across his lap and held her close.

"Your little friends heard a hover coming, so they took you outside and got you to climb a tree to see what was going on."

She drew in a shaky breath. "That sounds pretty mild."

He stroked her hair. "Do you remember what you saw? I couldn't get high enough up on the tree, but it looked like you had a pretty good view."

She shook her head. "I don't remember any of it."

"The hover never came that close to us, it was to the north, so I'm guessing it was making for the Caruson camp."

He had barely finished speaking when they heard the hover again, coming back the other way.

Neither of them moved.

"It didn't stay long," Ben said when it was long gone. "Dropping more soldiers off, maybe?"

"I don't feel any sense of worry when you talk about it, so I guess whatever is in me doesn't feel threatened by it."

She sounded so miserable when she said it, he tugged at her hair gently to distract her, and when she tipped up her face to frown at him, he bent his head and kissed her.

She opened her mouth beneath his, and kissed him back, and in an instant, what started as a gentle exploration ramped up into a hungry devouring.

He slid his hands up her sides, cupping her breasts and groaning at the feel of them under his palms.

She levered herself up on his shoulders, moving her legs so

she straddled him, so they were flush against each other, and then she rocked against him.

He lifted her thin shirt over her head, clamping his lips on a hard nipple and she arched back.

He had decided not to go down this path, and he forced himself to pull back, his breathing hard.

Tally looked at him through half-closed eyes. "What is it?"

"I don't know what my plans are, but I know I'll be stuck on Veltos for months, especially now." He could barely remember the reasons he'd given himself.

"I don't know if I'll even live to the end of the week." Her eyes gleamed in the moonlight. "I'm prepared to take a chance if you are."

He'd dropped his hands, but now he ran them up her naked back and pulled her a little closer. "You'll live to the end of the week, I'll make sure of it."

She sent him a smile, but there was something sad behind it. "It's not up to you, but for what it's worth, I have your back, too. There is nothing I'd like more right now than to make love to you, to feel good for a change."

Ben cupped her face in his hands. "Are you sure?"

She nodded, turned her head and kissed his palm.

The touch of her lips went straight to his cock, and he lifted her more fully onto him. "As it happens, there's nothing I'd like more, either."

CHAPTER 18

THEY WOKE and packed up their things in darkness, their bodies and hands brushing each other as they moved around, in a way that made Tally's blood sing, and made her regret they didn't have more time.

Dawn was still half an hour off when they left the cozy nest she'd made, working their way silently toward the Caruson camp.

The hover last night had definitely been headed in that direction, and neither of them wanted to move on without trying to see what the hover had brought with it, if anything.

Tally followed Ben, and he headed without hesitation to the east of the camp, where the ground rose in a series of small hills.

It was difficult going in the dark, but the sunlight had just started to filter through the branches when he stopped under a massive tree and pointed up.

The air was crisp, and the birds were calling in what seemed to be a morning frenzy.

As she found handholds and pulled herself up, she realized she felt good, despite the early hour and the danger they were in.

She was carrying her pack, unwilling to leave it on the ground, and when she looked down, she saw Ben had done the same. The weight pulled against her shoulders, but she didn't care, almost relishing the feeling.

Her body sang with contentment. Something inside her had relaxed. Ben hadn't held back as they'd explored each other's bodies last night, hadn't treated her like the alien thing she'd started to see herself as. He'd made love to her like she was the old Tally, and it had given her back a measure of calm.

No matter how fleeting their time together might end up being, she was deeply grateful for that.

She had been moving steadily upward, but a small sound from below made her stop.

She looked back, saw Ben wasn't able to climb as high as her. He was too heavy. He was looking up at her, his pack beside him.

She quickly descended, handed him her own pack, took the enhanced visor he handed her, and climbed again.

She found the Caruson camp easily. The hills put them above it, and the tree added a further boost.

It looked empty, though, the fire was smoking but looked like it had been doused, and there were no soldiers that she could see.

She worked her way back down, stepped in close to him, mainly because there wasn't very much space to begin with, but also because it felt nice.

His arm held her against him.

"Can't see anyone. They've already left for the day."

"Packed up?" he murmured in surprise.

She shook her head. "There's a few tents still up, but the fire's out and there's no one there."

He stood quietly, thinking about it, when Tally heard the crunch of dead leaves under boots below them.

She lifted a finger to his lips and pointed down, and after a moment, he seemed to hear it too.

There was no sound other than footsteps, and they stood, arms wrapped around each other on the narrow branch, absolutely still.

Then someone cursed.

Tally thought it was a curse, anyway. It was explosive and sounded annoyed, but it could just be how the Caruson spoke.

Someone else responded, and finally, there seemed to be a little group just out of sight through the thick, green branches, conversing with each other.

They kept their voices low, and it was hard to hear distinct words because of the rumble.

When she heard footsteps again, they came directly toward her and Ben, and she tightened her hold on him.

Someone spat something harsh and choppy almost directly below them, and then the sound of footsteps faded.

"Did you understand any of that?" She breathed it into his ear, as soft as a sigh.

"A little." He took the vision enhancers from her and angled them downward and to the south. "They caught our heat signatures earlier, and followed us. They don't know where we've gone, but they've made a decision to do something, and I didn't get what, but they've split up."

He went very still.

"What is it?"

"Two soldiers, headed back toward the cliff. I think they've decided to send a few back toward the supply station, just in case."

"We can't let them do that." There was no way she'd let Soo and Lenny fend for themselves while also trying to keep Frangi alive.

"No." Ben's instant agreement was comforting. "But we need to do two things. Stop the two going back, and give the others a reasonable belief that we're headed for Rainerville, or they'll give up and follow behind the two that are going south."

He was right.

"So which of us goes which way?" She didn't want to separate, but she couldn't see a way around it. They had two things to do, in opposite directions.

"I'll stop the two that went after Soo and Lenny. You keep making a trail, and lay low. Or high, rather. They didn't see us earlier on their heat sensors because they aren't pointing them up. They're too heavy to climb these trees, so they forget that we aren't."

She thought about it.

When he said he was going to stop them, he meant kill them. There was no prison to lock them up in, no other way to keep their friends safe. And of the two of them, she had to admit he was the one with the training for this. She drew in a shaky breath. "Okay. How do we meet up again?"

"I'll find you as soon as I've dealt with those two. Sleep in the trees at night if you can. And don't get caught."

She sensed the urgency in him, and knew every moment he spent talking to her increased the distance between him and the two soldiers. "I won't. Go."

He bent his head and kissed her. Lifted his mouth and then went in for a second, softer touch of his lips. "Please be careful. Don't take chances. I'll be as fast as I can."

She nodded, because anything else would take up time he didn't have, and then he crouched, pulled on his pack, and swung down.

Moments later, she heard the crunch of his boots as he jumped from the bottom branch, and then nothing but the wind in the leaves.

THERE WERE A LOT OF FOOTPRINTS.

Tally looked at them, and for the first time felt a dip in her confidence.

She'd enjoyed following the Caruso while they thought they were following her, but eventually they'd realized the trail Ben had set up the day before had disappeared, and that they were simply blundering around.

That's when they'd started hunting for her in earnest.

She'd managed to get ahead, create a trail, and then double back a few times. This time something felt off.

Things went very silent all of a sudden, the sound of the birds cut off, and a feeling of being in danger washed over her. Buzzing filled her ears, and every hair stood to attention.

She felt her control slip, and she forced herself to relax, to embrace it. There was just a hint of movement out of the corner of her eye, and she ran left, jumping down a small gully and then zigzagging through the trees.

She heard the hum of laz fire, had the sense of the air behind her brightening, and then heard the shouts.

She sprinted, and had the strangest sense of being a little outside her body, understanding she had never run so fast, never been so agile.

The gully had dropped into a fairly flat space, thick with trees, and then she heard the sound of rushing water, and, impossibly, found a little more speed.

She reached the stream moments later, and threw herself in, but instead of letting the water take her, she grabbed a rock that stuck out into the water from the opposite bank, and ducked behind it, crouching low so only her eyes and ears were above water.

Interesting choice, she thought to her little invaders.

Not obvious, and that might be a good thing.

Above where she crouched was a big fountain bush, like the one they'd slept under last night, and while it didn't extend over the water, it threw a lot of shade over the small cove between the rock and the bank.

The Caruso burst from the trees.

She couldn't see them, but she could hear them, their sentences a little breathless.

They were big and slow, she realized. They didn't move as fast as she could. The realization gave her a little comfort.

Another thing that helped bolster her was the icy water. It would definitely make it harder for them to find her with heat sensors.

Suddenly they were in the stream, splashing through the water, and she went very still.

One soldier passed her, and then a second, and she thought two more crossed the stream almost directly on the other side of her rock and climbed the bank, and then she heard them above her, following the stream on the other side.

That meant, if two had gone to follow Soo and Lenny, that the hover last night had brought soldiers to replace the three she and Ben had killed yesterday.

She waited until the sound of them faded, and then rose up, and quietly walked back the way she'd come. She needed to keep going toward Rainerville, and the way the Caruso were headed was south of her route.

She shivered as she went, but her clothes were VSC military issue and they dried quickly.

She made a point of snapping a few branches and choosing the rockiest paths, and even then doubled back and made more footprints, to make it look like she wasn't alone.

She'd been going for a few hours when she heard them again-- they were behind her, and she guessed they had picked up her trail.

She let herself feel a quick shiver of fear, and then she hitched her pack higher on her shoulders, and started to run.

CHAPTER 19

IT HAD TAKEN him over three hours, but Ben had finally caught up to the Caruso.

They had led him back to the clearing near the crashed runner, and he crouched down behind a tree and watched the soldiers examine the spot where the Caruson soldier he'd killed yesterday had died.

They were looking at the ground, and he realized they were examining the dark spot where Frangi had bled.

A wave of fury washed over him, and his grip tightened on the massive laz in his hands.

At least the dead soldier had been taken away, although his smashed up hover still listed drunkenly against the tree it had hit.

The hover that had disturbed them last night had probably been sent to fetch the bodies, as well as drop off more troops.

There had been at least five yesterday, and he guessed more likely six--one to guard the camp.

Three were dead, but there seemed to be six again. They'd received reinforcements.

The two soldiers straightened up and began searching the

outside edge of the clearing, looking for evidence of which way they'd gone.

One found his and Tally's deliberate path, but the other called out and pointed in the direction Soo and Lenny had gone.

They stood together for a moment, conferring, and more importantly, making themselves an easy target.

Ben raised the laz, leaning against the tree and angling his body, and opened fire.

He aimed high, going for their heads, because they were wearing anti-laz layers.

He saw one go down, but the other had dived to the side, and came up shooting.

Ben ducked, used the thick undergrowth to shield himself, and ran to the next tree.

He crouched beneath it for a moment, then started to climb.

He only went up a short way, but the tree was thick with foliage and it would be hard for him to be seen from below.

The Caruson shot wildly for a minute, the laz fire even striking the bottom of the tree Ben was in, causing shivers to run through its trunk.

The fire cut off, and the silence stretched out.

The Caruson was waiting for him to break cover, or start shooting again.

He could just see the body of the Caruson he'd hit through the leaves. The Verdant String version of a laz had a kill setting, but they didn't score flesh, they fatally disrupted the body's synapses. This Caruson version he'd stolen acted more like a real laser, burning as it went.

It was a shock to see the blood. Had been a shock when Frangi had been hit, too.

After a long break, long enough for the birds to start singing again, he heard the sound of footsteps. The Caruson walked toward him, stopping every few steps, and then moving again.

Ben tilted the laz downward. He would have to be very certain of his aim, or he'd be an easy target in the tree.

He could hear the rustle of leaves, but the foliage that was keeping him hidden also blocked the Caruson completely from his view.

He listened carefully, and when he thought the soldier had passed him, he moved down to the lowest branch and then dropped to the ground.

He landed almost on top of his quarry, who had his back to the tree.

Ben didn't know who was more surprised, him or the soldier, who turned, shock stamped on his face.

Ben got off a shot, but it went wide, and the Caruson reacted with a body slam, rather than using his laz.

He was massive, with the typically heavy frame and thick skin of the Caruso. Ben landed, winded, beneath him, levering the laz in his hands between them.

The Caruson grunted, lifting his hands to try to choke Ben, but Ben managed to get some momentum, and rocked them both to the left, and got the barrel of the laz under the Caruson's chin.

He fumbled for the charge release, while the Caruson got in a blow with his elbow to the side of Ben's head.

Dazed, Ben's grip on the laz slipped for a moment, but he got hold of it again and rammed it upward into the Caruson's chin a second time, with enough force to tilt the soldier's head back.

He slapped his hand down the barrel blindly, and eventually hit the charge release, but the Caruson wrenched his head to the side in time and the laz fire only scored along his jaw and ear.

With a shout of pain the soldier rolled away, and Ben rolled in the opposite direction, head still ringing from the elbow blow.

He stumbled to his feet, swaying where he stood, and tried to focus. The Caruson was doing the same.

Laz fire lit the gloom of the forest, and Ben threw himself back onto the ground, but not before he felt the pain of a hit along his side.

He landed, panting, and watched the Caruson shake his head as if to clear it and then stagger forward.

Ben couldn't lift himself up, and he could barely aim, but Tally was out there, all alone, and so he forced himself to wait, making himself look limp as he sprawled among the leaves, and then when the Caruson was almost on him, he fired.

He got the soldier's legs, and while it didn't break through his laz protection, it did knock him to the ground.

Ben struggled up onto his knees, and shot again, this time getting him in the chest.

The soldier grunted, but it wasn't enough to stop him lifting his own laz.

Ben's was already up, though, and he finally hit the Caruson in the face.

He realized after a while he didn't know how long he'd been kneeling, swaying like a tree in a strong breeze, and decided to just lie down for a bit, until he felt better.

———

HE BLINKED awake to the sound of sniffing.

Confused, he cracked his eyes open a little, and a long snout came into view. He felt the touch of a nose against his chest.

He sat up, and with a squeal, a long, sleek animal jumped, twisted in midair, and dashed off.

Ben swallowed back the nausea that rose up in him, and carefully removed the straps of his pack, wincing at the shooting pain from his side.

He should never have let himself sleep.

He forced himself to look down, saw with relief his uniform had helped minimize the damage, but he hadn't been wearing an anti-laz layer, and there was a deep score from his hip up to his waist. It was smaller than he thought from the feel of it.

He pulled out a heal-aid, slapped it on over the injury and almost sighed with relief as the cool gel started to numb the pain.

He managed to get to his knees, and glanced over at the Caruson. There was a big black beetle walking over the soldier's face, and Ben turned away.

When he'd drunk some water, eaten something, and swallowed a few anti-infection tablets, he got to his feet and forced himself to take a look at the other Caruson he'd shot.

He'd gotten lucky, he saw.

He'd taken him out with a shot through the eye.

With more effort that he thought possible, he hitched his pack on the shoulder on his good side and started to walk.

The sun was almost completely down, and he'd have to find a safe place to spend the night, but it wouldn't be near the bodies of his enemies.

He had known there was a chance Tally would have to spend the night on her own, and every time he thought of her alone, with Caruson soldiers trailing her, a spike of fear and dread gripped him.

He's secured Frangi, Soo and Lenny's safety for the moment, but he hoped he hadn't done it at the expense of Tally's.

CHAPTER 20

TALLY TIED HERSELF TO A TREE, as high up as she could go and still find a branch wide enough.

She put the thin heat-saver blanket over her first, and tied the rope just above her knees and under her breasts.

When she'd drunk almost a full bottle of water and eaten a few bars from her pack, which she'd hung on the branch above her, she lay back and listened to the sound of the forest sighing around her.

It was hard to work out where sounds were coming from with the hiss of the wind, and eventually she gave up and let herself drift off, only jerking awake when something small and furry landed in her hair and then dashed off with a squeak.

She must have fallen asleep because when she woke a second time, it was to the smell of a wood fire and the touch of the sun on her face.

She lay still, listening, and eventually thought she could hear the faint murmur of voices.

She carefully untied the rope, rolling her blanket as she went, and then stood up, stretching and carefully taking out more water and something to eat from her pack.

She'd kept close to the Trail, unsure of the way to Rainerville without it, and she'd crossed over from one side of it to the other as she created her false trail.

She was hoping Ben would find her more easily if she stuck to the Trail, as well.

She felt a sick, throat-clutching fear every time she thought of him.

He could easily have been unable to find her before nightfall last night, especially if the Caruso he followed were moving quickly, but he wasn't just following them, he intended to kill them.

That meant some kind of engagement, and anything could happen with that.

She tried to put that aside, digging into her pack for her vision enhancers and then easing out along the branch.

She went as far as she could, but the foliage was still so thick, she couldn't see what was happening below.

She listened instead, and felt her little invaders rise up into her consciousness, although she knew they'd been on some kind of guard all night.

The smoke was coming from the Trail, which was directly to the east, she realized, and the murmurs she could hear were Caruson voices.

Her pursuers had made camp a little way from her position.

She ran through her options. If she left now, she'd be ahead of them, able to continue making a false trail, but they'd be really close behind.

Or she could wait it out, let them leave, and follow behind them for a bit.

She eased back down the branch, hooked her pack on her back, still undecided.

Someone coughed, the sound really close, and she froze. There was a crash and suddenly a flock of tiny birds fluttered up from a tree nearby, tweeting madly.

She heard a hacking sound, frowned as she tried to work out what it was, and the birds settled back down on the branches of her own tree.

She held herself absolutely still, her gaze landing on the tiny brown feathered balls of fluff lining the branches all around her. They had a thin white line high across their chest and a yellow breast. Their eyes were ringed in white, giving the appearance they were all eyeing her with surprise. They were so small, they could have hopped through the space made if she put her thumb and forefinger together, and there were hundreds of them.

The cough came again, and then a rock crashed through the leaves. She bent to the side and it sailed just above her shoulder. The birds rose up in full-throated panic and then disappeared.

She felt panicked herself, pressing up hard against the trunk and standing in a sweat of fear. Was this an elaborate ploy to get her out of the tree?

The hacking sound came again, and her jaw dropped open. Was that *laughter*?

She felt a little dizzy at the effort her little helpers were going to, trying to work out how many Caruson were down below.

Another voice called out, even to her ears sounding more harsh and angry than the Caruson language usually did.

The soldier who'd thrown the stone answered back, with that hacking sound again, and was yelled at a little more.

Tally slid down, her knees close to her chest, and tried to look through the gaps in the foliage.

She caught a glimpse of a soldier adjusting his pants, and another lifting a clenched fist in anger.

He'd been answering a call of nature, and he'd thought it funny to disturb the birds.

She agreed with the soldier admonishing him.

They were supposed to be tracking her, and whoever else they thought was with her, not drawing attention to their location.

The VSC taught their soldiers better than that.

Finally, the choppy, harsh voices moved away from her, and eventually faded.

She forced herself to relax against the trunk, to sip more water and nibble at a fruit bar while she waited for them to pack up and go.

Her heartbeat slowed and she took a deep, cleansing breath, and closed her eyes. After ten minutes, she heard nothing but silence.

She made her way down, and after listening for a while to make sure she wasn't going to run straight into her pursuers, she set off parallel to the Trail.

She kept her pace slow but steady. She could go faster, but she wasn't going to lie to herself. She was hoping to give Ben more of an opportunity to catch her up.

She thought of the little helpers, and shook her head.

Well, not lie to herself more than necessary.

SHE HAD HEARD the Caruso on and off all day.

They were ahead of her, and she'd kept it that way until late afternoon, stopping when she needed to, slowing right down at other times.

But by the time the sun was low on the horizon, she'd left them far behind her.

Before she'd headed further from the Trail, she'd watched them from up a tree as they'd shot three animals that looked similar to kuyer but were smaller and a little plumper.

They'd dragged them to a nearby clearing and got a fire going.

Their pace through the day had been slow but relentless, and she could see they were struggling with their rations. She guessed the Caruso didn't have a lot of on-planet excursions and weren't well equipped for it, even though they'd tried to take Garmen and Lassa from the VSC just a few months ago.

They had failed.

Now it looked like they had set their sights on Veltos, and this must be their first genuine planet-side foray.

She had wondered through the day if they were going to turn back because of the lack of a trail, but they had forged ahead, and because they were headed in the direction of Rainerville, she guessed they had decided that must be her destination.

The camp near the crash site was just a temporary staging post, anyway, and she supposed there wasn't much to turn back for.

The path she was cutting through the trees began to slope upward, and she paused, thinking things through.

While she stood, trying to get the lay of the land, she heard the faint sound of running water, and turned in that direction.

Her own drinking water was running low, and it had been niggling at her since she'd taken a break at midday.

She knew her agitation about it was due to her time on the ghost ship, and she'd tried to keep the rising sense of panic down. She knew the sense of relief that swept through her at the sound of water tumbling over rocks was extreme, but she couldn't help herself.

She wanted to immerse herself in that water.

She could feel the prick under her skin as her little helpers stirred, and her senses heightened as she approached the stream. She wondered if it was because they picked up on something, or simply the latent, hindbrain instinct of every creature approaching water.

When she finally found it, it was a bitter disappointment.

It ran fast and clear, but it was so shallow, when she crouched down and rested her palm in it, the water barely covered the back of her hand.

She rose up and started following it, and when the bushes on either side became too thick, she stepped into the water, walking down the middle.

The flow picked up pace as it ran downhill, and then suddenly she was standing on a rocky ledge and the water fell down into a wide pool.

It shimmered in the dusk light, and she had to shield her eyes against the glare to see where the stream continued on, in a slow, lazy twist off to the north.

She took off her boots and socks, balancing on the slippery rocks at the top of the waterfall, then jumped down into the pool below. The water was cool and came just over her knees.

Her feet stirred up sediment, but as she got close to the left bank, the mud turned to rock and she had to step more carefully.

She set her pack and boots on some rocks and took out her standard issue wash gel and walked back in, heading for where the water left the pool and carried on its shallow, twisty way.

She took off her clothes piece by piece, washing each one before she peeled off the next, setting them on a rock before she rubbed gel over herself. She crouched down to rinse out her hair but before she could lift out of the water, her skin prickled and she felt the fizz of her little helpers in her blood.

She turned, still low in the water, and found Irwin standing by her pack, looking at her.

There was a strange beat of silence between them.

"Thank goodness you're all right." Irwin took a step forward, then hesitated as water lapped his boots.

"How about you turn around and let me dress, and we can catch up." She kept her voice neutral.

"Sure." He threw up his hands as if she'd accused him of something.

She kept her eyes on his back as she wrung out her clothes and pulled them on, grumpy because she'd planned to put on the clean, dry set in her pack, but there was no way she was walking up to him naked.

"So, where's everyone else?" Irwin asked, turning as she splashed back to where he stood.

"Where were you?" she countered. "We couldn't find you."

"Well." He rubbed the back of his head. "I woke early, wanted to check back on the crash site and no one else was up. I thought I'd be there and back before anyone knew I was gone."

He glanced at her and when she said nothing, he shrugged.

"I heard the laz fire, and ran back, but when I got to the clearing, everything and everyone was gone. I've been hunting for you all ever since."

It was as good a story as any, she guessed.

"Why did you want to go back to the crash site?"

He shot her another look. "Does it matter?"

She stared at him and he huffed.

"Fine. I forgot I needed to log the exact location for my report when I got back. I needed to get the coordinates."

"I'm sure Ben had them."

Irwin sneered. "*I* have to get them. Not get them secondhand from one of my group."

She lifted her brows.

His hand shot out, gripped her arm. "You don't seem very friendly, Tally."

"I don't feel very friendly, *Irwin*. You have a habit of disappearing, and coincidently, one of the times was when we were attacked. You're quite the group leader." She jerked her shoulder, dislodging his grip, and walked past him to sit on the rock next to her pack and boots.

Her little helpers were dancing away, urging her to run, which made breathing difficult, but she forced herself to look calm.

"Shit." He rubbed his hand over his head again. "Look, I screwed up, and I know it. I'll be lucky to still have the trail guide job at the end of this. But I swear I've been looking for you all ever since. And where the hell is everyone? You can't be the only one left."

She looked over at him, eyes narrowed.

"You're actually wondering how much to tell me, aren't you?" He gave an incredulous laugh. "Listen, I know someone was injured, I saw the blood. I know this is a fuck up. But please don't say you're the only survivor."

"Frangi's dead." Her voice wobbled a little, because it actually could be true, if her friend had taken a turn for the worse. She heaved in a breath. "Soo was seriously injured, Lenny less so." Tally pulled out a pair of dry socks and spread the wet ones next to her on the rock. "Lenny opted to stay with Soo, to hunker down with the supplies and try to keep her alive, hopefully heal himself. They found a place not far from the crash site. Ben and I were going to go for help at Rainerville, but we came under attack, got separated." She lifted her shoulders. "I'm hoping we find each other again."

He tipped back his head. "You sure he's still alive?"

She jerked her head up at that. "No. No I'm not sure. As I said, we came under attack." She knew she sounded a little too angry, but strangely, it seemed to settle Irwin down.

"Sorry. I'm obviously worried about . . . everyone. I'm sick that Frangi's dead. I hope Ben finds us."

She pulled on a boot to avoid looking at him when he said 'us'. Because as far as she was concerned, there was no 'us'. She didn't trust him enough to spend time with him.

"Were you planning on setting up camp here?" He looked around.

She rested her chin on a raised knee. "What are your supplies like?"

She knew he'd taken a lot from her stores. That was a huge mark against him.

He set his pack on the ground. "Just what was in the spare pack. I grabbed it rather than wake everyone by pulling down my tent." He kept a straight face as he lied.

She wondered if she should confront him. Let him know she knew he had stolen from her stores.

Decided against it.

She'd already played this wrong. Shown her distrust.

She mentally shrugged. It was what it was.

"What have you been living on, then?"

"I had enough energy bars to keep me going. Still have a few left. I know the forest pretty well, so I've supplemented with some berries and a few rodents."

"Okay, well, I'll find a tree nearby, and leave you to set up your tent. I'll see you in the morning." She smiled as she pulled on the other boot and stood.

"Where's your tent?" He frowned.

"In Ben's pack." She kept her tone light. She picked up her water bottle with its built-in filter and crouched beside the pool to fill it.

"You can share my--"

"No." She slid the bottle back into her pack. "See you tomorrow."

"Wait. Tally? You're going to sleep in a tree?"

She was already halfway across the small clearing and she looked over her shoulder and gave a nod. She didn't even want to tell him that much, but she understood she had to give him something, or he wouldn't leave her alone.

"I'll see you in the morning, Irwin."

She ducked through the thick bushes, and then put on a burst of speed, trusting her little helpers to keep her as quiet as possible.

Ten seconds in, she threw herself behind a tree and crouched down, pressing herself up tight against the trunk.

Irwin exploded from the trees, his head pivoting left and right. "Tally! Damn it!"

He ran on, and as soon as he was out of sight, she rose up and walked upstream, carefully picking her way to where the waterfall fell over the rocks, and crossing over.

She made her way back to the pool on the other side, found a tree two or three back from the bank with a view across the water to where Irwin had left his pack, and climbed it.

There was no way she was letting him out of her sight, and she hoped he wouldn't work out she'd crossed back over the river.

When she found a branch where she could watch the small clearing beside the water if she walked almost to the end of it, she settled in, securing her pack to the branch above again, and taking out one of her precious meal packs.

She ate it slowly, enjoying every bite, and then sipped some water, making a face at the brackish taste of it, which even the filter couldn't seem to get rid of.

Still, it was water, and there was plenty of it.

She heard Irwin come back to his pack about half an hour later, heard him muttering to himself, although she couldn't quite catch what he was saying.

She should feel a sense of achievement, getting away from him, doubling back, but his question about Ben was still reverberating in her head, forcing her to confront her fear that he *was* dead.

She thought about the logistics of going back, of retracing her steps and seeing if she could find him.

It was so tempting.

But that would still leave Soo, Lenny and Frangi in the lurch, and she had no guarantee of finding him.

They could pass each other in the dense forest and never know it.

At least, if he was alive, he knew she was headed for Rainerville. It made sense to continue on, and when she got to her destination . . . She smothered a sigh. She'd just have to figure it out when she got there.

She hadn't asked Irwin how far they were from Rainerville, but she didn't trust him to tell her the truth, anyway.

Before she tied herself up to sleep, she walked to the end of her branch.

Irwin was gone.

She huffed out a silent breath. So much for keeping watch on him.

She felt a rising sense of unease, as well.

She wanted to know where he was. Instead, he was sneaking through the forest.

She walked back to the trunk, sat down, and then faced the fact that there was nothing she could do about it. She wasn't going to run around in the dark looking for him.

She strapped herself to the branch, so wide she could fit one and a half of herself on it, and got herself comfortable.

She had dozed off, was almost asleep, when she heard the sound of footsteps.

She had come to recognize the Caruso's walk in the last few days, and fear caught her by the throat and her heart leapt like a wild cat in her chest. The little helpers seemed to come awake in a wave from her head to her toes, and her skin was suddenly freezing, icy to the touch, while her belly felt like it was on fire. Her heart rate sped up even more as she tried to make sense of what was happening.

Her little helpers kept her absolutely still.

The soldier moved past her, and she heard him stumble, and then a short, sharp curse.

He was answered by someone in a low, furious voice, and even though she didn't know a word of Caruson, she guessed he had been told to shut up.

Both of them must have entered the pool, because she heard the splash of water.

As suddenly as it turned icy, she felt her skin warm, felt the shift of temperature until it had evened out again.

She had to fight back a cough.

They had shielded her, she realized with an audible gasp. Her little helpers had shielded her.

They'd hidden her from the Caruson's heat sensor.

There had been a thick branch between her and the Caruson below, but she would bet that by concentrating the heat of her body in her core, if she had shown up at all, it would have been as something a lot smaller than a grown woman. She would have looked like an animal, crouched in the tree.

Her heartbeat leveled out, too, and she accepted there was no safer place for her than right where she was. They had cleared this part of the forest.

This was the first time they had hunted through the night. It was also the first time she'd seen Irwin, and given him an idea of where she was going to sleep.

She didn't think it was a coincidence.

But she'd have to deal with it, with him, in the morning.

She closed her eyes and began to inhale and exhale, using the slow, calming breathing techniques she'd used as a teenager in her exercise class before she joined the military.

It seemed ... familiar to her little helpers.

She could sense them sliding into it without a murmur, and she wondered if they had lived inside someone else, someone who had died on that ghost ship.

The thought hitched her breathing higher, interrupting the rhythm. It was both fascinating and horrifying.

Her mind skipped back to the moment she'd met Ben, when she'd been a little thrown by the sharp, handsome lines of his face, the intelligence in his eyes, and how she'd held out her hand and grasped Ben's to shake it in a greeting that she'd never used--never seen--before.

Was that the greeting once used by the people on the ghost ship?

She felt a stab of guilt because she would never tell that to the scientists combing the ghost ship right now. There was no way to verify it, but she had a strong feeling she was right.

There were no more sounds from the Caruso, and she let herself relax again, drifting off in a light sleep as she clung to the hope that Ben would finally catch up.

CHAPTER 21

BEN HAD SPENT the night sleeping in short, two hour snatches, alternating with moving through the forest.

He had the special forces training to sleep anywhere, taking what he could get and using it to his advantage.

His side still ached, but it was healing well, the skin knitting back with the help of growth gel and anti-infection dressings.

The cool anesthetic properties of the dressing helped him move more easily, and his only real worry had been the concussion.

But there was medication for that, too, and he knew it had probably been a mild concussion anyway.

He also hadn't come into contact with a single Caruson.

He'd found their camps, the ash of their fire pits blowing around, and the bones of whatever deer they'd caught and roasted scattered around.

It meant they were following Tally, which should have been a good thing. She was leading them away from Soo, Lenny and Frangi, and that had been the plan.

But it didn't feel good to him.

The only thing that calmed him was that they obviously hadn't caught her.

Yet.

After he'd come across the last camp yesterday afternoon, he'd pushed himself, following their trail, rather than waste time looking for Tally's, and he'd fallen into the two hours of sleep, three hours of walking rhythm he'd used on countless operations before.

He covered a lot of ground, but when he stepped into the new Caruson camp, he stumbled to a halt in disbelief.

This one didn't have a cold fire pit and a half-hearted attempt at clean-up.

This one had live coals still glowing in the pit, and dark, tunnel-like tents set under the trees, almost invisible until you were close enough to trip over them.

He shook himself out of his shock and eased back, a step at a time, until he was behind a tree, and then crouched down.

His wrist unit told him the only heat source was the fire, which meant they were not here, but they would be back.

He was considering his options when he heard the sound of voices, and slipped back a little further.

Four soldiers walked into the clearing. They spoke to each other in snappy, quick sentences, and then turned in, crawling into their tents and settling down.

Ben waited long enough for the first snores to drift across to him, and then climbed the biggest tree he could find that would give him a view of the camp the next morning.

He could keep going, looking for Tally, but in the dark, with no idea where she was hiding, it was a losing proposition. They had obviously gone out themselves to look for her, and come back empty-handed.

It wasn't much, but he'd take it.

TALLY SLID DOWN THE TREE, jumping lightly to the ground, and then worked her way along the thick line of bushes to the place where the stream left the pool. She used the dark, enclosed space of a fountain bush as a place to get out of her clothes, and walked into the water in her underwear.

She washed herself first this time, relishing her second bath in two days, then did a quick cleaning job on the trousers and shirt she'd had to put on wet the day before.

She went back into her makeshift changing room, and emerged in her spare clothes, her trousers rolled up to her knees as she washed the underwear she'd bathed in, and then set everything out on a rock that had full sun to dry while she crouched to get more water.

She was standing in the water, loving the swirl of the cool current over her bare feet, sipping from her bottle and eating a breakfast bar, when Irwin burst from the trees on the other side.

Her instinct was to reach down to the side pocket in her pants to pull out her laz, but something told her it would be a mistake to let him know she had it.

"You're all right!" He skidded to a halt just before he stepped into the water.

"As are you." She watched him with cool eyes. She was grateful, suddenly, for the lies she'd told him about Soo, Frangi and Lenny.

If he'd passed them on to the Caruso, they would hopefully decide it wasn't worth their while to send anyone else after the two who'd already gone looking for them.

And she could only hope Ben had managed to stop those two.

"Where did you go last night? I was looking for you." His surprise and delight at finding her had morphed quickly into resentment.

"I told you where I was going. To find a tree to sleep in."

"You had to have heard me calling for you." He crossed his arms over his chest.

She shrugged. "I heard you, but I'd already told you what I was doing, and I wasn't interested in more conversation about it."

He opened his mouth to respond, and then must have thought better of what he was going to say. "Look, I get you're low on trust, but your hostility isn't helping here." Irwin's eyes narrowed. "We'd be better off working together, and you have to know it."

She wondered if he'd practiced that slightly disappointed, slightly condescending tone and look.

She wanted to snort in amusement, instead she raised an eyebrow, then forced herself to relax and sigh.

Ugh! She hated even pretending to play nice with this asshole.

"Do you blame me?" she asked him--a hedge, because she couldn't bring herself to actually tell him all was forgiven.

One thing she knew, she'd have to get away from him at the first opportunity, even if it meant using her laz.

She guessed he'd gone to fetch the Caruso last night, had told them that he'd found her, and had given them an idea of where to look for her. She didn't think he had a way to communicate with them other than speaking to them face to face, but she didn't want to take the chance of him having some kind of Caruson comms unit.

He was watching her carefully, suspicious perhaps of her sudden change of heart.

"What?" She raised both hands and her voice. "You don't think you've screwed up at every point in this fun-filled excursion?"

"This isn't my fault," he answered, suddenly aggrieved. "*I* didn't shoot the runner down."

"No, but you're the one who knows the terrain, you're the one who's theoretically in charge of the whole thing, and you've been suspiciously missing in action."

He looked away from her, shaking his head. "That's true, but I've said sorry and I'm not going to keep apologizing. What's done is done. We've got to cooperate now, move forward and get out of this alive."

"You're right." She didn't have to feign the grudging tone of her voice.

She turned and walked to the rock to check on her clothes. They were almost dry, and she climbed onto it and crouched down, gripping the rock with her bare toes, and enjoying being barefoot for a little while longer. She sipped the last of her water and finished her bar, her eyes never leaving Irwin.

"You nearly ready to go?" he asked her.

She nodded. "Just another ten minutes, then my clothes should be dry."

He seemed to relax, and she tried to keep her face blank, but she was disturbed by how happy he seemed that she'd agreed to go with him.

No doubt in her mind. Irwin was going to sell her out.

CHAPTER 22

BEN HEARD the low murmur of voices over the sound of running water.

They were indistinct, but he thought one was higher, more melodious than the other, and he started into a shuffling run, pushing through the pain in his side.

He found the stream, a shallow, rocky thing that curved between the trees, and he used it as a pathway, stumbling a few times, and slipping more than once on the slick moss growing on the stones.

He came to a halt at the top of a bridge of rocks, and stood for a moment, caught in the tug of water flowing over his boots into a big pool below.

Across the glitter of light on water, at the far end of the pool, Tally was crouched on a rock beside some of her clothes, obviously laid out to dry, a water bottle in one hand.

She was talking to Irwin, who stood on the side of the stream, arms crossed over his chest, his pack on his back.

Something about the scene struck a wrong note, and he

jumped off the low waterfall. When he landed with a splash in the pool, their conversation came to an abrupt halt.

"Ben!" Irwin's arms dropped to his side, surprise and shock on his face.

Tally said nothing, but she rose up on her rock and he had to shade his eyes to see her over the sparkle on the water.

She waited for him, silent, as he walked toward her, although her expression was like pure energy to him; sustaining, uplifting.

When he reached her, she slid her arms around his neck, standing slightly taller than him thanks to the rock she was on, and bent her head to kiss him.

He vaguely heard Irwin's sound of surprise as he pulled her closer and let that energy engulf him.

She was alive.

Unharmed.

She pulled back, smoothing his hair with gentle fingers. "Where are you hurt?" she asked him quietly.

"Right side," he told her, murmuring it against her lips. "Irwin?"

"The little helpers and I are in agreement." She bent her head so her lips were touching his ear. "Do not trust."

"You finished?" Irwin's voice rose high enough to cut through their little bubble.

Tally dropped her arms, stepped back, and scooped up her clothes. Without a word of explanation, she jumped down into the water.

He noticed now she was barefoot and her trousers were rolled up to her knees.

He didn't take his eyes off her as she climbed the bank and then disappeared behind the hanging branches of a fountain bush.

"What is with her?" Irwin asked. "She--?" He made a twirling gesture over his head. "Not that there's any shame in that, after what she went through."

Ben forced himself to look over at the Trail guide. "What are you talking about, Irwin?"

"Her." Irwin flapped his hand at the bush. "She's hostile, she just goes off when she feels like it. I was hunting for her for over an hour last night. She had to have heard me calling for her, and she didn't answer."

"Why were you hunting her?" Ben asked. He kept his tone excruciatingly polite.

"*For* her. Hunting *for* her, Ben." Irwin's mouth snapped shut. His eyes narrowed. "What's with you two? I thought you didn't know each other."

"We didn't until this trip. We know each other now."

"Sure." Irwin rolled his eyes. "Won't be the first hook-up on the Trail, won't be the last." He gave a little sneer. "Never known one to last longer than two weeks, and sometimes, not even that long, which makes things a little uncomfortable toward the end of the trip."

Ben laughed. "What's your point?"

Irwin blinked. "Just, use your head, man. What is with that woman?"

Tally emerged from behind the bush, boots on, pack on her back. "I'll cross at the waterfall so I don't get my socks wet."

She disappeared again, and he kept watch until she appeared above them, then gracefully jumped the rocks to the other side.

He waded across the pool and stepped onto the bank just as she pushed through the bushes beside him.

He held out a hand to her and she took it, letting him help her through the thick foliage to stand beside him in the open space.

Irwin was fighting his own way through the bushes on the other side, but gave up and jumped into the water, wading around toward them, as if nervous to let them out if his sight.

"What's going on?" Ben's voice was low.

"We need to lose him. Soon as we can."

She'd just finished speaking when Irwin pulled himself up the bank.

"You injured?" he asked, looking Ben over.

"A little. Nothing serious." Ben couldn't remember if he'd favored his side, but he guessed Irwin would have noticed if he had.

"What happened?"

"I already told you." Tally's voice was icy. "Ben and I came under attack."

Irwin looked at her, then at Ben, in an exaggerated, *see what I mean* way.

"I don't know what more to tell you." Ben shrugged. "As Tally says, we came under fire. We got separated, obviously, and because I was injured, it took me a while to catch up."

She had been covering for him, Ben realized. Making it seem like they'd both been headed in the same direction.

She obviously didn't trust Irwin with the information that Ben had gone back to stop the soldiers following Soo and Lenny's trail.

"You just left him?" Irwin shot the question at Tally.

She shot him a cold smile and then turned her back on him to look up at Ben. "We need to go. There were Caruson hunting through here last night, and I'd rather not be around if they try again."

She adjusted her pack and started walking, and before he followed her, Ben looked down at the ground.

There were footprints all around, and he realized for the first time some of them were the big, heavy boot prints of the Caruson.

He didn't like having Irwin at his back, but for now, he forged ahead, following Tally.

As she said, they'd have to ditch him as soon as possible.

CHAPTER 23

THEY STOPPED WALKING when the sun was directly above them.

Tally had initially taken the lead, but Irwin had stomped irritably ahead when she'd led them unwittingly into a dense section of bush that had stopped their progress.

Even though she hadn't meant to, she was glad she had. It forced Irwin in front, where she could keep an eye on him.

She didn't think he had a way to contact the Caruso remotely, but she couldn't be sure, and as long as she was watching, he wouldn't dare do it.

She wondered what his move would have been if Ben hadn't found them.

Would he have incapacitated her? Led her straight into the Caruson's arms?

Or just killed her.

It depended on what the Caruso's plans were. And she didn't know enough to work that out.

It was irrelevant anyway. Ben *had* found them, and he would be a lot harder to kill. Especially when it was two against one.

Thinking of Ben, and possible death, she turned back, her gaze going to his side. He worried her.

He had a look on his face that was stoic, and she knew he must be at least uncomfortable, if not in actual pain.

She'd been in his arms, close enough to smell the crisp astringent scent of anti-inflammatory gel from the heal-aids. She knew it had an anesthetic effect. She only hoped their current pace wasn't doing him harm.

To help, she played the unfit invalid, rather than putting it on Ben. She made them stop more often than she needed to, and when they passed the entrance to a deep gorge, she got out of the midday sun and sat down on a cool rock that must live in perpetual shade with a sigh of relief.

She could hear water falling deep inside the narrow slash in the cliff. Trees grew thickly, like they did everywhere in this forest, but here they clung to the sides of the gorge, growing straight out of the rock in some places.

"Is that water close enough to go refill the bottles?" she asked Irwin.

He had moved closer to the entrance to the gorge, standing between the rock walls that soared nearly a full thou above them.

"I don't know. I've never been in before." He looked over at her, and seemed to be the most relaxed and friendly he'd been since they'd set off. "I've only seen this from the Trail, which is that way." He pointed east.

"We need to get water." She shifted on her rock, trying to hide the agitation that was rising in her at the thought of not filling up the bottles, and then finding nothing further along.

"The river cuts through about two thou from here." Irwin turned away to look back into the gorge. "It's probably not worth the time to go looking in there."

Anything could happen in two thou. They could walk straight into the Caruso.

Tally forced herself to take a deep breath. Her little helpers stirred, and she closed her eyes and counted down from ten.

When she opened her eyes again, she saw Ben was watching her. She winced internally, hoping that wasn't pity on his face.

"I'll just be a few minutes," she said decisively. "Give me your bottles."

Ben grinned as he stood. "I'll come along. I want to see what's down there, too."

Irwin scowled. "So do I, but this isn't a jaunt."

"No, but we need the water, and I'm enjoying being cool." Ben shrugged into his pack.

Tally touched his hand as she brushed past him, a light flutter of her fingers against his.

"It sounds really close," she said, and then started in.

Ben was right behind her, and while Irwin muttered and moaned, and pulled on his pack, they had a few moments of time to themselves for the first time that day.

"We need to ditch him." Tally said it as Ben crowded so close his chest pressed against the back of her pack as she stopped to squeeze through a narrow opening in the rocks.

"Agreed, but not yet. The longer he's with us, the more chance he'll slip up and reveal something. I want to know what he knows, and what the hell he's doing."

Tally shook her head. "Not worth the risk. He'll give away our position as soon as he can."

"He doesn't have a comms unit to talk to them, though. I've made two dives into his pack on the various stops, and I couldn't find anything."

Tally squeezed through and then looked back at him, eyes wide. "I didn't see you do that."

Ben winked. "I put my pack next to his. They're identical. It looked like I was going through my own stuff." He had more difficulty getting through than she did, and had to take his pack off and hand it to her before he could make it.

"As long as he's in sight, he can't tell them where we are. I agree that we ditch him tonight, though."

He stopped talking suddenly, looking over her shoulder, and Tally turned, and knew her mouth had dropped open.

They were in what seemed like a room with no ceiling, the walls soaring high overhead, completely covered in thick foliage and colorful flowers that hung down on long, delicate stalks.

Water fell straight down from the wall at the far end of the space, and then tumbled and frothed in white sprays into the stream that rushed toward them, and then disappeared straight into the ground.

"Wow." Irwin's voice jerked her out of her reverie. "Okay, this was worth a look."

Tally hopped down the steep rocks until she was standing where the stream disappeared into an almost perfectly circular hole in the rocky floor.

"Someone on the science team will be happy to hear about this." Irwin pointed his small screen up at the sky and took an image.

"I'm almost sorry to tell anyone else about it," Tally said. But she was a military science officer herself and she knew something like this was a treasure beyond price.

No VSC science officer or scientist would do anything to damage it. Especially as Veltos was supposed to be left alone, and had only become cleared for visitation because the rebels in the Faldine War had defied the Do Not Disturb order and done whatever damage the DND was supposed to prevent.

Not that more damage couldn't be done, but the VSC had decided it would be easier to prevent malicious interference if they were keeping a close eye.

Obviously not close enough, with the Caruso running around.

She glanced at Ben. Realized she was being unfair.

Ben had been here for a month, trying to find the Caruso.

He came to stand beside her, shoulder to shoulder, and they stood in the cool shadows, with the scent of exotic blooms and the color of a hundred different flowers around them. If they had been alone, they would have been in each other's arms. She knew that for a fact.

Instead, she tipped her head to briefly rest against his shoulder, and then crouched down, filling her two bottles, then lifting her hand to take his to fill.

When she rose up, he put an arm around her and pulled her close, kissed her forehead.

She looked up, saw Irwin was watching them, a tight look on his face, and then he jumped down to join them, jostling for position in the small space.

Giving him a look of disgust, she retreated up the rocks and sat, drinking in the view while Irwin filled his bottles.

She had felt in control, almost her old self, but suddenly, as she sat and looked over the scene, her heart rate picked up, and the hair on her arms and at the back of her neck stood on end. She couldn't suppress the shiver that ran through her.

She noticed for the first time that her arm was bleeding.

She tried to think of when it could have happened, guessed it might have been when she was climbing down the rocks.

"We have to go." She rose up, caught Ben's eye. "Now."

Ben looked up at her. "What is it?"

"I don't know." The sense of something very wrong constricted her throat, and her answer came out rough. "But . . . now, Ben. Now."

He pulled himself up beside her. "Okay."

His eyes asked questions, but he wouldn't ask them in front of Irwin. She was so relieved she had to fight back tears.

She loved this man, she realized. He accepted her more than she even accepted herself.

She started to clamber up the rocks, her nails tearing in her haste, and the only thing that soothed her nerves was the fact that Ben was right behind her.

She hated this. Hated that she couldn't work out what her own senses were telling her.

What was the threat? Where?

The little helpers didn't, or couldn't, answer.

"What the--?" Irwin's plaintive call rose up behind them, and he scrambled after them.

He didn't want to lose them, and maybe he thought they were trying to ditch him.

She almost laughed at the irony that his own bad faith reasons for keeping them in sight was going to save his ass.

Because the little helpers wouldn't react like this unless they were sure it was something bad.

Tally reached the narrow gap out of the gorge, a band of sweat prickling between her shoulder blades despite the cool of the gorge, and she stopped to take Ben's pack so he could go first.

He shook his head, and not willing to argue and waste time, although the panic had subsided a lot now they were away from the stream, she slipped through and then took the pack he extended out to her.

Irwin struggled through a minute later, red-faced, eyes bulging. "What the fuck, Tally?"

She had no answer.

And wouldn't answer to him even if she did.

She could feel a wash of embarrassment and anger rising up, so she shrugged, turned away, and started walking in the direction they'd been headed all day.

"Listen, man." Irwin didn't even try to lower his voice as he spoke to Ben. "I won't tell you your business, but you sure you want to be involved in that level of crazy?"

"She sensed a threat, she acted, what's crazy about that?" Ben asked him. "It's not like we were planning to hang around there much longer anyway."

"There was no threat." Irwin practically spat the words.

"I don't know," Ben's voice was calm, in huge contrast to Irwin's. "I'm willing to bet there's a chance something in that gorge meant us harm."

Tally's ears pricked up even more to see what Irwin's response would be to that, but suddenly, he had nothing to say.

CHAPTER 24

BEN LOWERED himself beside Tally and knew he was in trouble.

They were going to have to ditch Irwin tonight, and he was done.

His side ached, a hot, raw pain that throbbed in time with his heartbeat, and he knew he should have applied more gel during the day, but he hadn't wanted Irwin to see how injured he was.

They'd finally found a camp for the night, just moments before the sun set, and they'd risked a fire. He checked with his wrist unit that there weren't any Caruso nearby, and as soon as he was comfortable, Tally handed him a meal.

Irwin watched them from the other side of the fire, and there was a moment of awkwardness as he waited for her to give him one as well.

Ben remembered her disgust when she'd realized Irwin had taken some of her food supplies, and just managed to hide his smile behind a bite of something rich and spicy, and absolutely delicious.

There was no way Tally was giving Irwin any of their rations after that sin.

After a long beat, when he realized she wasn't going to hand him anything, Irwin pulled his pack closer and pulled out a meal of his own.

It wasn't the bars or high-energy fare that was standard in VSC military packs, it was one of Tally's requisitioned meals.

Ben wondered if Tally would call him on it, but she ignored him, focusing on her own food.

She hadn't said much since her panic in the gorge.

She had been sweating with fear, and it had made him afraid, as well. There had been something in that gorge. Or her little helpers thought there was. So far as he could see, they hadn't steered her wrong yet.

He glanced at her arm, and then did a double-take, because the long cut that had been there after the gorge was almost completely healed.

She'd used some of the gel from the medkit, but even so, that was an incredible level of healing.

He remembered her saying the little helpers had kept her alive on the ghost ship, and he wondered whether they were responsible for her disappearing wound, as well.

She folded the container her meal had come in, and fed it to the fire, her arms around her legs, her chin resting on her knees.

She looked deep in thought.

"Let's go to bed." She turned to look at him as she rose. "I'll put the tent up."

Ben knew she was initiating it so he wouldn't have to put the tent up himself. And he honestly didn't think he could.

Which made things very, very bad.

He couldn't be this weak.

He kept eating, taking his time to give him even more of an excuse not to stand up yet.

"Well," Irwin sneered at him. "She's decisive."

"True." Ben smiled. "I've always liked a partner who knows

what they want and isn't afraid to get it." He stretched out his legs. "Although, in this case, I think she's just tired."

"Whatever, man." Irwin threw his own container into the fire. "I better set up as well."

"Irwin." Ben kept his voice low.

"What?"

"What's with the attitude?"

Irwin struggled for a moment. Ben saw the dislike for him, and the even deeper dislike for Tally cross the guide's face before it went wooden. "I didn't like the way she ditched me last night, is all. She led me a merry chase."

"She's just keeping herself safe. And you gave up any right to being annoyed at people disappearing when you ditched *us*."

Irwin gripped the hair at the back of his head, blew out a breath. "I won't apologize for that again. And at least I did apologize. She does nothing but blow me off."

Ben stared at him, and with a huff, Irwin turned and grabbed his pack, dragging it to a flat space on the opposite side of the fire to where Tally was setting up their tent.

He wanted to be far from them, and Ben didn't think it was to give himself some space.

Irwin was going to try to sneak off. Because if he couldn't contact the Caruso using comms, he had to be going out to find them.

Ben wondered how he knew where to go.

He guessed they'd find out soon enough.

"He didn't go anywhere." Tally scrubbed at her hair with the scentless cleansing gel from her pack, and Ben tried to keep his attention on what she was saying, rather than the slick gleam of her naked body.

"Ben!" She snapped her fingers in seeming irritation, but her eyes were laughing.

He took that as an invitation, set his boots aside and pulled off his shirt gingerly, then jumped into the stream.

Pulling off the shirt had been a mistake, he realized, because Tally didn't look amused anymore. She looked worried.

"You dressed it last night in the tent," he reminded her. "And it's a lot better now."

He wasn't lying. It was a lot better. The careful application of more gel, the expert dressing she'd done last night, and a good night's rest, had made a huge difference. The score of laz fire on his side was no longer red and puffy, and the throbbing had stopped.

It still hurt to move too quickly, but after how he'd felt yesterday, it was an amazing recovery.

Tally bit her lip and crouched down in front of him, and he wanted to whimper a little.

"Sorry," she said, and he realized he might actually have whimpered. "I didn't think I'd touched you."

"That might be the problem."

She tilted her head up, eyes narrowed. Then they widened as she figured out what he meant. Her gaze went lower to the bulge in the front of his pants. "You're right," she said, rising up and stepping back. "You're a lot better."

He looked at her, absolutely naked, the late morning sun gleaming off the golden brown of her skin, and breathed in. "I think I'm a little lightheaded, suddenly."

She stared at him for a moment, then stepped in close, lips twitching. She put her arms around him, and kissed his neck. "Oh, poor baby. Are you not coping well with Irwin cramping our style?"

"No, I'm not." He nuzzled her forehead and let his hands trail down the wet, smooth skin of her back and cup the delectable cheeks of her butt. He groaned again and pulled her harder against him. Damn it, he really wasn't.

They had gone into the tent last night, and Tally had dressed his wound, and then they'd taken turns to be on watch, waiting for Irwin to sneak off and find the Caruso.

They hadn't even gotten naked.

Irwin was getting higher and higher on Ben's shit list.

"Well," she stepped back, "he's still cramping it, because no way are we doing anything with him lurking around. You know he only left us alone when we found the stream and I insisted on cleaning up because he couldn't exactly strip down with us. He'll be close by, though." She kept her voice so soft, even he could barely hear her over the sound of running water.

She was right.

He watched her for another minute, as she rinsed off the last of the lather in her hair, and then quickly washed himself, pulling off his pants and scrubbing down in quick, efficient movements.

Not even the cold water had much of an effect on his erection, though.

When he looked up, he saw Tally was dressed, sitting down to put on her socks and boots, but her gaze was on him.

He hardened a little more and her tongue came out and touched the corner of her mouth.

"You done?" Irwin's call was followed by the sound of him moving through the bushes.

Ben closed his eyes, hands shaking, and only just opened them in time to catch the clean shirt Tally tossed him. He was holding it in front of himself, more to hide the wound on his side than anything else, when Irwin stepped onto the river bank.

The guide's hair was wet, and he had his pack on his back.

"Give me a minute and I'll be right with you." Ben didn't know what was in his eyes, but Irwin stopped dead.

Tally stood, boots now on, and turned away, walking back to the small clearing where they'd left their packs.

Irwin hesitated, obviously torn as to whether he should follow her or not.

"This isn't a skin bar," Ben said, and his voice was lower and rougher than usual.

Irwin shot him a venomous look before following Tally.

Ben knew she'd headed back so Irwin would follow her, to give him a chance to dress in privacy. But he didn't like her having to be the bait.

He was off his game. He was a captain in Arkhoran Special Forces, and he kept getting distracted.

He was okay with that, because Tally was the best distraction he'd ever come across, but not when it put her in danger, or in a bad situation.

And leaving her alone with Irwin automatically made it a bad situation.

He moved his ass, pulling on his clothes and boots as fast as he could, scooping up the massive Caruson laz he'd hidden under a bush, and half-jogging to the clearing.

Tally was crouched by her pack, and he saw her hand was hovering near the pocket on the side of her pants were she kept the laz he'd given her.

Irwin stood over her, everything about his posture screaming intimidation.

"Problem?" Ben asked.

"No." Irwin stepped back, turned his back to them both to pull on his pack.

Ben exchanged a glance with Tally, trying to work out what had happened, but her face was tight and blank.

Irwin turned to face them again. "Let's go. This stop has already slowed us down a lot."

"Yes, all of fifteen minutes." Ben kept his tone light. "We need to shift direction, though. I think we're heading too far north. We'll miss Rainerville if we keep on this route."

Irwin shook his head. "You don't know the lay of the land like I do."

Ben forced down a surge of fury, and then breathed out, lifted his shoulders. "You want to go your own way, that's fine."

Beside him, he sensed Tally relax a little.

"You saying you're going to go against the route I suggest, even though I've worked as a guide on this planet for three years?"

"That's what I'm saying," Ben agreed.

"You're wrong."

"No. I've been tracking the sky every night, and taking an image of it, and my wrist unit data tells me we're going to miss Rainerville if we keep on this route."

Irwin looked down, fists clenched. "Except we're not traveling in a straight line. You're going to hit another gorge if you adjust further south east now. Sure, maybe we'll overshoot a little, but we'll take a sharp southerly turn after the gorge. I know what I'm talking about."

He sounded so sincere. So disappointed.

Ben knew he was lying.

"I must have missed that when I studied the Trail from the space imagery before I got here." He kept his voice soft.

Something crossed Irwin's face. Chagrin. Temper.

Before he could speak, though, Tally's hand shot out, gripped Ben's arm, and then she threw herself forward, pulling him with her.

Laz fire lit the late morning air, and Irwin gave a cry of pain.

Ben flipped himself onto his stomach and fired back, and he almost heard the shocked surprise as the Caruso came under fire with their own weapon. They did not return fire.

Whatever this was, he could see from Irwin's expression that he was as surprised by the attack as they were. He hadn't had a chance to let the Caruso know where they were and that Ben was carrying a Caruson laz.

He used the lull, jumping up into a crouch, and gesturing to Tally to run back to the river.

She hesitated, waiting for him, and in that moment, when she put him ahead of her own safety, he stumbled into love, and had to force his feet to move.

"Tally." He hissed the words, and she flashed him an annoyed look and ran, bending low, and he followed close on her heels.

He just had time to glance back, to see Irwin lying down, hand to his shoulder, groaning, and then the bushes closed behind him and he concentrated on catching up to Tally through the burning pain in his side.

CHAPTER 25

"THIS IS A BAD IDEA." Tally knew it was the third time she'd voiced this opinion, but damn it, it was a bad idea.

Ben shot her a look that said everything without saying a word.

She sighed, nodded, and stopped talking, following him through the thick ferns that grew in the narrow channel that must in wetter seasons be a shallow tributary of the river. She stopped under the tree they'd been making their way toward, and Ben boosted her up to the lowest branch.

Irwin was still shouting.

Not in pain, not even in fear. In anger.

As soon as they'd heard him, Ben had changed course from running away from where they'd been shot, to moving back toward it, and while Tally admitted it would be good to know what the deal with Irwin and the Caruso was, it would be better, in her opinion, to take the opportunity to head toward Rainerville while the Caruso and Irwin were busy shouting at each other.

She pulled herself higher, and then stilled when she caught a glimpse of a Caruson soldier walking, laz up, in the direction they'd run.

He disappeared.

Irwin was still shouting, and Ben joined her and then walked on silent feet as far along as he could get on the branch.

There was a low grumble of sound, a Caruson talking, and Irwin's diatribe came to a sudden end.

"I'll shout if I want to. You fucking shot me." Irwin's voice rose in tenor.

The Caruson rumbled something in response.

"I had her. Right here. And then you destroyed over a day's worth of earning their trust." He sounded like he was getting to his feet, and she heard him swear in a steady stream.

The Caruson's voice rose a little, too. She could hear him for the first time, and she realized he was speaking the common Verdant String vernacular.

It sounded like the Caruson didn't care much for Irwin and his outrage. And they were very unhappy Ben had acquired a Caruson laz. One of the soldiers had been injured.

Tally smiled.

"Fine. I thought you wanted the woman from the ghost ship. I put myself on the line to find her, bring her to you, and this is my thanks? Fuck you. The deal is off."

Whatever was said after that was impossible to hear.

The three remaining Caruson started moving, she could hear the whip of branches as they pushed through to the river, following the path left by the first soldier. One was hunched over, some kind of dressing on his chest. He wasn't carrying a laz.

Ben turned to look at her, signaled that she get moving.

She started down, swinging on the lowest branch and landing with a skitter of leaves.

Her skin prickled, and she turned her head. Saw Irwin standing staring at her, mouth open, his pack on the ground at his feet, and a medkit in his hands.

He was as surprised to see her as she was to see him.

She thought, just for a moment, he would let them go.

The Caruso had shot him, and he was obviously unhappy with them.

"They're here!" He picked up his open pack and ran backward, away from her, his gaze on Ben, hanging by one hand from the branch, the big laz in his other. "Here!"

He disappeared into the bushes, and Ben dropped down beside her.

He didn't need to say it, she ran the moment his feet touched the ground, heading deeper into the forest.

She could hear Ben's steady stride behind her, but she could also hear the crash of bodies slamming into low branches, and the thump of heavy boots.

The sound of water, strangely loud, made her veer left, and when she was faced with what looked like impenetrable bush, she shrugged off her pack and went down on her stomach, crawling under the low branches to come out the other side into a shallow pool, murky and slick with moss. The loud sound of splashing came from where water fell over the low rock embedded in the slope above.

She shoved her pack against the bush on the other side of the tiny pool, and grabbed Ben's as he pushed it ahead of himself, stacking it beside hers.

When he pulled himself through, he shook his head. "There's not enough room."

She ignored him, pulling him to the waterfall. The water was icy and brackish; it smelled of the earth, and she guessed it had bubbled up from an underground spring.

The pool was deeper in the middle, just enough to cover one of them, and she shoved Ben toward it.

"We won't both fit." He breathed it into her ear.

"It's okay."

He had gone down on his knees, and she made a motion for

him to lie down. He did it, reluctantly, and she wedged herself in with him. "Trust me. And get your head under the waterfall."

He shot her a look, but complied, wriggling back until the water fell onto his chest and his head and neck were behind the curtain of water. She lay against his side, putting as much of her body under the water as she could.

Her arms tightened around his waist. Her lips were already trembling with the cold, the icy water leeching all the warmth from her, but enough of her body was above the waterline to be dangerous.

If they used their heat sensor, they'd see her.

Except, if things went the same way they had the night before, in the tree, they wouldn't.

She couldn't hear the soldiers, now she was right beside the waterfall, until one of them gave a shout that rose above the sound of the water.

She was expecting the sensation this time but knowing it was coming didn't help. The fire started up in her belly, and she had to bite back a gasp of pain.

Her fingers were blue, she noticed, with her head resting on Ben's chest. She didn't feel like she was attached to her body anymore. Ben's arm tightened around her waist, tight and hard as a band. Her feet and legs felt as if they couldn't move. As if every muscle had seized.

She lay, sick and nauseous, until Ben sat up. He held her against him.

"They're gone." Ben tipped her back, an arm supporting her, his eyes wide with worry.

The little helpers were already spreading the heat back through her, and she twisted to the side and heaved up whatever she'd eaten that day.

Ben pulled back the thick rope of her hair, which had fallen forward, and eased his hold a little.

"What the hell was that?" His words were low and quiet, but she could hear the fear and anger in them.

"Little . . ." She retched again. Blew out a breath. "Little helpers."

"What did they do?"

He had seemed to be okay with her little helpers up until now. But he suddenly didn't seem so calm about them.

"Redistributed my heat." She swallowed down a cough, trying to keep as quiet as she could. "Changed my heat profile."

Ben was absolutely silent, his hands gentle as he stroked back her hair, and then he gave a shiver.

He must be as cold as she was. She fell forward on her hands and knees, awkwardly, because the rocks beneath the water weren't even, and then she pushed herself to her feet.

She was lightheaded for a moment, and suddenly Ben was there, arms around her, holding her tight against him.

She burrowed her hands under his shirt and pressed them against his back.

"Close call, but they've cleared this area now. They'll move on." He murmured the words, stroking down her back, and she realized they were taking heat from each other. She sighed, and put her head against his shoulder.

"One good thing in all this mess," she whispered.

"What?" His lips touched her ear.

"I met you."

"That's true." He pressed a kiss to her forehead. "You lucky thing."

She flashed him a grin.

His legs were longer than hers, and he could brace a foot on the other side of the tiny pond and reach her pack. He handed it to her, took up his own, and then pointed to a way out that didn't require squirming under a bush.

They were both soaked through, but it was only midday, so they'd dry off.

She heard the sound of shots fired, and froze, her gaze leaping to Ben's.

He shrugged. "Maybe kuyer?"

Maybe.

"Sounded like they wanted me alive before. Because Irwin told them I was the one in the ghost ship."

That's what the little traitor had been up to. Sticking close so he could hand her over.

Ben nodded, and she could see the cold, hard edge in his eyes when she mentioned it.

"If they're shooting indiscriminately, then maybe they're done with that." Or maybe they didn't care, either way.

They were most likely tired of running around after her and Ben in the forest.

That suited her fine. She didn't think she'd like being taken for questioning about the ghost ship.

The thought set her little helpers buzzing beneath her skin.

They didn't like the sound of it, either.

CHAPTER 26

THE CARUSO HAD PULLED BACK from actively hunting them over a day ago.

Ben had noticed the difference in the way they moved. They'd finally realized there was no sense wasting their time and energy when everyone knew which way they were going.

The soldiers kept to the Trail, killing a kuyer or two each afternoon and settling in for a rowdy time around the fire.

They were enjoying themselves.

He could hear it in their tone.

They obviously loved the meat and the fires and were making the most of it.

He and Tally, on the other hand, still had Irwin to worry about.

Their former guide was injured, but Ben didn't think he'd have turned around and gone back to the supply station.

There was nothing for him there.

He was limping along behind them, and that forced them to be constantly alert. They couldn't have the same warm fires and comforts at night as the Caruso.

They'd slept in the trees two nights in a row.

Even if Irwin had called off his deal with the Caruson, he was spiteful enough to let them know where Ben and Tally were if he happened to find them.

And the Caruson would most certainly stir themselves to go after them if they had a specific direction.

The only positive was their pace was good. They had managed to cover a lot of ground, and in the last half day he had the feeling they had left the Caruson soldiers behind them.

He heard the river long before they came to it.

He'd never seen it himself, but had read the reports. It was wide and swift, and rimmed with rocks, which explained the sound of pounding water.

Tally picked up the pace as they wove through the trees toward it and he put out a hand, touching her shoulder to stop her for a moment.

"What?" She breathed the word.

"Careful when we reach the river. It's deep and fast, and unlike the forest, there are predators in it that will attack us."

Her eyes widened. "What predators?"

"A long lizard, but with sharp teeth. The biologists at Rainerville have called it a legava. It grows about as long as a person, and its jaws are massive. There's venom on its teeth. It puts its prey into some kind of coma."

She shivered. "Should we even head there, then?"

He'd already weighed it up. "If there's a way to use the river to get to Rainerville faster, it's worth having a quick look." He couldn't help running a finger along her cheekbone.

It was sharper than it had been when they started the Trail. She was ruthless with their supplies, making sure they had enough to keep going for another week. And they had been in constant motion, keeping up a pace even his special forces team would have found taxing.

She smiled at him, sliding a hand around to grip his neck and going up on her toes to kiss him lightly.

There hadn't been much time for shows of affection these last two days, and he closed his eyes to savor the brush of her lips on his.

The snap of a branch behind them had him going absolutely still.

He eased back, and saw Tally was staring behind him, eyes scanning the woods.

She shook her head. "Can't see anything." She mouthed it without speaking.

Carefully, she slid behind the closest tree, and he followed her, moving in fluid, easy increments.

Jerky or too-fast movements always attracted attention.

He slid his pack off and eased it to the ground, then peered around the trunk.

A Caruso soldier walked through the trees to his left, laz held in front of him, two handed, at an angle, from shoulder to waist.

He looked less ragged than the four who'd been following them. Ben realized with surprise he'd come to recognize those four, and this soldier was new.

He waited until the Caruson had disappeared among the trees.

"They found us?" Tally asked. "I thought we'd pulled ahead."

He shook his head. "It was a guard. We're closer to Rainerville than I thought. Either that, or their patrol radius is much bigger than I estimated."

That gave him pause.

"What are they protecting?" Tally asked.

"That," he turned and pulled on his pack, "is what we're here to find out."

THEY HAD CUT out a large loop of the Trail when they'd made for the crash site, and then headed north east, but Tally was still amazed they were already so close to Rainerville that they'd encountered Caruson patrols.

She moved through the trees silently, and felt the tingle of her little helpers under her skin. She felt every touch of the light breeze blowing through the forest, heard every rustle of the leaves.

It was muted enough that she could concentrate, but every now and then the feeling spiked, so intense she imagined the top of her head blowing off.

She stepped out onto the river bank.

She'd never seen a river so wide with her own eyes.

The part of Raxia she came from was cool and dry, and it would be almost impossible to live there without the technology that created water enough for their needs.

Standing beside the roaring, tumbling beast as it snaked through the landscape, she understood the need some Verdant String citizens had for travel; for exploring the planets of the String and visiting each one. She had traversed the whole Coalition airspace, but she had seldom had the chance to go on-planet, and now she knew she would insist on it in the future.

She wanted to see more wonders.

Her body sang with energy, and a strange memory--an unfamiliar excitement.

Whoever the little helpers had once been a part of, before her, they had stood beside a river like this, and felt at home.

"What is it?" Ben was suddenly at her shoulder.

"I've never seen something like this," she said.

He looked at her, a hard, quick search of her face, then nodded down the river. "This isn't a good place to stay. We need to go back into the protection of the forest."

She knew he was right. The noise of the water overrode everything else, and anyone watching from the forest would easily see them but keep hidden themselves. She wished it wasn't so, even as she turned and made her way back to the treeline, annoyed at feeling someone else's nostalgia.

This has to stop. She thought it forcefully, and sensed the little helpers' resistance, almost sadness, and then it was gone.

She breathed a free breath. Felt a twinge of guilt, which she suppressed.

"Sure you're all right?" Ben frowned.

She nodded, breathed again, nice and easy.

He gave her a final, worried look, and then began moving again.

They worked their way along the curve of the river, deep enough in the forest to take advantage of the cool shadows, but close enough to the river that she caught glimpses of the sun shining off the water.

Ben stopped, easing up against a tree, and putting his hand behind to signal a warning.

She crouched beside him, and there, just through the trees, she saw a small section of a white building.

A guard walked in front of the wall, and disappeared from view.

They had made it.

CHAPTER 27

TALLY STARED down on the buildings that made up Rainerville and tried to rein in her shock.

It was tiny, and made up of low-slung white domes that were similar to the supply station building at the start of the Trail. What she guessed was new were the big tents that had been erected in the field beyond.

Caruson soldiers were busy working next to the small launch pad beside the domes, building an even bigger pad. She could hear them shout to each other as they pulled massive tree trunks into place, obviously using what materials they had to hand.

Something big was happening here. She looked down at Ben, standing on the ground below, and saw he was keeping watch, body tense as his gaze did slow sweeps of their surroundings.

The only tree tall enough to give them a good view of what was happening had branches too high up for either of them to reach, so Ben had given her a boost up. She didn't like him down there, out in the open, and she focused back on the numbers of Caruson, the buildings and the big open space beyond them, trying to memorize everything so she could climb back down quickly.

Ben had told her Rainerville had been built at the edge of the forest, but until she saw it, she hadn't realized how abruptly the trees cut off, a solid line that switched to open plain.

The Caruso moved between the tents and toward the buildings without any great hurry, but they weren't aimless. She thought they looked grim, and compared to the four soldiers who'd laughed and joked each evening after a hard day of hunting her and Ben, they seemed devoid of humor.

She guessed the reason for their attitude was the one Caruson who snapped orders from a large tent closest to the construction area.

He was obeyed instantly, and she guessed he didn't approve of laughing or jokes.

She counted numbers, again felt the sink of dread in her stomach, and then headed down. Ben was crouched, hand out in the 'keep silent' signal, and her heart sped up as she slid quietly beside him.

His broad back was tense, and as soon as her feet touched the ground, he stood, pointing back the way they'd come in, and she could see the worry on his face.

She caught a glimpse of movement through the trees to their right.

She moved in the direction he pointed in the fluid, easy way she'd learned from watching him, sliding from shadow to shadow, keeping to the cover of the thick tree trunks. She glanced back at Ben, saw he was moving backward, laz up, covering her back.

She pulled her own laz out and then the little helpers fizzed through her. She stopped, lifted a hand toward him, not sure what was wrong. As her gaze met Ben's, her throat closed, rendering her mute. His head snapped right and then her muscles bunched, without her permission, and she was flung deep into the bush beside her.

Laz fire exploded before she even hit the ground, and Tally

fought herself, fought for control, so she could look out between the leaves and see where Ben was.

He was lying, arms thrown back, and she hoped that his uniform had protected him. That even if he was injured, he was alive.

Two Caruson guards walked cautiously up to him, and one picked up the big Caruson laz that had fallen beside him.

A second one bent over him and checked his pulse. When he straightened, he spoke in hard tones to his friend, and they picked Ben up by the feet and under his arms.

She didn't think they'd hold him like that if he was dead.

She wanted to believe that so badly, she was almost afraid to trust it. She was crying, she realized, as a tear dropped off the tip of her nose.

Ben looked broken, and she could do nothing about it.

A loud hum suddenly rose up and two Caruson on hovers roared into the clearing. The two holding Ben dumped him on the back of one of them, and it raced off.

The pilot of the second one spoke with the other two for a moment and then powered off toward the river.

Tally heard the hover turn to the left when it reached the river bank.

She waited, barely breathing, while the two soldiers spoke quietly to each other and then began looking on the ground.

For traces of her?

They seemed to give up and walked straight toward her, and she held her breath.

One of them was taking something out of a side pocket, and suddenly Tally knew what they were about to do.

She was lying on the ground, and the moment she recognized the thermal imagining device, she dropped her cheek to the loamy, dark soil, spreadeagled her arms, and closed her eyes. Braced.

Her skin seemed to boil for a moment, to actually ripple, and then bright, hot points of pain flared up along every limb, and all over her torso.

She bit down on her lip to keep from crying out, and felt her teeth draw blood.

The Caruson walked past her.

Her body slowly reset itself, but she couldn't move. Her muscles trembled and she gagged, trying to fight her nausea, to keeping absolutely quiet.

The sound of their footsteps faded.

She didn't know how long she lay; miserable, sick and panicked, but eventually she pulled herself up, slid out of the protective shield of the bush, and started walking.

She was headed for the river but she had no plan.

No good idea in her head.

The shout behind her almost didn't register at first. She turned her head, and saw the Caruson on his hover speeding toward her with a strange detachment.

And the little helpers, as worn out as she was, she guessed, suddenly sprung back to life.

She was standing near the river, and she turned toward it.

Some part of her was horrified at the thought of going in. She couldn't swim. Had never even been in a river. And yet, some other part of her, the part that had died a little at the sight of Ben lying still as death on the ground, didn't feel that worried about it.

She cooperated with the little helpers as they bunched the muscles in her legs and flung her into the fast moving water.

She moved her arms, kicked her legs, and found herself moving in strong, sure strokes.

She considered shrugging out of her pack, but rejected the idea immediately. She would not throw away her food--the things she needed to survive.

This was swimming, she realized as she hit the halfway mark

of the river. The little helpers' last host had been good at it. She was a few strokes from the opposite bank when the hover pulled up next to her.

A hand came down, grabbed her pack, and pulled her up.

The Caruson guard was incredibly strong. He lifted her straight out of the water as if she weighed nothing, setting her beside him. He dwarfed her, his broad body almost blocking out everything else.

She bent, coughing, her hands going to her thighs, and he turned to cut off the hover's power before they reached the bank.

When he turned back, she shot him in the eye with the laz Ben had given her.

She kicked him off the hover, and then swallowed as he sank straight down.

She thought she caught a glimpse of movement under the wash the hover had created. She swallowed again, this time, to fight back the nausea that had risen.

She'd never shot anyone until this trip. Not even in the Caruson attack at the ghost ship.

This was the second body she was personally responsible for.

The hover hit the grassy bank, the shudder snapping her back to her current predicament, and she started it up, rising above the water and heading into the trees on the other side of the river.

She hoped the Caruson patrols were less frequent on this side.

She needed time to work out what to do.

CHAPTER 28

TALLY WRIGGLED to get comfortable on her branch and felt a return of the terrible weight that had pressed down on her earlier after Ben had been shot and taken.

She couldn't see a way in to the Rainerville buildings--there were Caruson soldiers everywhere--and she needed to sleep, so she'd forced herself to rest for at least a few hours.

Her view of the small settlement was limited from this side of the river, but she remembered clearly what she'd seen earlier, and the night sky was bright with lights as the Caruson carried on with their construction of the launch pad.

They seemed to be working around the clock.

She finished tying herself to the branch, and listened to the sound of the river. It should have been soothing, but all she could think of was the Caruson soldier sinking like a stone, the water closing over him in seconds, and the quick, sinuous movement of something predatory beneath the surface.

She breathed in and out, trying to find some equilibrium, and slowly drifted off.

She woke up standing on the hover she taken from the

Caruson soldier, her hands on the controls, speeding through the trees.

It was like old times, she thought grimly.

Darkness all around. Unaware of how she got to where she was.

Her pack was at her feet, her hair blowing back in the breeze.

She had a sense the speed had roused her from her sleep, and she looked at the controls to see how to slow the hover down.

She felt the little helpers fight her, the hardest they had since she left the ghost ship.

Until earlier today, she'd almost forgotten this. The terrifying lack of control of her own body, the pull and tug as she tried to take herself back.

Her mind had been too full of fear for Ben to really care earlier. But now that the little helpers were steering her away from Rainerville--from Ben--she cared. A lot.

She wrenched free, easing back on the speed, and then looked ahead, suddenly realizing she was now fully in control of the hover.

She had the impression of an astonished face, and then the hover slammed into a body and she fought again for control as the little helpers tried to force her to keep going.

She won again, just barely, coming to a stop and then turning the hover around, creeping it along at its slowest speed to return to find out who she'd hit.

Not a Caruson, she was sure of that. It had been a Verdant Stringer.

She stopped when she heard groaning, and hopped down, laz out, moving carefully toward the man. She switched her light to its lowest setting and lifted it.

"Irwin!"

The guide raised a hand to shield his eyes from the light.

She didn't come any closer.

"What are you doing on this side of the river?"

"More open on this side. Faster." He wheezed his answer, his hand on his side.

The collision had either bruised or broken his ribs, she guessed. And there was a nasty score of laz fire across his right shoulder from where the Caruson had attacked them a few days ago.

It looked bad, but she guessed he had antibac gel, because it wasn't infected.

She studied him for a long moment and then took a step back and pivoted toward the hover.

Irwin's eyes widened. "Wait." His call was outraged.

She stopped, looked over her shoulder.

"You're not going to help me? Where's Ben?"

She hesitated. Thought through the implications, because whatever she said, she knew it would end up repeated to the Caruson. "He's dead." She didn't look at him as she said it, she kept her back turned. "I'm going to see if Lenny and Soo are still alive, and if I can help them."

She let the weight that had pressed down on her earlier infuse her words.

She felt the fizz of the little helpers coming back to life, and her body turned and her hand holding the laz lifted. Irwin shielded his eyes as the light hit him again, and for a moment, shock held her frozen.

The little helpers wanted him dead.

She drew in a deep breath, and her arm shook.

They were right. The safest thing to do would be to kill him.

And even so . . . she would not.

Her fingers tightened their grip on the laz. And she gasped, for the first time really, really frightened she'd be forced to do something she refused to do.

"No." She said it through gritted teeth.

"No, what?" Irwin had hunched over, his eyes full of defiance and resentment.

"I don't want to kill him." She enunciated each word.

"Who are you talking to?" Irwin looked around and then focused back on the laz in her hand.

Sweat dripped down her face and trickled between her shoulder blades. She needed air in her lungs but she couldn't seem to get enough.

Irwin stirred, rising to a crouch, and she read on his face that he thought he had nothing to lose anymore. That he was going to try to grab the laz.

The little helpers fought a moment longer, and then gave way as he started to stand. She turned and ran to the hover, fumbled for the starter button, and roared off.

When she looked back, she couldn't see Irwin in the dark.

She switched off the light, and tried to slow the hover again, tried to turn right to loop back to where she'd gone to sleep earlier.

The little helpers wouldn't let her.

She fought, teeth gritted together, a sound coming from her throat that was part rage, part wounded animal.

For a moment, she overrode the messages they were sending to her hands and she wrenched the controls back.

The hover headed straight at a massive tree.

She cried out with dismay as they reasserted themselves, but it was only to flip the steering up, so the nose of the hover lifted up vertically moments before impact.

Tally was thrown back, and air exploded from her lungs as she hit the ground.

She lay, winded and exhausted, and saw the hover had tipped on its side, as well.

"This can't go on." She whispered the words, and the little helpers shivered through her.

The forest was alive around her, sighing and rustling. The stars above her, just visible between the trees, were strung across the black sky as thick as the leaves on the forest floor, and from behind her, the bright lights of Rainerville, where they must still be working on the launch pad, lit the sky with a faint glow.

She decided it didn't matter if she moved right now or not, and so she stayed where she was.

"I'm not going to leave Ben behind. Even if it puts me in danger." Her voice was a little louder, this time.

She could almost hear the hum of the little helpers' response.

She would not, could not, accept this situation any more.

The anger and helplessness that had gripped her since the first time she'd woken in the ghost ship, unable to say where she was or how she got there, suddenly exploded out of her. She cried in loud, wracking sobs. "Let me be. Just let me be."

There was a response, a tentative touch she could almost believe was an apology.

"*I* get to be in control. If you want to help me, that's fine, but you ask first, and you never, never override me." Her voice cracked. "Otherwise, get out and go find someone else." She rested her hand, palm up, on the ground, waiting for the metal ball to appear.

There wasn't so much as a shiver under her skin.

"This had better be an acceptance of my terms." She waited a little longer, and then curled her fingers into a fist.

She rolled over, onto hands and knees, and then struggled to her feet, so tired, she decided to move just a little further away from Irwin, and find a place to sleep that didn't include a tree branch.

Her pack had been thrown from the hover as well, and she set it back in place and started the hover again, going the slowest speed so that it made almost no sound at all.

She was about to seriously look for a place to sleep when the little helpers prickled again.

Her heart rate sped up. She didn't know if she could trust their truce, but she was about to find out.

Her hearing became more acute, and she caught the sound of someone shadowing her on the other side of the trees, running in parallel with the hover.

She pulled out her laz, and put on a spurt of speed, shooting the hover forward at an angle across the trees, to intercept whoever was there. The hover spun as she braked, and she stood, laz raised, pointing in their direction.

"I'm armed. Show yourself." She flinched as a light shone straight in her eyes.

"Who are you?" The voice came from her right, not in front of her, and she saw a man in VSC military fatigues standing between the trees, a weapon in his hand.

"Put the laz down." The command came from her left, and with a sinking sensation, she saw there was a woman standing there, also dressed in military gear.

The man in front of her moved, and she saw all three of them now had weapons in their hands.

Tally slowly put her laz in her pocket. Thought it through.

"I'm Tally Riva. Are you Ben's team?"

"Now, how," the man in front of her stepped closer, "do you know that?"

CHAPTER 29

"YOUR FOOD LOOKS BETTER THAN OURS." Handel glanced over at her as the sunlight crested the treetops and spilled over the camp. He swallowed another spoonful of what looked like standard VSC readies to her, and then crumpled the box in disgust.

"It is." She scraped the last of her food out of its container and then threw it into the small fire he'd lit when they woke up.

She'd slept well.

They'd given her a tent when they'd seen she was too exhausted to make much sense to them, and shared the other two between them, taking turns with guard duty throughout the night.

Sari came back from the stream, face still dripping water. Garner pulled himself out of the tent he'd slept in, and scratched at his chest as he stumbled to sit across from her.

The small stand they had set up over the flames to heat the jah rattled as it boiled, and everyone held out a cup as Handel lifted it carefully and poured.

"So." Sari took a sip of her jah. "All we got for sure from you last night was that Ben has been captured?"

She nodded.

"Where?" Garner's voice was a deep rumble.

She looked at him for a long moment. She knew it would be difficult to explain how she was at least two thou from where he'd been shot. "He was taken at Rainerville."

"And what happened to you?"

"I managed to get away, but I was chased by a Caruson guard. That's how I got the hover."

There was surprised silence for a moment.

"You took down a Caruson guard?" Handel leaned back on the stone he was sitting on. "What part of the Raxian military are you?"

"I'm a science officer in surveys. I'm part of the forward expeditionary force."

"So no real combat experience." Sari said it like the fact it was.

"No. But the Caruson thought I was no threat, and he turned away. When he turned back to look at me, I shot him in the eye with the laz Ben gave me."

Garner gave a half-laugh. "That'll do it." He held out his hand. "Let's see the laz."

She took it out of her pocket, amazed that they hadn't taken it from her last night, and handed it over.

"It's Ben's," Garner confirmed. "Why'd he give you his weapon?"

"He got hold of one of the big laz the Caruson use, so he gave me his."

"Let's just back right up." Handel tapped his mug in the palm of his hand. "What were you and Ben doing here, anyway?"

"You don't know?" She stared at them, then blushed, because how could they know? The comms satellite was down. She shook her head, and lifted a hand. "Sorry. Of course you don't know. We were walking the Trail when we saw the runner that brought us to Veltos shot down by a Caruson warship. When we tried to send out a message, we found the comms satellite had been taken out as well."

There was silence.

Tally looked at them one by one. "You must have guessed about the satellite."

They stared back, giving nothing away.

"What happened after the runner was shot down?" Garner broke the silence.

"We raced over to it as fast as we could." She clenched her fists. "No one made it."

"That's when Ben told you he was a plant on the Trail?" Handel asked.

Tally shook her head. "I caught him sneaking off on his original mission to find the downed 'weather' satellite."

"You caught him?" Sari sounded skeptical.

Tally shrugged. "It was by mistake."

They didn't seem convinced.

"And then?"

"Then we came under fire by the Caruso and Frangi was injured. Lenny and Soo volunteered to take Frangi to the supply station, because it's much closer to where she was hit than Rainerville."

"And what was the Trail guide doing in all this?"

Tally's lips set in a thin line. "He disappeared sometime in the night, before we came under attack. He's been in the pocket of the Caruson all along."

"And then you and Ben headed for Rainerville. Why?" Sari leaned forward.

"Because Ben said he needed to find out what the Caruson were doing."

"You didn't have to go with him," Handel said.

"No, but I wasn't going to let him go by himself."

"So, Ben was shot, you were chased, and you got the upper hand. Then what?"

"Then I ran into Irwin on the hover, completely by mistake. I hurt him, but he's still out there."

"A lot of things seem to happen to you just by mistake." Sari was watching her over the rim of her mug.

There was silence for a moment.

Garner cleared his throat. "Irwin spent the night at a place about a thou away." He stretched. "I doubled back to see where he was, and she's right," he tipped his head at Tally, "he's injured. He won't be a problem. But he's got some laz burn, not just internal injuries." He looked at her expectantly.

She sighed. "He was with us when the Caruson attacked us a few days ago. He got in the way, took some laz fire. We heard him shouting at the Caruso for it afterward, and he broke with them, told them he was out." Her lips twisted. "Except, how can he be out? How's he going to get off-planet without their help?" She lifted her hands. "He might not be a problem in a fight, but when he meets up with the Caruson again, he'll tell them that he saw me. I lied before I left him last night, and told him I was going back to the crash site. I hope he believed me."

"Why would he?" Sari set down her mug.

"Because I told him Ben was dead." She eyed Sari with interest. The Arkhoran Special Forces soldier was short and trim, her dark, tight curls cut close against her skull.

"The Caruson will know he isn't," Handel pointed out.

"Sure, but they don't know that I know that. If I think he's dead, it's a solid reason for me to head back to find Lenny and Soo. The Caruson might decide we aren't worth going after, at least not yet."

"So what did you and Ben see at Rainerville?" Handel started cleaning up around the fire.

"You haven't been there yet?" Tally tilted her head. "Where did you come from? Ben didn't know you were here."

They were silent for a moment, sharing a look with each other.

"What did Ben tell you about our mission?" Sari asked.

"He said you've been here a month, that you were trying to find evidence the Caruson were on-planet. That he specifically was going to check on a location where you suspected the spy satellite you dropped into the atmosphere had been shot down."

They shared another look.

"That's more or less it." Sari lifted her shoulders. "Except the day after that big earthquake, we didn't need to speculate about whether the Caruson were here. Four big hovers of them passed our position, moving toward Rainerville, dragging rough pallets of injured Caruso behind them. There were a few smaller hovers like your one buzzing alongside."

"You followed them?" She thought about it. "Isn't a special forces team usually made up of six? Where are the rest of you?"

There was a gleam in Handel's eye as he watched her. "Yes. Two of the team went in the opposite direction, to see where the Caruson had come from, and what they were doing there. The rest of us followed behind the hovers."

"And they came here." Tally frowned. "You followed them on foot?"

Garner gave a brief nod. "We couldn't keep up with them, even though they were traveling slower than usual because of the injured. The pallets left a nice trail for us to follow."

"Why would they need to bring their injured to Rainerville?" Tally asked.

Sari shook her head. "No idea. But they were in a hurry."

"And now we've got all that out the way," Handel packed the last of the equipment into his pack, "what did you see at Rainerville?"

"The Caruson are building a landing pad. There are some

hovers and a lot of tents out on the open fields beyond the forest." She stood herself, picked up her pack. "Maybe the injured are in the tents. I wasn't able to see inside."

"They want to get off Veltos. I'm assuming the injured soldiers need a quick extraction." Sari spoke softly. "But why come all the way here? Why not get picked up on the plains?"

"You don't think they have a ship on-planet already. How did they get here?" Tally asked.

"They were probably dropped in small one or two person carriers," Handel said. "That's the only way they could have gotten so many down here without us knowing about it."

Garner nodded, looking grim. "And they've shot down the VSC runner, and have taken out the comms satellite, so they can get off-planet without any witnesses."

CHAPTER 30

"HOW'D you come to be on the Trail team?" Garner shifted a little. He was lying on his stomach beside her as they watched two Caruson soldiers move between the domed buildings of Rainerville. When he glanced over at her, it was with curious eyes.

Tally knew he was watching her as much as he was watching the Caruson. Ben's team obviously decided they couldn't leave her on her own, and Garner had been saddled with the job.

They'd all left their packs under a fountain bush, and Sari and Handel had left her and Garner in the forest to crawl through the high grass of the open plain to get a better look at what was happening around the launch pad. They'd disappeared with the same silent, professional skill as Ben.

"You don't already know why I was picked?" she asked. "I thought you had our files."

Garner's eyebrows lifted. "Ben probably did. They would have debriefed him before he started the Trail."

She was relieved he didn't know. She preferred it that way.

To avoid answering, she lifted the vision enhancers to her eyes, zooming in on a Caruson walking toward the building at the far end of the complex. No one had come out of it yet, that she'd seen.

"You see that one?" she murmured. "He's the first one to go near that building." She zoomed even closer, just caught the movement of his fingers as he keyed in the code next to the door.

"I see it." Garner lifted his own vision enhancers to his eyes.

The soldier disappeared inside.

"So." Garner glanced at her. "You were saying about how you got recommended for the Trail . . ."

"No, I wasn't." She ignored him.

"Why won't you tell me?" Garner lifted his enhancers again, did a slow sweep of the area.

"Because I don't like talking about it." She gave him a smile. "And it's none of your business."

"It *is* my business if you're going to freeze up if we come under fire or you have some triggers I need to know about."

Tally shook her head. "I've taken down two Caruson soldiers since this started, helped Ben take down a third. I'm guessing that's more than you've done."

His eyes met hers, startled and wary. "Maybe."

There was a shout, beyond the buildings, toward the launch pad construction, and Garner rose into a crouch, laz in hand.

Tally blinked. He'd gone from affronted to deadly in moments.

They were lying under bushes at the very edge of the forest, and the moment he stepped forward, he'd be visible.

"You think they've seen Handel and Sari?" She couldn't think of another reason for a shout like that.

"I'll see. Stay here." He stepped back, melting into the foliage.

She barely even heard him move away.

She lay still for a moment, then movement from among the buildings caught her attention and she lifted her enhancers again.

The soldier who'd gone into the building earlier stepped out, then stepped to the side, his laz raised.

Two women and a man stepped out.

They looked a little dazed, and one of the women stumbled as she moved into the bright late morning light.

They stood for a moment in front of the soldier, as if unsure what to do.

The Caruson said something to them, motioning with his laz, and they started to walk, moving toward the other end of the complex, the Caruson following behind them, laz still raised.

Tally was lying on the edge of the forest between the third and fourth buildings, and worried her bottom lip when the three disappeared from her line of sight.

They had to be the scientists who were stationed here to study the flora and fauna of Veltos.

They would theoretically only have been allowed on-planet years from now, after a full sentient life and planetary development study had been done, but the Faldine rebels had landed here, had shot down VSC craft here, and had rendered the careful steps the VSC employed before settling a life-supporting planet useless.

They had changed the planet for good.

When the VSC won the Faldine War, they'd set up a small research station at Rainerville, and Tally had heard the competition to get a place on the team was fierce.

While their access was as a result of bad circumstances, no scientist wanted to pass up a legal look at a planet this early in its evolution.

Whoever those scientists were, they would be bright, and she hoped they'd be able to keep their wits about them.

She swung the enhancers back to the building they'd come out of, and saw the Caruson soldier had left the door open.

She also became aware that since the shout she and Garner had heard earlier, she hadn't seen any other soldiers, and she wondered if they'd all gone to see what was happening.

If they'd put an injured Ben anywhere, it was most likely that building.

For a brief moment, the little helpers locked her muscles as they realized what she planned to do, and then, as her panic and anger rose, released her and gave her an extra spurt of speed as she raced from the treeline toward the door, as if to make up for their lapse.

She slowed as she approached the building to her right, peering cautiously around it. There was no one visible, and she darted through the open door of the dome to her left.

Ben lay, eyes closed, on a bed placed near the back of the room, which looked like a communal lounge. There was an open door through which she could see a corridor with doors off it, which she guessed led to the living quarters.

She pulled the door behind her so it was only open a crack and then ran over to him, putting a hand to his forehead.

His eyes opened with a snap, his hand coming up to grip her wrist.

"Tally?" He darted a look at the door. "They caught you?"

"No." She touched his face with her free hand. "They left the door open when they took the scientists out, and I took a chance to see if you were in here."

"You shouldn't be here. I want you safe. Leave me and get as far away as you can." He winced as he tried to sit up.

She made a sound as he went white with effort.

"Don't move. I'll go, but I just wanted you to know I'm here, and some of your team are here, too."

"What?" He lay back in surprise. "Who?"

"Garner, Sari and Handel."

"What happened to Enn and Va-Laya?"

"They were together when a big group of Caruson passed them. Enn and Va-Laya went to see where they'd come from, the other three followed them all the way here."

"So where the hell are they, and why are you here by yourself?" His words were almost a snarl.

"I think the Caruson might have spotted Sari and Handel when they were working their way closer to the launch pad the Caruson are building. Garner went to see what was happening, but so did all the Caruson." She shrugged. "They left this door open when they took the scientists out, so I saw a gap and I took it."

"Tally." He sounded exhausted. "Please. Leave things to my team."

She shook her head. "When it makes sense I will. But if I'd followed orders, I'd still be watching this door instead of talking to you."

He made a face. "Well, go now, before they come back."

"Where did they take the scientists?" She didn't move, instead lifting his shirt to see what injuries he had.

She sucked in her breath at the sight of the big bandage that covered his torso. It was higher than his older laz burn, and this time on his left side. Almost over his heart.

He looked down at his wound. "It's actually not bad. That bandage isn't covering much damage. The problem is my system is fried. My motor neurons aren't firing properly, but Dr. Lenar says they'll suddenly come right. We've overplayed my injuries so they think I'm too incapacitated for them to question me."

"Dr. Lenar?"

"She's a biologist, but she's also the med tech for Rainerville. She did a good job. I'll live, apparently." He tried to smile. "The scientists managed to get permission to get more supplies and to stretch their legs. They've been cooped up in here for days and eventually Dr. Kilmer convinced someone it would be one less thing for the guards to do if they were able to collect their own supplies."

"What should we do to get you out?"

Ben was shaking his head. "I can't walk properly yet, let alone run."

"I've got a hover now." Tally dismissed his argument with a wave of her hand. "You won't have to run."

His eyes narrowed. "How did you get a hover?"

"After they shot you, one of the soldiers came after me." She sent him a lopsided grin. "I won."

"Tally." It was the second time he'd said her name, but this time his voice was full of regret.

"Shh." She leaned over him, hands brushing back his hair, and then she leaned over him and kissed him.

At that moment, the door opened, and a woman in a pair of trousers and a colorful jacket almost stumbled at the sight of her.

Tally had turned her head as the door swung open, and she saw the Caruson soldier who'd been there earlier was standing to one side, laz up, his gaze outward, rather than inward.

He hadn't seen her yet.

She dropped down and rolled under Ben's bed, coming up on the other side in a crouch, laz in her hand.

The door closed, and then after a moment of absolute silence, someone said: "You can come out now, it's safe."

She rose cautiously, the little helpers buzzing through her like supercharged adrenalin, and she could sense their disquiet that they hadn't heard anyone at the door until it was too late.

She tried to calm them as she looked at everyone in turn.

The woman who'd entered first had stopped closest to Ben, her shock still apparent.

The other two must not have seen Tally before the door closed, because they looked completely astonished at the sight of her.

"Everyone, this is Tally. Tally, Dr. Lenar, Dr. Kilmer, and Dr. Bey." Ben had managed to get up on one arm, although Tally saw it shook.

"Where did you come from?" Dr. Lenar stared at her.

"I was watching from the forest and when they took you off and left the door open, I decided to see if they might be keeping Ben in here, so I took a chance."

There was silence, as if they couldn't conceive of someone running toward the Caruso, not away.

"You're military trained?" Kilmer asked at last.

She nodded. "I'm not in Ben's team, but I am in the Raxian Expeditionary Force. I was on the Trail when this started."

That seemed to make sense to them.

"Of course, you're on the Trail because you've seen action with valor," Dr. Bey nodded.

Tally decided not to contradict her, but before she could make any response at all, her little helpers, who had amped up her senses, went on alert.

She felt a subtle push for permission to act, and gave it.

She put a finger to her lips, and ran toward the wall to her right.

There was a chair, a table, and a shelf, and she jumped, using each one to get herself higher, before she leaped up onto the wide beam above the door.

"The supplies," Dr. Bey said suddenly, eyes wide as she turned to the door. "They wanted to check them first to see if we were trying to sneak something dangerous in."

She'd barely finished speaking when the door opened again and a Caruson soldier stepped in with a large box in his arms.

Tally hesitated a moment, unsure what the little helpers had in mind, and then relaxed into it. She dropped straight down onto his shoulders, put the laz against his ear, and shot him.

He went down silently, but the box dropped from his lifeless fingers and thumped onto the floor.

Tally was off him before he'd hit the ground, spinning to stand behind the door as the guard from outside stepped in, his gaze taking in the shock on the three scientists faces, and Ben, lying in bed, eyes burning with some emotion she couldn't read.

The guard must have been as confused as everyone else, because he didn't even raise his laz as he stepped into the room. Tally stepped out in line with him, and shot him in the ear from where she stood.

She pushed the door closed as he went down, and then, at the last moment, remembered it probably couldn't open from the inside, and grabbed the handle before it closed completely.

Wordlessly, Dr. Kilmer handed her a rock that she'd knocked off the shelf when she'd jumped to her position above the door. She used it as a prop to keep the door open a little way.

"Take what you need, we're going."

She looked around at three blank faces and one that said more than she wanted to hear.

"Listen to her," Ben snapped, and suddenly they were moving in swift, efficient steps, loading up packs, taking supplies from the box the soldier had dropped.

"What about Ben?" Dr. Lenar asked.

"You and I are going to support him," Tally told Dr. Kilmer.

He nodded, and gave his pack to Dr. Bey. "Ready."

Tally looked out the door. There were soldiers moving around at the far end of the buildings, closest to the construction, but none were looking their way.

"See the treeline over there?" She pointed, and Bey and Lenar nodded. "Run. Now."

She didn't watch them go, she turned immediately and got beneath Ben's arm as he swung himself upright on the bed. Kilmer had already taken his other side.

She looked into Ben's eyes, saw he was wearing his special forces face.

"I'm sorry," she said, and then she and Kilmer heaved him off the table.

He was heavy, but she could feel the little helpers . . . helping. Strengthening her somehow.

Kilmer sidled through the door first, and then they ran toward the forest, with Ben's large frame between them, his feet dragging on the ground behind them.

Tally could hear Ben breathing through the pain, and had to force herself to keep running. She was hurting him, and yet, she couldn't leave him behind in that room.

They reached the treeline and passed Lenar and Bey, who were waiting for them, eyes wide.

She led them to the place where she and the rest of Ben's team had left the packs earlier, stepping inside the fountain bush. It was a big one, more than big enough to fit everyone.

She and Kilmer laid Ben down, and then she pulled her thin mattress out her pack and they lifted Ben onto it.

He looked at her through eyes narrowed with pain, and she knelt beside him.

"I'm sorry," she whispered again.

He shook his head, looking like he'd have a lot to say if they weren't surrounded by strangers.

"I should check him over," Dr. Lenar murmured beside her, and Tally ceded her place.

Her muscles were screaming at her. The little helpers had redirected energy and strength where she needed it to carry Ben and run at the same time, but now it was payback time.

"How did you do that?" Dr. Bey asked. "Back in the residential dome? How did you react so fast? I didn't even really catch exactly what you did. It seemed like you climbed the wall somehow, and then you were just on that Caruson's shoulders and . . ." She petered off.

"She jumped the chair, the desk and then the shelf," Dr. Kilmer said. "I've never seen such quick reactions. Whatever division you're in in the Raxian military, my bet is it isn't the Expeditionary Force."

Tally opened her mouth to deny it, then closed it again. Better they think her some special forces prodigy than know the truth. They were all looking at her, now, even Dr. Lenar had twisted around from her position next to Ben, her gaze thoughtful.

She couldn't read Ben's expression.

Her hands had been trembling for a while, but now her legs started to, as well. She reached into her pack and pulled out water, drinking it in big gulps. Then she grabbed some bars, shoved them into her pocket.

"Who do these packs belong to?" Kilmer asked.

"The rest of Ben's team. I think I need to go see what's happened to them." Tally glanced at Ben's face, saw he was about to tell her no, and unwilling to fight with him in front of an audience, she stepped through the curtain of leaves, back into the forest.

Where no one looked at her with curiosity and far too much interest.

CHAPTER 31

THEY WERE FINALLY HERE. Not that it was going to do them much good.

Soo sank down onto one of the old, dusty couches in the supply station's communal lounge and realized her hands were shaking.

That fucker Irwin had pulled out the transmitter on the spare set she knew she'd seen in here and had either taken it or hidden it somewhere.

She'd thought Irwin had been doing a final check of the place before they left on the Trail. He'd been doing a final check all right. To make sure no one could use the spare comm set.

She rubbed a hand over her face and leaned back against the cushions.

The supply hover couldn't make it through the door, so she and Lenny had lifted Frangi up and carried her to a bed, and then Lenny had gone out to bring in the rest of the gear.

She could hear him outside, and was grateful he was seeing to it.

Frangi worried her.

There was a sickly gray tone to her skin, which was the warm shade of brown common in most Verdant Stringers.

Frangi's gray-tinged pallor told her she needed far more medical assistance than Soo and Lenny had managed to give.

It worried her sick.

She forced herself to her feet as Lenny began stacking boxes just inside the door, and carried them deeper into the room.

She didn't bother with anything more than sorting them by stacking the same things together.

"All done. You all right?" Lenny leaned against the doorjamb to look at her with tired eyes ringed with black.

Soo knew she looked no better. She nodded. "You hide the hover, I'll search for the transmitter. Maybe Irwin hid it somewhere here." Although that would have been stupid of him.

"We don't have to look right now," Lenny said. "You need to rest."

But Soo was already shaking her head. "The sooner, the better, Lenny. Who knows what's happened to Tally and Ben."

He nodded, and ducked out, and Soo closed her eyes, stretched to get out the kinks, and then started looking.

At least tonight they'd have hot water and a bed to sleep in.

It had been a hell of a run from the crash site to here. They hadn't been able to go as fast as they wanted to.

They'd ended up moving at night, too afraid of discovery to risk moving during the day, and even then, they'd had to go slow to keep the sound of the hover down, and to keep it from jolting Frangi.

Still, they were here now. And she had a job to do.

LINN FRASER STOOD in front of Captain Harris on the VSC warship *Galaha* and tried to keep his gaze steady.

"Let me get this straight. You gave your lover this warship's call signatures?" Captain Harris had walked out in front of her desk, and leaned back against it, arms crossed over her chest.

"No, Captain. I gave her the call signature for my station at the comms desk."

"And you did this because . . .?"

"Because I miss her. She was badly injured in the mess after Cepi, and she earned a place on the current Trail team. I knew we were close enough for the Trail comms equipment to reach us, and it was a good way to keep in touch without giving away our position or any details about the warship." He could feel the back of his neck heating up, and risked a quick glance at the captain's face.

She didn't seem as angry as his lieutenant had made out.

"So, the timeline is, she sent a message the morning the team was starting the Trail, and everything was fine. Then we went out of system on maneuvers, and today when we came back in range you got a delayed message which is timestamped the afternoon of the second day. A message that says the runner that brought them to Veltos was shot down by a Caruson warship, to send help, and by the way, your friend Ben Guthrie says hello."

"Yes, Captain." He shuffled his feet.

She said nothing for a moment. "You obviously tried to reply. There was no response?"

"It seems the comms set is either off, or no longer operational."

Captain Harris pushed away from her desk. "And contact via the Veltos comms satellite?"

"It appears the satellite is off-line, or down."

"It would be," Harris said quietly. "If the Caruson shot down the runner, they shot down the satellite."

Linn lifted his head. "Captain--"

Harris held up a hand, and he realized she was listening to something through an earpiece. She gave a grunt of displeasure, then fixed him with her dark eyes. "Confirmation from Situ that the runner is not responding, and the satellite appears to be gone." The captain tilted her head. "We would never have known about it this quickly without those messages from your friend, Fraser. It seems true love might have saved the day."

Linn's neck felt white hot but he held her gaze. "Yes, Captain."

She grinned at him. "I like you. I want you to keep trying the Trail team's call signature until I tell you to stop. If I know Captain Guthrie, he'll be working to get the comms equipment back up again, and we're going to be there, listening, when he does."

As Linn had been doing that anyway, he simply nodded.

Harris laughed. "You're already doing it, aren't you?"

"Yes, Captain."

"Well buckle up in that chair of yours, Sergeant, because we're heading full speed for Veltos."

She made a shooing motion out the door, and he escaped, his step much lighter as he jogged back to his station.

He would keep calling the signature Frangi had given him until he heard from her. There was no other outcome he would accept. And they were coming for her. Weapons hot.

CHAPTER 32

THE DOCTORS SETTLED AROUND HIM, sipping water and getting comfortable beneath the cool green of the fountain bush. It would do nothing to hide them from any heat sensors, but there was nothing Ben could do about that.

He could feel the cool of the numbing gel, knew he was much better today than he'd been yesterday, but he'd nearly passed out when Tally and Kilmer had carried him from Rainerville. He wasn't going to be able to keep the Caruson from getting the scientists back if they came looking for them here.

His muscles trembled and spasmed at strange times, and he hoped that meant he was recovering, that he'd be able to shake off the laz hit soon, but that wasn't any help right now.

He looked at the scientists who'd been so helpful since he'd woken in their care yesterday, and forced himself to be honest with them. "If the Caruson come looking, you'll need to run. They have heat sensors."

"Hopefully Tally will be back by then." Bey set her water down. "I always thought Arkhoran Special Forces were the top military unit, but . . ." She shook her head. "She's something else altogether."

Ben didn't say anything to that. It was true.

He wanted to know where his team was. Why they'd left Tally alone near Rainerville. What the hell they'd been thinking.

He forced a breath in, then out.

Suddenly, the leaves parted and Garner stood there, face stone cold, laz raised.

When he caught sight of Ben, his eyes went wide. "Captain."

He stepped into the protection of the foliage curtain. "How did you get here?"

"Tally broke into the dome where they were keeping me and the doctors and rescued us all." He kept his tone dry, but he saw Garner wince, and was glad he'd heard the unspoken 'you fucking idiot'.

"Where *is* Tally?" Garner seemed to realize there was one missing.

"She went looking for you, Handel and Sari." He kept his voice clipped. "She seemed to be worried the Caruso might have captured or killed Handel and Sari."

"They almost did." Garner crouched down beside him after giving the doctors a respectful nod. "They ran, and I think they got away. I watched them head for the far treeline, away from my and Tally's position, so my guess is they'll work their way back here."

"We're pretty close to Rainerville here. We should probably move deeper in when Tally gets back." Ben wouldn't be moving until then.

"We have a hover, thanks to Tally, so moving you will be pretty easy." Garner moved even closer, lowered his voice. "How bad is it, Ben? What happened?"

"Caruson laz fire runs hot," Ben said. "But my uniform did a fair shielding job. I'm guessing Tally filled you in. She said you and the others caught a hover train of Caruson going past, and

Enn and Va-Laya worked back to the origin point, and the rest of you followed them here."

Garner nodded. "We followed the hovers. My guess is their injured were caught in a rock fall when the earthquake hit."

"That's correct," Dr. Lenar interrupted. "They arrived four days ago and took us by surprise."

"Why did they come to Rainerville, though?" Ben suddenly realized he'd been in too much pain to ask the most important question until now. "Why not get picked up out on the plains?"

"They haven't said anything to me about it." Lenar lifted her hands, palms out.

"I don't know why they came here, but I don't think they'd have done it without a good reason," Kilmer said. "Some of the injuries look critical. I don't think they were supposed to reveal their presence, but I guess their commander decided he had no choice but to signal for help, and he wouldn't have moved them to Rainerville unless he felt he had to."

Ben still wondered why, but he'd find out eventually. He flopped back against the mattress. He remembered how the earthquake had shaken loose the trees of the forest, caused a kuyer stampede.

"That last sector we were surveying," Ben looked at Garner, "that wasn't particularly mountainous. Where would they have been under a rockfall unless they were underground?"

Oh, yes. It was making sense.

Their inability to find any activity from their satellite shots, the invisibility of the Caruson presence. All explained by the Caruson being underground.

If the Caruson had built quick and dirty mine tunnels, then yes, they would most definitely have been in trouble when the tremors hit.

Garner tilted his head in agreement. "That's the best explanation I've heard. Handel, Sari and I thought up a few colorful ones on the run here to Rainerville, but my bet is that Enn and Va-Laya have ended up at a mine site."

"I wonder what they've been mining?" Ben didn't expect an answer, but Dr. Bey lifted a shoulder.

"My guess is they found a deposit of high-grade tinria. They brought some of it with them in the hovers."

Ben hadn't heard of it, which must have been clear from his expression.

Bey grinned at him. "It's not well known, but some of my colleagues have been studying it, trying to see if it has useful properties. I think we can safely say the Caruson beat us to the punch there. They obviously have an important use for it."

"How did they find the deposit, though?" Garner asked.

"They must have been searching for some time. Sneaking down here and doing surveys." Which meant they could have been visiting Veltos for years, and the VSC hadn't known it.

He'd been fooled by Caruso's attempted annexation of Garmen and Lassa, Ben realized. He'd thought this latest Caruson incident was a result of their recent boldness, but if they'd been here on Veltos, a VSC planet, for years, then this wasn't a sudden surge in aggression from them. It was part of a long-term strategy.

This was really not good.

If the Caruson had been planning for this for a long time, they would have made sure they had the supplies, the trained troops, and the means to wage war with the VSC.

And they had almost caught the Verdant String completely by surprise.

He forced himself up into a seated position. "You have some comms equipment in one of these packs, Garner?"

His teammate nodded. "But the comms satellite is down."

"As it happens, I have the *Galaha's* call signal."

Garner frowned. "You have our warship's signal? How--?"

Ben managed a grin. "The power of love."

CHAPTER 33

TALLY PRESSED herself up against a thick tree trunk and watched the Caruson soldiers filter back out of the treeline that curved to her right and jog toward the almost completed landing pad.

It was clear they'd been recalled from their hunt for Sari and Handel, and she was relieved Ben's friends had managed to escape.

She wondered why the search had been called off, why they'd given up, when she finally noticed a sound in the distance, getting louder.

The little helpers perked up, and she lifted her gaze to the skies. Her view was blocked by thick branches and leaves, but she caught the glint of metal as a big runner came in to land.

As it settled on the landing pad, she saw it was about the same size as the runner that had brought her and the others to the head of the Trail, but that the landing pad it settled down on had been built for something much bigger.

The runner didn't switch off its engines, and as the door at the back lowered, Tally saw movement from the tents set up in the open field.

Caruson soldiers emerged, some carrying stretchers between them, some driving hovers with stretchers on them. They headed for the runner.

The Caruso who were being transported were all bandaged, and she could see blood seeping through some of the dressings.

Some of them had limbs missing.

She and the others had managed to survive the earthquake unscathed. The Caruson had obviously not been nearly as lucky.

The earthquake must have been the catalyst for this whole nightmare.

She was so busy focusing on the injured being ferried to the runner, she missed the confrontation at the runner's open doors until the first shout.

The big commander she'd caught a glimpse of the day before when she and Ben had been spying on Rainerville strode across the field, face set in lines of unspeakable fury, and Tally turned to see what could have put him in such a towering rage.

The pilot was blocking access to the open doors of the runner, refusing the injured Caruso admittance.

He did something using a small device in his hand, and the door, which doubled as a ramp, lifted up a little, making it almost impossible for the stretcher carriers to get inside.

She wished she could speak Caruson, because the commander descended on the pilot with a blistering verbal attack, and the pilot yelled back in turn.

They were big men, both of them. The thick skin on the faces of the Caruso made it difficult for Verdant Stringers to intuit expression, but there was no doubt in her mind that they were both angry. Their big hands chopped the air, and she could hear their harsh breathing even from her hiding place.

Eventually, the pilot threw his hands up, turned to the men carrying the stretchers, and pointed back to the tents.

He snarled a last retort at the commander, turned on his heel, and stalked back to the runner, using the device to lower the door back down so he could get in.

He got three, maybe four, steps, and then the commander lifted his laz and shot him in the back of the head.

He pitched forward, his head lying at an odd angle on the wooden planks of the landing pad.

For a moment, no one moved, but suddenly, the whine from the runner's engines picked up, and with a roar, the commander sprinted toward the runner's ramp, leaped inside, and then moments later, came back out dragging another pilot with him.

He threw the man down beside his colleague.

The co-pilot said something, his hands moving much like the original pilot's had, the invective clear and taunting. Whatever he said, the white hot rage that flashed across the commander's face made Tally shrink back, her fingers pressing against the rough bark of the tree.

He lifted his weapon and fired again.

Then he lowered his laz, and stood, staring at the two dead men in front of him.

He rubbed a hand over his eyes, then lifted his head and shouted.

At first Tally thought it was some kind of cry of frustration, but she realized when the soldiers around him began to move, that he was barking commands.

The stretcher bearers carried the injured up the ramp and then ran back to the tents to get more.

In the end, at least eighteen where carried in, and two were brought who obviously couldn't fit. There was a little juggling, as one was obviously considered more severely injured than another already on board, and they were swapped, and then the two extra were taken back to the tents.

There was something wrong, though.

The commander moved through the camp, the sound of his voice grating on Tally's nerves as it seemed to ramp up.

His temper was clear, but he seemed to lack a focus for it, and when he glanced over at the dead pilots, it seemed to be with regret.

Had he killed the only two people who could fly--?

The prickle under her skin happened only moments before she felt the press of the laz against the back of her head. She froze, her fingernails digging into the tree bark.

A grunt of satisfaction sounded right in her ear, and she flinched.

She slowly turned her head, and met the eyes of one of the soldiers that had tracked her through the forest for days. He smiled as he stepped back so she could stand, and she could read the triumph at having found her on his face.

He shoved her forward, out of the forest and toward the commander.

Tally stumbled a little as she stepped out of the cover of the treeline, and felt the little helpers desperately try to find a way out, ramping up her heart rate, making her skin prickle.

She couldn't see any options, and neither, it seemed, could they.

And she'd just seen what happened to people the commander really didn't like.

THE COMMANDER TURNED to the soldier pushing Tally toward him with a snarl.

The look in his eyes said he'd happily kill her just to check one more thing off his list.

His words landed in harsh, quick whips, and even though she couldn't understand, she had the sense the commander wasn't pleased at all that his underling had gone looking for her.

To him, it was a waste of time.

The soldier responded, trying to look obedient, but even to her untried ear, he was failing.

The commander waited until he was finished, and Tally saw his massive hands curl into fists, his eyes on the ground as he fought for control.

The little helpers buzzed. If the commander attacked her captor, they could maybe run.

But his hands uncurled and shot out, grabbing Tally by the front of her jacket and hauling her close.

She could see the blue-green-brown swirls in his eyes, and smelled the sour, spicy scent coming off his skin.

"You ghost ship girl." He gave her a shake.

She blinked. His Verdant String vernacular wasn't great, but it was a lot better than her Caruson.

"No," she said.

"Lie." He shook her again, and this time her teeth rattled. He tossed her to the ground. Lifted his laz.

She stared straight into his eyes, refusing to look at the bodies lying near her, and knew he no longer gave a damn about whether she was useful to the Caruso or not. He was clearly no longer a Caruson team player.

She was just one more problem, and he'd eliminate her without a second thought.

So she needed to be useful to him.

She had no wish to offer herself as a hostage, and it was clear that whatever the Caruso had planned for her in that area, this commander was no longer onboard.

But there was something he needed.

"Wait." She held up her hand, keeping her gaze steady. "You can't find someone to fly this runner, can you? But I can."

The little helpers approved. A lot.

She felt the surge of energy, felt every sense heighten.

The laz dipped a little, then pointed down. "How?"

"I am ghost ship girl," she said in response.

He frowned. "How?"

She made a gesture to get him to back off. "I'll show you."

He stepped back, motioned for her to stand.

She did, although her knees dipped a little and she had to force them to lock.

What was she doing? Her breathing accelerated.

The little helpers promised her they were good at learning systems. That they would show her how.

She hoped to the stars and back that they were right.

CHAPTER 34

BEN SHOVED himself forward as the massive Caruson commander hauled Tally toward the runner.

A hand grabbed the fabric of his jacket and pulled him back.

"Have you lost your mind?" Garner shoved him deeper into the forest. "What are you going to do, run into their laz fire?"

"Not likely. They aren't even looking this way." Ben had taken a full step out into the open before Garner had grabbed him, and no Caruson had even glanced their way.

"That's just dumb luck," Garner hissed.

"I can't let her be taken." Ben leaned back against the tree Garner had shoved him against, and faced the fact that he wasn't yet up to full strength. He was getting there, though.

"Ben!" Sari stepped out of the shadows, face alight with relief. "You escaped."

Ben looked over at her. Saw his teammate was filthy, her uniform torn, and she had a scratch on her cheek. "Tally rescued me."

She went still, and her expression turned thoughtful. "I thought there were too many things that 'just happened by accident' to her for her to be as harmless as she pretended. What are you doing here?" She glanced over the field.

"Tally was just captured," Garner said.

"She got caught looking for you and Handel." Ben tried to keep his voice level.

Sari lifted her hands. "I wish she hadn't done that. We can look after ourselves."

That it was true didn't ease the terror in his gut.

"What's this about your little Raxian?" Handel moved out of the shadows behind Sari. He looked worse than she did, his one sleeve was wet and it stank of mud and was dripping slime. "Captain." He nodded to Ben. Looked over at Garner.

"Tally rescued him." Garner crouched down, looking out over the field through the trees. "But she's been captured."

Handel raised his brows at the news that Tally had rescued them, and Ben could see he thought it must have been luck or chance.

"Where'd they take her?"

"To the runner." Ben straightened. He was feeling stronger. He tipped the last of the energy solution Dr. Lenar had given him down his throat and then crouched beside Garner.

"You think they're going to fly her up to the warship?" Sari was watching him carefully.

"What else?"

"And what are those two dead guys doing in the middle of the field?" Handel moved closer to the treeline, joining them in the growing shadows.

"I don't know. We got here as they were dragging Tally to the runner." But Ben wondered what had happened. Who had killed the men.

"Maybe Tally killed them before they got the better of her," Garner said.

Handel looked over at him and scoffed.

Ben didn't tell him she'd taken down two Caruson in about five seconds when she'd rescued him, but this looked different. The men were laid out on the ground as if it was some kind of execution. They didn't look like they'd died fighting. "Whatever happened, they have her now. And we have to get her back."

"Not to state the obvious, but how?"

Ben glanced at Garner. "You go back and signal to the *Galaha* that she's on that runner, so if they encounter it, they don't shoot it down."

"Signal?" Handel's voice rose in hope.

"We have the *Galaha's* call signature." Garner grinned at Ben. "I can get word to them."

"The Caruso haven't even taken off yet," Sari said.

"The delay in direct signaling means they could be long gone before the *Galaha* even gets the message." Ben shuffled back and then stood once he was deeper among the trees. "Garner, go. I'll stay here and see if there's a way to get her out."

"And us?" Sari asked.

Ben looked at her and then Handel. "I'm not going to ask you to risk yourselves to free Tally. If you want to help me, I'll take it, but this is personal for me. You can wait for the *Galaha* to get here, help protect the scientists Tally rescued. I'm happy that's a good use of your time and skill. But I'm going after Tally."

Handel rubbed a filthy hand over hair that was too short to even grab. "Why?"

"Tally has saved my ass more times than I can count in the last week," he said.

"But it's more than that, isn't it?" Sari asked.

His lips quirked and he inclined his head in acknowledgment. "Oh, yes."

BEN LEANED AGAINST THE TREE, watching the field.

Garner and Handel had gone back to the scientists, but Sari had stayed. She was wiping herself down with the thick wipes from her pack, stripping the mud and grime off her face and arms.

"You go into a bog, or something?" Ben asked her.

She snorted. "The river bank. Just managed to avoid being lunch for a legava, too. Had to kill it."

They sat in silence, the clean, pleasant scent of the wipes swirling around them as Sari pulled off her shirt and scrubbed at her neck and chest.

"That runner is just sitting there. Not going anywhere." Ben was confused. His worst fear was they would take off immediately, but they hadn't moved, and he didn't understand what was going on. He still couldn't see a path to getting onboard without being seen, though. There were Caruson soldiers all around the runner.

"Maybe they're waiting for someone." Sari pulled a clean shirt over her head. "The soldiers don't look comfortable, do they? They're twitchy."

Ben had noticed that, too. "They're expecting trouble, maybe?"

"Trouble from whom?" Sari's eyebrows rose. "They don't know we have a direct call signature. They think they've killed the comms and they've taken down the only ship that could have sent word about them. Who could they be scared of?"

It was a good question.

"Well, look there." Ben tilted his head. "Here comes someone familiar."

Irwin stepped out of the treeline on the far side. He was limping, and he didn't look good.

The Caruson soldiers standing around, fidgeting, reacted immediately as he made his way toward the runner, running toward him, shouting instructions, weapons raised.

He gave them the sign every sentient species knew to go fuck themselves, and kept coming, and when they reached him, Ben wished he could hear the exchange, because it was heated.

Eventually, they half-carried him toward the runner and disappeared inside.

"They were waiting for him, you think?" Sari asked.

Ben lifted his shoulders. He was crouched, gaze trained on the runner. Irwin's appearance had woken the soldiers up a bit, but most still looked at a loose end. "Irwin told them to go to hell a couple of days ago, and he's been limping his way here ever since."

"Looks like that's still his position, given the shouting and the gestures." Sari sounded slightly amused.

Ben thought Irwin looked in worse shape than when he'd seen him last. Almost gray, and moving with far more difficulty than before. He'd been trailing Ben and Tally through the forest relatively well after he was shot. Either something had happened to him, or his wound was infected.

"Garner was right when he said Irwin looked bad," Sari said, almost as if reading his mind. "Tally really did some damage when she ran into him on that hover."

Ben grunted, not commenting. But it explained a lot.

He'd have to find out the circumstances of how that happened from Tally.

"Why are they still sitting there--?" Sari cut off as a massive Caruson soldier ran toward the runner.

Ben looked behind him, saw two other soldiers, looking very much the worse for wear, following him at a slower pace.

They looked like they'd been pushing themselves for days. He'd bet a lot they'd come from the mine, and they'd had to make the journey without hovers.

The Caruson commander strode out of the runner, and he met the front-runner halfway across the field. They spoke, heads together, and then turned to wait for the other two to join them.

"Something's happened at the mine," Sari said.

"Yes. Maybe there's been another cave-in." Ben checked the distance between where he was crouched and the door of the runner. Wondered how distracted the Caruso were, and then suddenly the sound of the runner's engines changed. Idled down, and then revved up.

The commander turned, pointing toward the entrance, and one of the Caruson soldiers jogged up the ramp.

He had just disappeared inside when, out of nowhere, an explosion shook the ground.

Ben was thrown back, ears ringing, and from his position on his back, looking straight up, he caught the glimpse high up of a warship.

The Caruso were firing on their own?

Another strike hit the ground.

"How come they keep missing?" Sari shouted. She was crawling toward him.

Good question. The runner was the perfect target. Unmoving, unarmed.

"On purpose," he guessed. Because whoever was in command of the warship would be acting under orders from a distant authority, but it was hard to kill your own.

Very hard.

He had gotten his feet under him, and tried to see if the chaos was enough to give him the chance he needed.

Before he could do anything more than straighten up, the runner's ramp began to lift.

The Caruso had scattered as the bombing had started and there was a clear path.

Ben ran.

He heard Sari shout behind him, but Tally was in that runner, and he had a chance to get in there with her.

He was less than halfway across the field when the door snapped shut.

With a shriek of its engines, the runner lifted, wobbling side to side, and then shot up into the air as a third explosion ignited up ahead.

And Ben was left standing exposed in the field, with absolutely nowhere to go.

CHAPTER 35

TALLY'S HEART seemed to be lodged in her throat, which meant she couldn't respond to the Caruson soldier screaming at her.

He followed up his tirade by lifting his massive laz and putting it to her head.

The little helpers were like lightning under her skin, and she shivered with fear and adrenalin as she tried to keep the runner level.

As she banked away from the latest explosion, she thought she caught a glimpse of Ben standing below her and gasped, her hands lifting off the control panel.

The runner dipped, and the laz dug into her temple as the soldier screamed instructions she couldn't understand.

She lunged back to the panel, giving control to the little helpers so they could smooth out the flight.

She had a sense, a flicker of awareness, that it didn't have to be like this. That she and the little helpers could merge somehow into a single entity, and that she didn't need to feel this separation within her.

But if that was possible, it wasn't going to happen right now.

If she wanted it to happen at all.

She let them use her hands and fingers, moving over the controls, so they accelerated away from Rainerville and left any glimpse of Ben behind them.

The Caruson soldier who'd walked on board just moments before they were all fired on from above adjusted the grip on his weapon, and now his words were more of a hiss than a shout.

She forced herself to go still, and turned to look at him, eyes hot with rage.

"I. Can't. Under. Stand. You." She spat each syllable separately. "Now either stop shouting at me, or communicate in a way I *can* understand, or I'll land us again."

Irwin, who ever since he'd come aboard had stood gaping at her, as if she was the last person he expected to be in the runner, stepped forward, speaking in rough Caruson.

The soldier lowered his laz, and answered, his voice suddenly less strident.

"He says go southeast. He keeps saying southeast to 'something', but I don't know the word he's using." Irwin rubbed at his chest as he spoke, and she felt a tiny lurch of guilt at the sight of him.

She'd really hurt him with the hover. He looked terrible.

She let the little helpers tell her exactly which way southeast was, and she adjusted their trajectory. "Who was shooting at us?"

Irwin laughed weakly, leaning back against the wall. "The Caruso were shooting at their own people. So on every level, this is now officially a fuck up."

"Nowhere to run to now, huh?" She kept her voice neutral.

"If it were just you who knew about me," he said, "I'd kill you the moment it was possible for me to do so, but there's Ben, and at least one of his team came circling around me last night, and I'm guessing more saw me walk across to the runner, so it wouldn't be worth my while to silence you. Too many people know."

"How nice," she bared her teeth at him. "And after I walked away from shooting you."

He pressed his lips together and shrugged.

"Why? Why did you do this?" She assumed she was still going the right way, because the soldier beside her was carefully watching the ground below them, his stance at ease.

"My family is from Faldine. Part of the resistance. And while the war may be over, I saw an opportunity to stick it to the VSC without any blow-back on myself. If the Caruson hadn't shot down that runner and taken out the comms satellite, no one would have even known what was happening. But it seems they skimped on the safety measures when they dug their mine and that earthquake wiped out their whole operation." He looked over at the Caruson soldier standing beside her with ill-concealed dislike.

"Why come all the way to Rainerville, though? Why not lift their people out from the mine?"

"They were told the med ship they needed was too big to land near the mine, they needed a launch pad, and wood from the forest was the fastest way to build one. They were also told the med ship wouldn't come until everyone on the Trail team who saw that runner go down was dead."

Before she could say anything to that, the soldier tapped Tally's shoulder and pointed to a low range of hills in the distance.

She altered direction.

"How did you know how to fly this, anyway?" Irwin asked.

"I'm part of the Raxian Expeditionary Force." She lifted one shoulder.

He narrowed his eyes at that, but didn't respond, and she released some of the tension she held in her shoulders.

The hills slowly took on more definition as the runner got closer. They rose out of a dusty plain, the rocky folds of their cliffs gray and brown against the bright blue sky.

The soldier pointed due south when they got close enough to see the deep folds in the rock, and the lush, dark green of the plants and trees that grew in the deep shade.

She followed along the front of the range, and wasn't surprised when at last, up ahead, she could see tents and movement.

She guessed they had moved up into the open since the earthquake, because no way would Ben and his team have missed this.

She looked around for a place to land, but the soldier had that covered, too. He pointed to a small, flat-looking piece of ground, and with no other good options, she let the little helpers show her how to lower them down.

The runner slammed down a little hard, jolting everyone and earning her a shout from the soldier.

"Then you fly it," she told him, keeping up eye contact.

Irwin shook his head, as if she was foolish to provoke him.

She ignored him. "What now?"

The soldier turned to Irwin, rattled out a long diatribe which had him lifting a hand to stop it and sputter out what she guessed was a request for him to repeat it and speak slower.

Tally ignored them. She got up and walked to the window, and leaned against it, looking out.

There were bodies lying in a long line to one side, and three Caruso digging a trench.

She could see the ground had been disturbed to one side, and guessed that represented the bodies already buried.

They had lost a lot of people.

A few Caruson stepped out of the tents, looked over at the runner and then ducked back inside, only to emerge carrying a makeshift stretcher with a limp body on it.

Did they have room for more injured on the runner?

And where exactly was she taking them, if the warship was firing on their own people, and they'd originally been waiting for a med ship, not a small near-space runner with no equipment?

Somewhere out there, Ben's other two teammates were watching.

The thought made her straighten.

She gnawed at her lip, thinking about that quick glimpse she'd had of the field as she lifted off. Had it been Ben, or one of the other members of his team?

She wanted it to be Garner or Handel, but she knew the shape of him. Knew how he stood. She was terrified he'd been there because he was coming after her. Trying to save her.

She was suddenly shoved to the side, and she fell with a cry.

She looked up, eyes wide with surprise and fear, and saw the Caruson solider who'd pushed her seemed almost as surprised.

He shouted at her.

She stared at him for a long moment, then gave the little helpers full permission to do their thing as she looked all around her, searching for options.

She was done.

She jumped up, the little helpers giving her a boost as she landed on her feet and then she used the Caruson's knee like a step to propel her up to the narrow sill of the runner's massive front window. She launched herself into the air over his head, and flipped over to land behind him.

She was fast.

So fast that he didn't realize she had snatched his laz when she'd boosted up on his knee until she landed behind him and stuck it against his ear.

"Say that again, this time in a reasonable tone." She looked over at Irwin as she spoke.

There were two other Caruson soldiers who'd been in the back with the injured, and they stepped in behind Irwin, weapons raised.

Irwin was staring at her, face slack.

"Irwin." She made her voice sharp. "What was he shouting at me and why the hell did he shove me down?"

Irwin stuttered out a word, cleared his throat and then said something to the soldier she was holding hostage.

The soldier answered, his head swiveling a little toward her, until her sharp tap of his laz against his ear stopped him dead.

"He says he was telling you to open the door." Irwin's words tripped over each other. "He didn't mean to push you so hard. He forgot you aren't as sturdy as a Caruson."

"If he wants me to do something in future, you tell him to do so politely."

Irwin nodded, stumbled out a few sentences in Caruson, but she had a suspicion he hadn't passed on her ultimatum. She decided that probably meant he didn't know the word for 'polite', or he was too scared to give the Caruson orders.

She stepped back, lifting the laz away from the soldier's head, and the Caruson turned and put his hand out for it.

She hesitated, giving him a long, hard look.

They stared at each other, and eventually she handed it over, but she thought the message had been received and understood.

She moved to the control panel, and the little helpers showed her how to open the door.

As soon as the ramp lowered, Caruson soldiers brought the first stretcher in.

Tally walked to the door, standing beside Irwin.

It was the first close-up look she'd gotten of the injured. And they were in a bad way. She guessed there were others who were not hurt as severely who hadn't made the cut, and now, the decision was whether to take some of those from Rainerville out and replace them with those whose injuries were worse.

"How did you talk your way onboard?" It suddenly occurred to her that Irwin had taken a valuable spot.

"I persuaded them that if you were flying, they'd need a translator." He sent her a humorless smile.

"You didn't know I was flying it until you came aboard."

He inclined his head. "True. I saw the runner and I ran for it,
and I was prepared to say anything to get a ride. In the end, you
being there made it easy for me."

"And where will you go? Where will this lot go? Did they forget
their warship fired on us?" She was surprised the warship hadn't
been ordered to fire on the mine, too, but then, maybe the
Caruson still hoped to sneak back here when this had blown over.
They couldn't know that some of Ben's team had followed the trail
back here, and knew all about it.

"There is something called '*fraknvos*'." He pronounced it as a
Caruson would. "It means 'all family', I think. It stipulates help for the
injured, no matter what the circumstances. I think it's from the wars
the Caruso fought amongst themselves for so many millennium."

"So if they go meet the warship with a demand for this
fraknvos, they think the injured will be taken in and helped?"

Irwin nodded.

"And everyone else on the runner?"

Irwin shook his head. "Good question. When I got on the
runner, I had no idea we were about to be attacked by the Caruson. I'm trying to decide what gamble to take now. Stay. Or go?"

He still looked gray and there was a tightness around his eyes
that told her he was in a lot of pain.

As if aware he wasn't going to get far, even if they'd let him
leave the runner, he slid down the wall and sat, eyes closed.

She was sorry she'd done that to him.

She reminded herself he'd tried to kidnap her. Had sold them
all out.

An argument had started between the Caruso onboard, and
the those from the mine, and eventually they fitted in two more

injured miners, and the Caruson soldier in charge asked her through Irwin to close up and head off-planet into near-space.

"Last chance to run," she said, not sure if she would help him if he decided to chance it, but he curled over his knees and simply shook his head.

They'd all have to take their chances with the warship.

One that'd just tried to kill them all.

CHAPTER 36

QUIET DESCENDED.

After the deafening explosions and the screams of the runner's engines, it felt like sound had been sucked out of the world.

Then Ben heard a bird chatter in the trees, someone moaned from one of the tents, and things snapped back into place.

He stood alone in the open, and while he had a clear run back to the treeline, there were Caruson to his right, standing in front of the tents, and to one side of the landing pad.

The runner was just disappearing on the horizon, dipping and swerving more than it should.

He watched until it disappeared completely, and wanted to shout his fury at the sky.

Tally was gone.

A few Caruso began to move toward him, and he forced himself to concentrate on what was happening right in front of him. He had to judge whether he could make it back to the forest, and whether he should even try, because he'd be leading them straight to his team and the scientists.

He also had no weapon.

He'd given his to Tally, and the Caruson laz he'd had before had been taken away from him when he was captured.

He glanced at the treeline again and a flicker of movement caught his eye. Sari stood in a shooting stance, her laz raised, just a step out from under the cover of the forest.

He closed his eyes for a moment.

She needed to get back. To disappear amongst the late-afternoon shadows.

The Caruso were gathering speed as they ran toward him now, but a shout cut the air, stopping them in their tracks. The big commander strode through them, his laz held across his chest.

At least it wasn't pointed at him. In fact, Ben wondered why he hadn't been shot already. They hardly needed to be near him to do that.

The commander slowed as he got closer, and then stopped.

"Surrender," he said.

Ben tilted his head to one side, confused. Because he'd have to be fighting first to surrender.

Then the commander held out his laz with both hands. "We surrender," he corrected.

Ben reached out and took the weapon, and the commander knelt on the ground and put his hands behind his head. His expression was calm and unreadable.

But Ben read it anyway.

They'd just been fired on by their own people. They were done.

Injured, without transport or supplies.

Their only chance was to throw in with the VSC.

"Captain?" Sari called from the edge of the forest, but she was out in the open herself now, moving toward him.

"Go call the others," he said. "We've taken Rainerville back."

Sari stopped dead, looked around at the Caruso, most of

whom looked as confused as she did, and then finally she gave a nod, turned, and disappeared.

It was never a good idea to predict the outcome of conflict, Ben reflected. Because unless you controlled everything, there was no telling.

No telling at all.

And now he was in control, he was calling that runner right back.

"THEY JUST HANDED over their weapons and rolled over?" Handel watched the Caruson soldiers as they took the wood they'd gathered and started up the evening fires that were clearly part of their routine.

"What else are they going to do?" Ben leaned against the building closest to the field, and watched as two kuyer, already skinned and dressed, were lifted onto roasting spits.

He still had both his and Tally's meals. But the smell of roasting meat drifted over to him, and he had to admit, there was something about it that made his mouth water.

"You're just going to let them wander around?" Garner asked, coming from the forest himself, arms loaded with wood. He dropped it into the fire pit nearby.

"We don't have enough people to hold them captive, and where are they going to go?" Ben shook his head. "You want to find someplace they can all fit, with a working bathroom and medical facilities?"

Handel made a face. Shook his head. "Point taken."

"What about the runner?" Garner asked. "Did they get in touch with it?"

Ben shook his head. Dread gripped him, because the commander made it clear he was no longer in control of that runner. It had left before he could give the soldiers onboard instructions.

They were on their own.

"Commander Vrk says he was given the warship's call signature, but they didn't exactly have a two-way communications system. They were supposed to be invisible here. They had a set time to transmit once a week. He can contact them, ask them to order the runner back, but as they just fired on him . . ."

"And the bodies in the field?" Handel asked, face sour at the news.

Ben shrugged. "He seems a little reluctant to talk about that."

"Maybe he didn't like what some of the crew had to say, and shut them up," Handel said.

"All the more reason for the warship to ignore any requests he makes. The runner didn't exactly hang around when the shooting started." Garner turned to watch Sari come out of the accommodation building, hair slicked back and wet, with a new uniform on.

Ben gave a tight nod. "Except, the runner flew off in the direction of the mine, which means at least some of the people onboard are Commander Vrk's. They might have control of it."

"Even if they did go pick up more of the injured," Sari said as she joined them, "how will it help them to come back here, whether they're loyal to Vrk or not? Those people need the kind of medical treatment they're only going to get on a med ship. I don't know that a warship will be able to cope with that number of injured, but surely it's better than nothing?"

"Even a warship that just shot at them?" Garner asked.

Sari shrugged. "I'm not saying it'll be an easy decision, but they may think it's worth it."

They might just think exactly that. And that had Ben terrified. Because wherever they decided to go, they were taking Tally with them.

CHAPTER 37

TALLY COULD SEE the warship up ahead.

It hunkered beside Veltos's small moon, still and unresponsive.

The big Caruson hailed it again as they approached, his frustration ramping up as the minutes ticked by with no answer.

They could have been onboard already, but the soldier had told her to wait until they had permission.

When it was clear that was never going to come, he insisted she go forward anyway.

Tally headed the runner toward the big landing bay on the under side of the ship, but a sudden warning light pulsed red on the bridge.

Irwin swore.

"What is it?" But she was afraid she already knew.

"Their weapons just went hot." Irwin finally sounded a little more like himself. A little more energized.

The Caruson soldier's tone changed, and he started to repeat the same word, over and over.

"*Fraknvos.*"

A sudden blast of static had Tally wincing and covering her

ears, and then the warship lifted up and away, disappearing behind the moon.

The runner was really only a near-space vessel, built to go from the warship to the planet below, and it didn't have sophisticated tracking, but even so, she knew the ship was gone. She had never seen a ship move that fast.

The Caruson swore and hit the side of her control panel, then he walked away, fists clenched.

"What now?" She looked over at Irwin.

He shrugged, still sitting with his back against the wall. "Go back to Rainerville, maybe? What else can we do?"

"What was that about?" She could see all of the Caruso looked more than just unhappy, they were furious. She'd almost say betrayed.

"They didn't honor the *fraknvos*." Irwin spoke as if he was feeling his way. "I don't fully understand it. I said before it's like family, but I think it's also a bit like our surrender. If you surrender, the other side is honor bound to give you medical assistance, and treat you well."

"So it's hard for them to do? They have to put aside their pride?" Tally asked.

Irwin nodded. "And after they bent the knee, so to speak, instead of help, the warship pretended not to hear them, and then ran away."

Tally looked through to the hold. Recalled the urgency in the Caruson soldier's calls to the warship. There was no possible way they hadn't understood the severity of the situation.

"Maybe it was the best the captain of the warship could do," she said. "If their orders were to attack, pretending not to hear and then running away was as much *fraknvos* as they could give."

Irwin nodded, and they drifted in silence for a long moment. Their only option was to go back to Rainerville. She dreaded what she'd find there.

If Ben had been hurt . . .

The Caruson who'd been directing her stepped into the back, and went into a huddle with the other two soldiers, talking quietly.

The runner drifted closer to the moon and she turned it around, back to face Veltos. She didn't care now where anyone else wanted to go, she was going back to Rainerville.

As they came about, something slid from the far side of the moon, and Tally froze.

She stared at it as it moved into view, sleek and sharp. They were so close, she could see the name of the ship, the VSCS *Galaha*, along the side.

She was still looking at it when the red glow of the warning light started flashing. The warship's weapons were hot.

She heard Irwin swear behind her, heard the thump of boots as the Caruson ran to the big screen to have a closer look.

But all she had eyes for was the cannons as they came around.

TALLY WATCHED the reactions of the Caruson soldiers to whatever message was being transmitted from the VSC warship.

They stood, faces and bodies tense.

Whatever was being said was in Caruson, and she decided it was time for her to get in a word.

"Hello," she said. "This is Tally Riva of the Raxian Expeditionary Force. I am on board this runner. There are at least twenty Caruson onboard who are severely injured, and they need immediate medical assistance."

There was absolute silence for a moment, and even the Caruso turned to her with faint smiles at how thoroughly she'd flipped the situation on its head.

"Tally Riva, this is the signals operator on the Verdant String

Coalition Ship *Galaha*, Sergeant Fraser. Is anyone else from your group onboard with you?"

Tally remembered the name Fraser. This was Frangi's friend, Linn, talking.

She closed her eyes briefly. But she found she didn't want to tell him how badly Frangi was hurt. "The trail guide, Irwin, is with me, and he requires medical attention as well."

There was a pause. "No one else?"

"I'm afraid not. Frangi is--"

"Tally Riva, this is Captain Harris of the VSCS *Galaha*." The commander's voice cut across both of them. "What are you doing onboard that runner, and what is going on?"

"It's a very long story, Captain." She held the runner in place, too afraid to move and get shot at. "Whatever the reasons for my being here doesn't detract from the fact that there are people dying on this runner, and their own warship just raced off and left them."

"When was that?" Harris's voice rose.

"About ten minutes before you came around the side of the moon."

"Is that so." There was a cold edge to her voice.

Tally imagined the captain was directing all sorts of long-range tracking searches in the silence that followed.

"So, let me get this straight. Their people have abandoned them, and you want me to take them in after they shot down the runner that was meant to take you home, took out our comms satellite, and attacked our people."

"Yes, Captain."

She didn't say any more. She didn't need to.

The VSC would not leave these people to die.

"Tell the pilot to approach the landing bay," Harris said at last. "And every laz had better be on the floor, or we will not hold back."

"Thank you." Tally turned the runner toward the landing bay on the *Galaha*, and let the little helpers float it in.

When they landed, she had Irwin tell the Caruson to put their weapons on the floor to one side, and go sit up against the wall on the other.

She opened the door, and moved away from the control panel, standing just inside the hold as it lowered.

With any luck, no one would realize she had been the one flying the runner.

There would be way to many questions about that.

The soldiers who stepped inside the runner as soon as the door was open reeled back a little at the sight of the injured Caruson.

One of them touched their ear and muttered something, and Tally heard the sound of boots running toward them.

"Tally Riva?" One of the lieutenants asked, her hair pulled back in complex braids from a stern face.

"That's me." She raised her hand.

"Come."

Tally picked her way through the Caruso, and when she reached the lieutenant, she stepped in a little closer. "Irwin, the trail guide, needs medical attention, but he was also helping the Caruso."

The lieutenant gave her a hard look. "Meaning?"

"Meaning, he's not an ally. He sold out everyone on the Trail. Don't trust him."

"Hmm." She stepped away, spoke quietly into her comms. "All right. Follow me."

Tally sighed and did as she was ordered. "Am I going to speak to Captain Harris?"

The lieutenant didn't turn around, didn't answer her.

Tally guessed the answer was yes.

CHAPTER 38

TALLY STEPPED into what was clearly a conference room and noticed there were only four people present beside herself and the lieutenant who'd brought her.

One was clearly Captain Harris, a short woman with dark hair and big dark eyes, wearing the VSC uniform.

A sergeant stood beside her, and she guessed he was Linn Fraser.

She could see from the desperation in his eyes he had a personal stake in this.

She liked the fact that Harris had allowed him to be here. He was by far the most junior officer present, and she guessed he'd been allowed to participate because of Frangi.

The other two looked like older, more grizzled versions of Ben. Both the man and the woman held themselves in a way that shouted Arkhoran Special Forces. They wore plain black with just a single stripe of rank on the left side of their chests.

"This is Sergeant Fraser," Harris said. "I'm Captain Harris, and this is Commander Reskit and Commander Veniur. Let's hear your report."

Tally hesitated a moment, battled the ingrained resistance to taking orders from someone other than her own commander, then gave a nod. She began to relay what had happened, and when she got to Soo trying to fix the comms at the supply station, she stopped.

"Have you gotten a message from Soo?"

Linn shook his head. "Not yet." He looked over at Harris, as if requesting permission for something, and she inclined her head slightly. He walked out of the room, and as soon as the doors closed behind him, Tally heard him break into a run.

Tally hoped he was off to order a med runner down to fetch Frangi.

"Let's move this along." The Special Forces commander, Reskit, a tall, spare man with a brutal haircut, crossed his arms over his chest. "What did you find at Rainerville?"

"There were a lot of Caruso there. They were building a landing pad out of the wood from the forest, and they'd taken the scientists prisoner. There were tents in the open fields behind the forest, and they were full of injured Caruson miners."

"And Ben?" Reskit watched her with hard eyes.

She hesitated, wished she knew exactly where Ben was, and that he was safe.

Reskit made a sound of impatience, and she raised her chin.

"Ben was captured. I got away and ran into some of his team."

"Who?" The Special Forces woman, Venuir, spoke for the first time.

"Sari, Handel and Garner. They'd been searching for signs of the Caruso when they saw them moving toward Rainerville with their injured and followed." She paused for a moment, trying to think how to word it without drawing any attention to herself. "Some of Ben's team distracted the Caruson soldiers and we were able to free Ben and the scientists. But I was caught shortly after that. I'd just been taken into the runner when the Caruso warship attacked from near-space. They shot at their own people at least three times, then the runner took off. We went to the mine to get more injured, and then came up here to find the warship to get them the help they need."

"The same warship that just sped off?" Harris asked.

Tally nodded.

"There's a mine, you say?" Veniur asked, her voice thoughtful.

"Yes. On our first day on the Trail there was a very strong earthquake. It appears the mine walls collapsed and either injured or trapped the Caruso working there."

"So they needed to get their people off Veltos. They tried to eliminate all witnesses by taking out the runner and satellite, and those of you on the Trail, and then they built a landing pad for what, a ship to come down and get their people out?" Harris was nodding as she spoke.

"Yes, but something changed. My guess is the Caruso in charge of the operation weren't happy the Caruson commander on-planet made the decision to bring attention to themselves. They shot at their own people, and they've left them here without help."

"Why did they put you in the runner? Why bring you to the warship?" Veniur tilted her head.

Tally lifted her shoulders as she thought through her answer. They would know about her. They were the ones who had probably given Ben his file on her. "I don't know for sure, but Irwin said they wanted me because I was the one on the ghost ship. He tried to grab me for them. They wanted to debrief me on what I saw on that ship."

All three went still at that.

"And Irwin came in on the runner with you?" Harris spoke first.

Tally nodded. "He was caught in the crossfire between Ben and I and the Caruso, and then later I hurt him, accidentally, when I ran into him on a hover. He had some deal with the Caruso which broke down when they shot him, but he had no other way off Veltos, so he persuaded them to take him with them as an interpreter between me and them."

Harris and Reskit exchanged a look.

"We need to make contact with Ben, get the lay of the land before we go in," Reskit said, looking across at Harris.

Tally lifted a hand, then forced it back down at her side. "They may have recaptured Ben." She bit her lip as they all turned to look at her. "I thought I saw him on the field as the runner took off, and if it was him, then he was in the open, with no cover."

"Why would he have done that?" Reskit asked, voice harsh.

"To try and rescue me." She felt her shoulders hunch under their scrutiny and forced herself to stand straighter.

"What about the other members of Ben's team? Enn and Va-Laya? Where are they?" Reskit eyed her with suspicion.

"I was told they followed the Caruso trail back to its source. So theoretically they are watching the mine site."

Reskit gave a grunt Tally assumed was of approval.

"We need to get down there and see," Veniur said. She turned to look at Harris. "With your permission, Captain."

Harris nodded, and as the two commanders jogged out, she turned to Tally. "Lieutenant Sentko will show you to a room, and we'll call you if we need more information."

"I'd like to go back down," Tally said. She should have anticipated this happening. She wasn't part of the *Galaha's* crew, and she was an unknown entity. They would treat her politely, but she was at best a witness, at worst an annoyance.

"What do you think you can do that our own people can't?" Harris asked.

The little helpers vibrated a bit at that, but Tally kept herself still. "I know where the mine is, for a start."

"If we need you for that, we'll let you know," Harris said.

"Captain, I know I can be--"

"Science Officer Riva, let me be blunt. I don't know you. I have a feeling you glossed over parts of your report, and I don't trust you. You will not be allowed to do anything more as it relates to this incident, other than answer more questions. Have I made myself clear?"

Tally stared at her, and then the lieutenant with the beautiful braids appeared in the doorway, and gestured for Tally to follow.

Captain Harris swept her arm in the direction of the door, and Tally realized she had no choice but to come to heel.

She followed the lieutenant out and they were a few steps down the corridor when the lights suddenly dimmed and then came back up, and a siren began to sound.

"Incoming enemy warships," someone said over a speaker. "Prepare for evasive action."

Lieutenant Sentko glanced over her shoulder, her face tight with frustration.

"Go, I'll take care of myself," Tally said, and with a nod, Sentko ran off.

Tally followed behind her at a slower pace, and found what she was looking for a few doors down.

A room full of screens, and Linn Fraser and some colleagues hunched over their control panels.

"What's happening?" Tally asked.

"There are two Caruso warships coming in almost faster than we can track."

"Did you get a runner off already to rescue Frangi?"

Linn looked up, face grim. He shook his head. "They were loading one up with medical supplies when the warships were spotted."

"What's going to happen now?"

"The orders are to move out of range, arm shields and wait for the reinforcements we called in before we came here." Linn stood suddenly. "Where was Frangi hurt? What did she look like the last time you saw her?"

Tally didn't move back when he stepped into her space. "She was hit in her leg. The one that had been injured before. She was unconscious last time I saw her, but we had a supply hover, and Soo and Lenny made sure she was lying comfortably on it, and Ben circled round when the Caruso sent soldiers after them and killed them, so they had a clear run back to the supply station."

Linn's eyes had widened when she mentioned Caruson soldiers. "They were hunting her?"

"They were hunting all of us." Tally held his gaze. "When we couldn't avoid them, we had to deal with them."

He nodded. Then noticed the light blinking on his control panel. He sat, and began to tap at the controls.

"What now?" Tally leaned over him.

"Two Caruson warships have just arrived. They've launched runners into Veltos's near-space."

"Where are the runners headed?"

"Too soon to tell, but I think we can guess."

Yes, she could guess. Rainerville and the mine. It had to be. And they would either wipe out everyone there, or take their people and kill the Verdant Stringers. She couldn't see any other reason for them to come back.

She wouldn't let that happen.

"Are we out of their line of sight?" Tally asked.

Linn looked up, his brow creased in a frown. "Yes."

"Okay. Thank you. I'll leave you to it, now."

"Thanks." Linn had already turned back to his control panel, his focus on what was in front of him.

Tally made her way back out into the passageway.

If she was locked out by Harris and distrusted by Ben's commanders, then she'd have to take her chances on her own.

If there were Caruson runners in near-space, no one would notice one more.

She'd flown the Caruson runner into the *Galaha's* launch bay. And she could fly it out.

CHAPTER 39

THE CORRIDORS WERE full of people moving from job to job, but Tally was still in her military uniform, no matter that it was not the cleanest it had ever been, and she blended in well enough.

She made her way back to the launch bay and caught a glimpse of Commanders Reskit and Veniur standing in a small circle of men and women in the same black uniform, talking quietly together.

They were in front of a sleek runner that looked like it was Special Forces property, rather than part of the *Galaha's* standard vessel allocation, and Tally was pleased to see the Caruson runner was at the other end of the bay.

She tagged along behind a group of crew who were headed for the small, agile fighter ships in the middle of the bay, and then broke off and made her way to the Caruson runner.

There was no one around it now. All the Caruson had obviously been moved out of the hold to the med bay.

It was her lucky day.

The little helpers sort of got the joke. She could sense a stirring of amusement, and then a single thread of query about whether this was a good idea.

Probably not, she told them. But I'm not letting the chance go.

She stepped into the runner and settled into the pilot's chair.

Another fear gripped her.

This was going to out her. She had no explanation as to how she knew how to fly this runner. Eventually whatever she was about to do would come out, and if she was alive to face the consequences, she was going to have to tell them about the little helpers.

She blew out a breath and touched the controls, closing the door before she started the engines so there was no chance someone would notice what was happening and jump onboard.

Then she let the little helpers have the wheel, and they showed her how to start the engines in a soft, launch bay mode, so the runner rose up more like a hover and then drifted forward toward the flexi-screen that sealed in the ship's air.

Just before the runner hit the semi-liquid curtain, she caught movement from her left, saw Reskit and three other special forces officers running toward her, shouting.

She judged the distance and kept the gentle speed as the runner slid through the pale blue wall, and out onto the other side.

Then she bent over the control panel and let the engines rip.

The comms squawked and then a string of unintelligible Caruson came over it.

She hesitated. If this was from one of the Caruson warships, they had caught on to her very fast. And if she answered in VS vernacular, she'd be made. But it was most likely the *Galaha*, who thought a Caruson was flying the runner.

If she didn't set them straight, they'd shoot her.

"I don't understand Caruson," she said at last.

"Is that Tally Riva?" Captain Harris's voice was a hiss.

"It is. Sorry, Captain Harris. You shut me out, and I didn't feel I could share my idea with you. I'm going to blend in with the runners the Caruso have launched into near-space and see if I can retrieve my friends."

"Come back right now." Harris's tone was harsh.

"Sorry, no. I don't report to you, Captain. And I have a good idea what your plans for me would include if I did come back. There's no time to waste, anyway."

She cut off the comms over Harris's reply, and concentrated on piloting toward the dark green, gold, and red planet below.

She didn't have time to find the warships and slip amongst them, she realized. They would be heading down to wipe out every single witness, so she needed to be the first one down.

She just hoped the Caruso didn't notice.

"COMMS SAYS there are two warships coming in." Garner called from inside the building that housed Rainerville's communal lounge and dining room.

Ben was standing just inside the door to avoid the heavy rain, and he looked up. There was nothing to see but dark purple clouds. "We'll have to take their word for it."

Garner must have left the comms unit because suddenly he stood shoulder to shoulder with Ben. "Shit. We're blind."

Handel and Sari ran toward them when Ben gestured to them, slowing when they saw the direction of Ben and Garner's gaze.

"Caruson warships," Garner explained. "Two."

"Why come back?" Sari asked, making room for herself in the doorway and wiping the rain from her face. "Especially when they'd gotten away."

"Because they didn't want any Caruson left to talk about what they've been up to." Handel's eyes were on the tents just visible through the curtains of rain. "Someone over there probably knows what use they're going to put the mineral they're mining to back on Caruso."

"Vrk does, I'm sure," Ben said. He looked over at the field, and saw Vrk walking through the downpour toward him.

This time, he was willing to bet, they'd have sent Caruson warships that were prepared to fire on their own people. Not like the last one, the crew and captain of which had probably known Vrk and some of his people personally.

The comms unit behind them emitted a high pitched squeak, and Garner rushed back to it.

They all turned toward him.

"The warships have launched at least four runners each at Veltos." Garner tapped out a confirmation of receipt, and then went still. Lifted his gaze and when it met Ben's, he flinched away.

"What is it?" Ben knew he wouldn't like it, whatever it was.

"The runner that took off when they were shooting at us? It got taken by the *Galaha*. Tally was onboard."

If it had been any other time, Ben knew he'd feel the weight of worry for Tally lift. But those two Caruson warships meant the Caruso didn't want any witnesses, and that included the *Galaha*.

The *Galaha* had no way to transmit what was happening to the rest of the VSC--the comms satellite was gone. If the Caruso could destroy the *Galaha* and everyone on Veltos, they could get away with what they'd done.

He forced himself to shrug. "She'd be in as much danger down here as she'll be on the *Galaha*."

He looked back toward Vrk, who was still jogging through the rain toward him, and it suddenly hit Ben. If there were runners coming, the injured Caruso in the tents were sitting out in the open, completely vulnerable.

He started running.

"Ben, wait!" Garner called behind him, but Ben waved his hand.

"Later!"

Handel and Sari had obviously come to the same conclusion as he had, because with a burst of speed, they drew level with him.

They met Vrk at the edge of the field.

"What is it?" Vrk asked.

"Your people are back." He pointed up, shielding his eyes against the rain.

Vrk frowned as lightning lit the dark, bruised clouds.

"We've been told there are eight runners coming."

Vrk stared at him, and Ben had the impression he was thinking the words over, trying to understand them.

"Eight?" He held up his fingers, showing seven.

"No. Eight." Ben showed him eight fingers.

Vrk's mouth formed a grim line. "Need to move."

"Yes. Into the forest. It isn't going to save everyone, but it's better than sitting out in the field," Ben said.

Vrk gave a nod of agreement.

"Let's start." Ben turned to Sari. "Get the scientists here to help as well. We'll need everyone."

She nodded, turned, and ran toward the buildings.

Vrk turned the opposite way, running toward the tents and shouting the news to the Caruson who weren't hurt.

As Ben followed him at a jog, Handel put out a hand and gripped his arm. "We're going to try and save them?"

Ben glanced over. "They surrendered to us, so we are obliged to save them. But I would have tried anyway."

Handel smiled cynically as he nodded. "Vrk knew what he was doing, all right. But if they hadn't surrendered? Even if they'd left us alone and stopped hunting us down, I don't know that I'd have tried to help them."

Ben lifted his shoulders. "I don't think anyone who's injured should be attacked. But if you want to look at it another way, who keeps the moral high ground here?"

Handel shot him another look. "Even if they don't care about the moral high ground?"

"We don't worry about what they do or don't do. The Verdant String has to work with a lot of other people from a lot of other planets. Who are they going to prefer to ally themselves with when the Caruso get more aggressive with their attacks? Us, or them?"

Handel conceded the point with a nod, and took his side of a stretcher with good grace when they got to the first tent.

They started running the first wave of injured miners across the field and into the forest. With only four hovers, all the stretchers needed to be used, as well. Ben was paired with a Caruson soldier, and he was glad of it, because the Caruso they were carrying was heavy.

They all were.

He was also near death.

The rain pounded down on them and the injured Caruson didn't even turn his head.

Ben wondered if they needed someone to walk through the tents and choose who was most likely to live, so those people could be moved first.

He would have to raise it with Vrk.

His people. His call.

"Ben." Sari reached him as they were loading the second Caruson onto the stretcher. "Garner got word Tally stole the Caruson runner out of the *Galaha's* launch bay, and she told Captain Harris she's on her way down here to get us."

Ben stilled in shock, looked up. The clouds were too thick, and the rain still too heavy to see anything.

Suddenly, he frowned.

"How's she flying it?"

Sari shrugged. "They don't know. But she cut them off and she's gone dark for now. All they know is she said she's coming to get us."

"Is she ahead of the runners the Caruso sent?"

Sari shrugged. "That's all I know." She ran toward a stretcher being dragged by a Caruson soldier, and he stopped to let her pick up the other end.

Ben picked up his own end, and then he was running across the field, arms burning, injured side stabbing him with pain, mind spinning.

Tally had stolen a runner.

He didn't understand why she hadn't discussed it with Harris before she left, but he was sure he'd find out soon enough.

She was coming down. Coming to get them. And she didn't realize there were a lot more of them to get than she thought.

CHAPTER 40

THE CARUSON RUNNERS were just behind her.

Tally felt them like a hot breath against the back of her neck. They were racing down, and on the screen she could see the two warships had left their original positions and were moving toward the *Galaha*.

She'd gotten away just in time.

Veltos was no longer a sphere in front of her, she was close enough to see the large swathes of green forest, the red sand and gold grass of the plains.

A runner edged into her peripheral vision, over to her right, and she turned to follow it.

Somehow its pilot had caught up with her, knew how to go faster than she did, which was no surprise, but as she had no sense of where Rainerville was precisely on the vast planet in front of her, it would surely be quicker to follow someone who looked like they did know where they were going than guess.

A quick look at her tracking system showed her they were the front runners by a lot.

She pushed the runner more than she was comfortable with to

keep up, and then felt her stomach cramp as she saw they were headed not for Rainerville, but the Caruson mine site.

She gnawed at her lip as she kept up her speed, wondering what to do, whether to veer north, toward Rainerville or follow along. Because Ben's colleagues were still down there, too.

But they wouldn't have any idea of who she was. Would certainly not come toward the runner if she landed. It might be a huge waste of time when every minute counted.

Any ideas? She asked the little helpers.

They were silent, and she tapped her fingers nervously on the control panel. Her gaze sharpened on a few of the controls near her drumming fingertips.

There were lights underneath the runner. She'd used them before when she'd entered the *Galaha's* launch bay.

With nerves tightening her breath, she made her choice to at least try and pick Ben's friends up.

She activated the lights, and then began using Verdant String Switch Code as she approached the mine.

She'd had to learn it because she was part of the Expeditionary Force, which meant theoretically she could be stuck somewhere without access to tech. Switch code gave her the ability to still send out a message. She hoped the Arkhoran Special Forces learned it, too.

She kept it simple, flipping the switch on the same message over and over, and then took a careful look at the landscape as she lowered the runner closer to the ground.

The little helpers told her where they thought the best place to watch the mine site would be, and Tally agreed with them, setting down in the closest open spot.

Her comms unit buzzed, and she kept the engine running as she checked her tracking system, saw the runner she'd followed down was circling the site.

It hadn't opened fire yet, and Tally wondered if that was to fool the Caruso hiding in the tunnels and tents into coming out, so they could shoot them down in the open.

The buzz on the comms set was probably the other runner trying to contact her to ask what the hell she was doing.

She ignored the hail and opened the door, walking through the back hold to stand at the top of the ramp.

The runner's engines were whipping up the dust from the dry plain, the red swirl making it hard to see.

She hesitated, searching through the flying sand for any sign of Ben's people. She couldn't stay. She was only just ahead of the other runners as it was, and every second was a second she wasn't headed for Rainerville.

Suddenly two figures dressed in black appeared, heads bowed against the blast of dust from the engines.

She waved, gesturing them in.

They hesitated.

Frustration roared through her. She pointed to the other runner, and then gave the VSC military standard sign for 'we have to leave now'.

They stayed were they were, and Tally took a step toward them, and then stopped, looked back to the bridge.

She didn't have time to persuade them. Regret held her for another beat, and then she broke free of it. Hardened her heart.

She turned back to face them, gave them the one minute signal, and ran back inside.

She started closing the door, and almost sagged with relief when she heard the clatter as the two soldiers threw themselves inside.

Then she lifted up, to the near constant buzz of her comms unit.

The other runner was still circling, and the technique was working. Some of the Caruso had come out of the tunnels, and more out of the tents.

She wanted to warn them, but--

She looked down at the panel, and engaged one of the laz on the underside of the runner.

She took aim at a point out in the open, where there was no one that she could see, and she took her shot.

The Caruso flinched back, and she shot again, this time a little closer to the tents.

"What are you doing?" The voice behind her was a little rough, as if they had been breathing in dust.

"I'm warning them to keep under cover, because the runners that are coming are here to wipe them out." She lifted the runner up and banked to the left, heading in the direction of Rainerville, which she remembered from her earlier trip in the other direction. Last time, she'd had to do it at laz point.

She glanced over her shoulder and couldn't help the laugh that escaped. Looked like she was doing it at laz point again.

The two members of Ben's team who'd gone to watch the mine stood on either side of her, both with their weapons drawn, covered in red dust, faces streaked.

She couldn't remember either woman's name.

"I'm sorry, Ben told me your names but I've had so much happen to me, I can't remember what they are."

That threw them a little.

"How do you know Ben?"

"We were on the Trail together." She turned back to the control panel, even though the little helpers were buzzing, were telling her all the ways she could turn this situation around, so she was the one with the laz.

"So what's going on and what was that message--"

"Listen." Tally flicked a glance their way. "I don't have time for a long explanation. I risked a lot to pick you up. While I don't expect you on your knees with gratitude, there are two Caruson warships in near-space, and they've released eight runners to come clean up the mess they made. That means killing their own people, and us. I'm going to grab Ben, Sari, Handel and Garner and the three scientists at Rainerville, then my three friends at the supply station, and try to get us all off this planet, or at least find a place to hide until the *Galaha* and those two warships finish facing off with each other."

There was silence for a moment and Tally concentrated on checking to see what the other runner was doing.

It had begun to follow her, but after a minute, it turned back.

"I'm Enn, she's Va-Laya." The woman with hair that gleamed almost as red as the dust caked on her cheeks gave the Arkhoran greeting, and her companion tucked a long, dark braid behind her ear and did the same.

"Tally Riva." Tally nodded back, and tried to coax a little more speed out of the runner.

There were head winds, and the vessel was buffeted, rattling a little.

She went higher, and it eased off a bit.

"So, you were on the Trail with Ben. How did you get this runner?" Enn started wandering around, and Tally noticed her laz was no longer in her hand.

The little helpers stopped buzzing as much.

"I was captured by the Caruson, and they were going to take me to their warship." She would stick to that story. It was simple, and at one point, it had been true.

"You escaped in it?" Va-Laya asked, surprised.

"No, their warship abandoned them, and then the *Galaha* arrived and the Caruson soldiers on this runner surrendered to them. I took it out of the *Galaha's* launch bay when the Caruson sent in those two warships, because I hoped the Caruso wouldn't notice one more runner in near-space. I was hoping to pick everyone up and get away."

There was silence from both of them after that, and she was glad to have no more questions.

They were getting closer to Rainerville--Tally could see the edge of the forest far in the distance, as well as clouds as black and thick as any she'd ever seen.

She checked the tracker screen.

The runners headed toward the settlement were only going to be a few minutes behind her.

"What is it?" Va-Laya must have been watching her face.

"Look," Tally offered, indicating toward the screen.

The special forces soldier leaned over, her face grim as she realized what she was looking at. "You can't go faster?"

Tally shook her head.

"Enn and I will jump out straight away, start looking for everyone. Where will they be?"

Tally raised her shoulders. "Last time I knew for sure, they were in the forest close to Rainerville. But I thought I caught sight of Ben on the field as this runner took off."

"What does that mean?" Enn asked.

"It means he was out in the open, with the Caruso standing all around him." She could barely say the words. It was like she had no air left in her lungs.

Va-Laya gave her a quick look. "So he's maybe a prisoner, maybe hiding out in the forest. This isn't going to be a quick extraction."

No. It wasn't. And Tally couldn't do a thing about it.

CHAPTER 41

BEN LOOKED up as thunder crashed and the world lit up with the one-two flash of lightning. The runners seemed to fall toward him, the lightning illuminating them as they came in fast. There were four of them, ranged in a pattern that was too precise to be mere chance. They were in some kind of attack formation.

He stumbled in the mud, just righting himself before he pitched the injured Caruson he was carrying out of his stretcher. The soldier he was paired with growled at him, and he inclined his head in apology.

He was trying to do too much at once. Carry the injured to whatever dubious safety the forest afforded them, and still keep watch for Tally, as well as a lookout for their enemies as they came in.

As he jogged back out to the field, his shoulders and arms aching from the strain, Sari sprinted over to him.

"Look." She pointed south. Coming in low and fast through the curtains of rain was a runner.

Tally. It had to be.

He ran further from the trees, right into the middle of the field, and waved his arms.

The runner dipped lower, and then skimmed the trees before it lurched to a landing on the launch pad which lay in what was now a quagmire of mud.

The back opened, and Ben stumbled for the second time at the sight of Enn and Va-Laya running down the ramp.

They were covered in the dust of the plains, which the rain instantly turned to streaks of red mud. They grinned when they saw him.

"Where are the Caruso?" Enn asked over the roar of the engines and the pounding rain. Then she blinked and put her hand on her laz as a few of the Caruson soldiers jogged through the trees toward them, carrying empty stretchers.

"They surrendered to us. And we're about to be attacked. We're getting their injured to safety." Then he couldn't stand there any more. He left them standing, open-mouthed, and ran toward the runner as Tally stepped into the cargo bay.

She put a hand against the wall, as if to steady herself when she saw him, and then he was up the ramp and had his arms around her, lifting her up for the few steps it would take for them to be back inside the runner's small bridge.

She was kissing his jaw, his temple, and then, as he lowered her down, his lips, and he pulled her closer for a brief moment.

"We don't have time." His voice was raw, a rasp of dry gravel on stone.

"I know." She pressed herself against him, held tight for a beat, and then stepped back. "You got the better of the Caruso?"

"They surrendered." He lifted his shoulders. "I think their commander, Vrk, has defied Caruson orders to get his people to safety. And now he's got no one but us."

She nodded slowly. Then her gaze snapped to his face. "We can't take them all."

That was true. "I'll have to ask Vrk what he wants."

And then, as the words left his mouth, they ran out of time. The first laz strike rattled the runner, and Tally flung herself into the pilot's chair. "I'll have to move."

"Hop the buildings and land between the accommodation hut and the forest. They won't get an easy strike on you there."

She glanced back at him, eyes wide, and nodded, and he ran out as the door closed up, jumping off the ramp as it rose.

What neither of them had said was that if the Caruson runners managed a direct hit on the building, they could still take another shot at the runner, but why waste time? This was as good as it was going to get.

Even if Tally flew away now, one of the runners could follow her and shoot her down.

He heard her lift off behind him as one of the tents burst into flames, and caught Vrk's gaze from the last tent in the line.

There were two stretchers making their way toward the forest, and Handel was holding up one of them.

A Caruson, injured but on his feet, staggered out of the tent beside Vrk, and Vrk hooked his arm around him and began dragging him to safety. "The last one," he called to Ben.

Ben ran to help, bending over as the ground was hit behind him. A hot rush of air and flame sizzled the rain and turned the air steamy. He reached Vrk, got a hold of the soldier's other side, and they ran for the cover of the trees, the tent alight behind them.

When they'd laid the soldier down, the Caruson commander kept his gaze on the tents burning in the field.

"Tally's in the runner that just landed. She's here to fetch me and my team, but we can take some of your injured, as well." He had to shout over the sound of thunder and the rain hammering against the leaves and branches.

Vrk shook his head. "Not moving again." He made a sharp chopping motion with his hand, and Ben couldn't blame him. It had been agony for most of Vrk's people to move the first time.

"You won't get them to your warship." He pointed up to the sky. "If there are two warships . . ." He looked frustrated, made a gesture with his hands.

"They'll block the way."

"Yes." His face relaxed a little.

That was true. The Caruson warships would make it impossible to get aboard the *Galaha* and would make it impossible for the *Galaha* to send down runners of its own.

They may have gotten a few off before they were surrounded-- Tally got out, after all--but there'd been no sign of them. And even if Tally's runner could somehow get back onboard, the *Galaha* was not the safest place right now.

"We'll hopefully draw some of the runners away when we leave."

"Can you leave?" Vrk looked up at the descending runners, and Ben wondered the same.

Handel had come to stand beside him as he spoke to Vrk, and some of his team, as well as Bey and Lenar, picked their way through the pallets of injured miners toward him.

"Vrk doesn't want to move his people into the runner, especially seeing as we can't get them to the *Galaha* safely right now anyway."

Lenar nodded her agreement. "It's better to leave them here than try to move them again."

The tents were ablaze, burning despite the rain because of the material they were made from, but while at least two strikes had been aimed at the trees, and had ripped them up, the forest had not caught alight.

"What are the tactics they'll use now?" Ben didn't think they'd keep circling, taking wild shots at targets they couldn't see.

"They land. Three." Vrk held up three fingers. "One stay up." He circled a finger.

Ben nodded. He'd have done the same. "Before they do that,

hopefully we can draw one away, so you only have two runners' worth of soldiers to deal with."

Vrk gave a little bow, and Ben responded with a bow in kind.

"Good luck."

They nodded to each other. No longer enemies, not exactly allies.

"Let's go." He looked around at everyone, saw only Garner and Dr. Kilmer were missing, and he knew they were closer to where Tally had put down the runner, still communicating with the *Galaha* on Garner's small comms unit.

He jogged through the forest, with Handel on one side, the two scientists behind him along with Enn and Va-Laya, and Sari taking the rear. He took them to where Tally had set down, using as deep cover as he could.

A runner flew overhead, the growl of the engines clear through the rain and the thick branches above, and then a boom shook the ground. It galvanized him into a sprint, and when he caught a glimpse of flames up ahead, he ran even faster.

There was another strike, one that made a thump that rattled his bones and the ground beneath his feet shudder.

Handel glanced over at him, face tight with worry, and he had to suppress an urge to shout at him that Tally was fine. That she hadn't been hit.

He dodged trees, even running into the open for a few steps because it would get him to Tally faster, but when he reached the small area she'd managed to squeeze into, it was ablaze.

He circled it, desperate to find any way in.

The building had come down on the runner on one side, and it was burning like there had been some accelerant involved, and three big trees had come down on it on the other. They weren't burning, but they almost covered the runner completely.

He saw the back door was open a small crack, and he clambered along a branch to put him closer to the top of it.

"Tally?"

"I can't get the door to open."

He could just see the top of her head and her eyes.

The branch he was standing on was part of the reason. The tree it was attached to had fallen at an angle, pressing the door closed at its base.

Ben jumped, grabbing the top of the door and pulling down with his full weight.

The door opened a little bit more.

"I still can't." Tally shoved a hand and her head through, and looked at him with massive eyes. "They could shoot again. You need to get out of here."

He shook his head, swung his legs onto another branch, braced and heaved with everything in him.

Sari was suddenly on his left, pulling with all her weight, as well, and then Handel took the other side, his bigger mass angling the door a little more open on his side.

Tally put her arms out, finding a grip on Ben's shoulders, and then levered herself out, jackknifing her body so she stood in a handstand on his shoulders, and then she flipped, landing on the branch below.

Her gaze went straight upward. "They're coming back," she said, turning to him with her face set.

He jumped down to join her, grabbing her hand to race for the trees, with Handel and Sari running beside them.

The third strike lifted them off their feet, but by then, they were in the forest, and the landing was on spongey ground covered in dead leaves.

He twisted in the air, trying to cushion Tally's landing, and they rolled a little way until they fetched up against a tree trunk.

"I failed." She glanced back through the trees at the pyre that had been the runner. She met his gaze solemnly. "I was supposed to rescue you, and you've had to rescue me."

CHAPTER 42

THE DELAY at the mine site had cost her.

Cost all of them.

Tally ran behind Ben as he led them back to Vrk and his people, her arms tingling as strength returned to them.

The little helpers had worked overtime from the moment the first runner strike had hit the building beside her, collapsing it on her runner's roof. She'd tried to take off, but the second strike came almost straight away, damaging the one side of the runner and dropping three massive trees on top of it. With no choice but to get out, she'd opened the door, and had stared in dismay when it barely opened at all.

The little helpers had hardly requested permission before they'd propelled her into a run, giving her enough momentum to jump up and hold onto the very top of the door.

They'd also given her the strength to support her whole body-weight with her arms, and then, when Ben had forced the door open a little more, they'd taken over to lever her through the narrow space.

Handel had asked her how she'd managed it as they ran, his

face set with suspicion, but Dr. Bey, who was running in front of them, had turned with a smile when she heard the question.

"She's Raxian Expeditionary Force," she said, as if that explained everything. "I've seen her run up a wall."

Handel had gone quiet after that, giving her strange looks.

They arrived at Vrk's little makeshift hospital under the trees at the same time as Dr. Kilmer and Garner arrived on the hover, with everyone's packs loaded onboard.

Vrk must have guessed why they were back, because he didn't seem surprised. "We stand together?"

Ben nodded.

Vrk glanced at Tally. "Ghost ship girl, what you doing back here?"

"Your warship ran away when we approached it. Your soldier called for . . ." She tried to remember what Irwin had called it. "He called for *fraknvos*, but they did not help. They sped off."

There was an audible reaction from the Caruson.

"He said *fraknvos*?" Vrk asked.

She nodded. "That's what he said. Many times."

"And then?" Vrk lifted his hands.

"And then the VSCS *Galaha* arrived, and I asked them for our version of . . . *fraknvos*." She said the unfamiliar word carefully after hearing how Vrk pronounced it. "And they took your people to the med bay."

There was another murmur through the miners and soldiers.

"So, you helped my people." He inclined his head. "What do you say about this fight?" He turned and waved toward the field, where the runners were landing, one by one.

It felt like every eye was on her, and she snapped her spine straight. "I say tell us why you are here. The whole reason, including what the Caruso are using those minerals you're stealing for. Use that to make yourself safe, because they're trying to kill you to stop the information getting out."

There was a beat of silence, and then an argument broke out among the Caruso--not just the soldiers, but some of the injured miners as well.

She guessed it was hard for some of them to come to grips with being under attack by their own.

Vrk watched her while the argument raged around him, but eventually he gave a shout, and everyone was silent.

He said something in Caruson that had all his soldiers turning to the field, and Tally could see the doors of the runners were opening.

This was happening.

And she just remembered she didn't have a laz.

Ben must have noticed her patting her pockets. "Where's your weapon?"

"Vrk took it before he put me in the runner." She crouched down, watching as Caruson soldiers ran out of the three runners that had landed. They formed into three units of eight.

As soon as they were in position, they moved forward.

The weather had darkened the sky, and it was already late in the afternoon, so it wouldn't be easy to see through the trees, but they must be using heat sensors because they were headed in exactly the right direction.

Ben crouched beside her. "There's no time to find you a weapon now. You need to hide." He rose up, hand still on her shoulder, and faced the scientists. "That goes for everyone with no weapon. You need to hide. Now."

The doctors hesitated.

Tally pointed to the hover. "Take it back to where we hid before."

Dr. Kilmer nodded, and when he moved toward the hover, the other two followed him.

Ben's lips were right against her ear as he grabbed her hand

and pulled her up. "You can't help without a weapon. Please go with them."

She shook her head. She would not.

She was not leaving again.

"I'll hide up a tree, where I can see what's going on and help if it's possible." She put a hand to his jaw, frustration and worry mixing together in a potent blend. "Don't tell me otherwise."

His mouth formed a tight line, but he gave a nod, then stooped to make a step with his hands. She put her foot in it and he boosted her up the tree they'd been crouched behind.

She pulled up onto a branch and looked down at him for a moment, but he was already turning away, laz raised in the direction of the units moving slowly toward them.

As she climbed a little higher, she heard Vrk call out to the Caruson sent to kill him, his voice raised to be heard over the rain.

He called for *fraknvos*.

The units stopped, and she saw a few of the newly arrived soldiers give each other uneasy looks.

Her gaze drifted back to the runners, sitting with engines idling in the field, and she realized there was no obvious guards around them.

They were just sitting there.

Unless there were pilots still inside.

As she thought it, a Caruson walked out from behind the middle runner and made his way around the front, to watch the units as they moved forward.

She didn't know if it was her imagination, but since Vrk had called out to them, they seemed to move even slower than they had before.

Vrk shouted something else, and the pilot rubbed at his face in a way that spoke of deep unease.

Tally looked up through the leaves, the rain forcing her to shield her eyes. She found the fourth runner.

It was no longer circling the field, it had moved with the units and was hovering over them, waiting like one of the legavas in the river to explode into action when someone broke cover.

One thing it wasn't doing was guarding the runners that were on the ground.

Maybe the Caruso couldn't conceive of the idea that someone might steal one from under their noses.

The first line of soldiers stepped under the trees. The thick canopy of leaves blocked most of the rain, and so many of them shook the water from their eyes as they came under its shelter.

Sitting above them she noticed the almost imperceptible stumble as they took in the miners lying on their pallets, at least thirty people with severe injuries.

Ben had obviously spoken with Vrk again since he'd tossed her into the tree, and they stood on either side of the injured, their weapons pointing down.

The other Caruson soldiers under Vrk's command stood behind the wounded at the back, also with their laz held across their chests, ready to lift and fire, and Ben's five teammates covered the middle ground, two on one side, three on the other, the injured miners making the center of a rough square.

Vrk spoke again and then looked at Ben.

"I want you to know I agree with Commander Vrk. You will regret any harm you do now until the end of your days." Ben raised his voice so the Caruso could hear him clearly, even those at the back of the units, most of which were now fully under cover of the forest.

She understood Ben's reasoning. What choice did he and Vrk have but to try to appeal to the soldiers' consciences first? If they fought, the injured miners would be the first to die.

They had nothing to lose.

The leader of one of the units took a step forward, and shouted at Vrk, his hand lifting off his laz to chop at the air.

Vrk answered, calmer, and swept his hand toward the injured miners. Explaining why he'd done what he'd done, she guessed.

She wondered what trouble the warship he'd originally called in to help him was in. They had shot down the runner, they'd destroyed the comms satellite. And they'd refused to kill Vrk and his team.

The commander challenging Vrk obviously didn't like what he was hearing. He pointed to Ben and the other Arkhorans, chop, chop, chopping away with the flat of his hand.

Vrk responded, arms out in a gesture that Tally thought must be universal. It said, well, then, kill me if you have to. Go ahead.

He smacked his chest with his palms. Opened his arms up again.

She gripped her branch so tightly it hurt as the commander slowly raised his laz, took aim at Vrk's head, and then jerked back.

For a confusing moment, Tally didn't understand what had happened, until she saw the raised laz of one of Vrk's soldiers, and the hole between the eyes of the Caruso who'd raised his weapon at Vrk.

It seemed she wasn't the only one in shock.

There was a single, quiet moment where the only sound was the hammering rain, and then the gloom under the trees lit up with the staccato flare of laz fire.

Her gaze went straight to Ben.

He had leaped to the side, rolling toward her tree as the Caruson aimed at their own people.

"Ben!"

He looked up at her, and she pointed to the runners. There were no Caruson soldiers below her anymore and she jumped, grabbing a lower branch and swinging herself forward to land on the ground.

Ben ran, bent over, toward her, and she took off across the field.

It was almost completely dark now, and she had to hope no one would notice them as they ran toward the runners.

Ben caught up with her after a few strides.

"One pilot outside," she gasped, pointing at the middle runner. She pushed back hair plastered to her face by the rain and ran around the runners, coming in from the back.

Ben moved ahead of her a little, and took the ramp first. He slowed as he made his way through the cargo hold, and she stopped completely, mouth open, at the rows of smooth metal cylinders lined up and secured to one wall.

There was no one on the bridge, and Ben gestured her in, standing aside to let her take the pilot's chair. She hit the sequence to close the door first, and noticed from the corner of her eye that Ben took up position in the cargo bay, laz trained at the door, to make sure no one jumped in as it lifted off.

The sizzle as he fired made her flinch, but she didn't look back and see who he'd had to shoot.

The engines had been set to a low idle, not turned off, and she revved them as she pulled up.

Ben came to stand behind her, one hand on her shoulder.

Her first target had to be the runner in the air, and she fired over it, to get its attention.

It turned on its axis, something she hadn't worked out how to do yet, and she shoved her runner into reverse, drawing her target away from the treeline, from the forest.

If she hit it and it went down where it was hovering, it could kill everyone.

It followed her, and she felt a quick flash of guilt as she realized the pilot must think she'd simply been trying to get his or her attention. Whoever was flying it thought she was Caruson.

The comms unit beside her lit up and someone spoke Caruson in quick sentences, the volume getting louder.

By now, they were a safe distance from the forest, and she shoved down her guilt and fired.

The runner exploded in a ball of flame, veering off to one side. She couldn't help the sound that came out of her throat, and Ben's hand squeezed her shoulder.

She drew in a deep breath and forced herself to move on, to aim at the runners on the ground. It was almost too easy.

"They're both hit," Ben told her. "Are there search lights on the front of this?"

She looked for them, letting the little helpers have their say, and then switched them on.

Caruson were pouring out of the forest, and while it was difficult for her to read their facial expressions, she had to think they were shocked.

She fired again, this time just in front of them, and some threw down their weapons.

It seemed strange to her that they would give in so quickly, but then Vrk came from behind them, and she had to assume the Caruson leader had somehow gotten the better of them, trapping them between the runner and his soldiers. He was bleeding from a shoulder injury, but he still carried his laz.

Tally slowly lowered the runner. She still hadn't mastered the landing and she wobbled them down to the ground.

She went limp against the chair, tipping back her head.

Ben looked down at her, slowly lowered his forehead to hers.

"How are you flying this?"

"The little helpers. They seem to . . . understand technology."

He lifted his head, brushed a kiss on her forehead, and stepped back.

"I don't know what we're going to do with the Caruso. We can't keep them prisoner. And the *Galaha* still has two warships circling it."

"Go out and speak to Vrk." She patted the control panel.

"Signal me if I need to open fire again." She wouldn't let her voice wobble. She lowered the door, and he nodded and brushed a last kiss on the top of her head before he walked out the back.

"Ask Vrk to ask one of the other Caruson what those cylinders are," she shouted after him over the hammer of rain, and he turned to look at her again, nodded, and disappeared into the night.

Tally sat for a moment, just looking blindly out of the big window.

It was more or less light now, thanks to the burning wrecks on either side of her, as well as her own search lights.

She caught a glimpse of Sari, and then Enn, and felt a little lighter with relief.

The sound of boots up the ramp got her out of her chair, looking wildly for a weapon.

"It's me." Handel lifted both hands as he walked through the cargo hold.

She shook a little as the adrenalin subsided and leaned against the pilot's chair.

"Ben asked me to give you an update."

"How bad is it?" She didn't understand how any of them were okay after the way the Caruso had opened fire.

He lifted his shoulders. "It was mainly between Vrk's soldiers at the back, and the units that were lined up at the front."

Something in his voice told her he wasn't exactly broken up about that.

"We hit the ground, and neither side seemed interested in us, or the injured miners." He turned thoughtful. "Even then, I don't think their hearts were in it a second after they started shooting. They regretted it almost immediately.

"When the runner moved away, they stopped firing altogether." He shrugged again. "I don't think they know what to do. They're very conflicted."

"What's going to happen to them?"

Handel shook his head. "I don't think anyone knows what to do now. Ben's suggested all the weapons be transferred to this runner. It'll make killing each other harder. And we'll go off to the supply station."

"Yes." She should sound more enthusiastic about that. It had been her plan all along, but she didn't want to know if Frangi had made it. Right now, she could have. She could be fine.

Going to the supply station would tell her for sure.

And all she could remember was the gray under the golden brown of Frangi's skin. The blood.

"Vrk wants you to go check the mine site."

She bit her lip, and wondered what there was to find there now. She shook her head. "We need to get to Frangi and the others."

Handel nodded. "So, Raxian Expeditionary Force." He was staring at her.

"Yes." She couldn't help the defensiveness in her voice.

"I didn't know it was a special forces unit."

She shrugged, although her heart was beating double-time at the thought of his scrutiny. "We aren't Arkhorans."

"Meaning?" He crossed his arms over his chest.

"You have a reputation for being a bit . . ." She lifted her hands. "Boastful."

"Boastful?" He tilted his head.

"Arrogant," she clarified.

"How did you pull yourself out of that runner into a hand-stand?" He shook his head. "A fucking *handstand.*"

"It was hard, my arms were jelly afterward, but I didn't have a choice. That was the only angle I had. The only way I'd fit through." That was the bare truth. Even if she was leaving what he really wanted to know out.

He shook his head, still unconvinced, but she turned away,

suddenly aware she hadn't been keeping watch on what was happening outside.

She heard Handel jog back out behind her, and lifted her shoulders to get rid of the tension she felt talking to him.

She saw Garner on the hover, moving out of the forest toward where Ben and Vrk were standing.

Vrk had one of the new soldiers with them, and they were in urgent conversation. The soldier pointed to her runner, and Vrk turned to look at it, a deep frown on his face.

Garner started waving one arm around, steering with the other. Ben was staring at him, listening, and then he turned toward her, but Vrk put out a hand, stopping him, and said something that made Ben wrench himself away and sprint toward her.

She frowned at the look on his face, glanced down at the scanner, and saw it was registering something big moving down through near-space.

She froze.

The Caruson warships must have been monitoring what was happening here. And at least one of them was going to finish the job themselves.

CHAPTER 43

SECONDS. Ben had seconds to warn her.

And instead of getting out of the runner, Tally was lifting off. What the hell was she thinking?

The ramp was closing, but he leaped up, hooked a hand at the top, and swung his body up, slid down the other side.

The runner lifted and banked left, and he staggered to his feet, and ran to the bridge.

Tally was hunched over the controls, her face a tight mask.

"Why?" he asked.

"I was hoping the warship would follow me, and everyone could scatter."

Ben gripped his hair in frustration, because she was right. It was following her. The scanner told the story all too well.

And she didn't even know the worst of it.

"Those cylinders are a new bomb the Caruso have developed. They can torch a whole planet."

"They were going to burn Veltos to the ground?" She almost whispered it.

"Vrk said they wanted to be sure they'd killed everyone. It was just lucky the bombs were on your runner, not one of the three you hit, or we'd all be dead."

She was silent for what felt like a long time.

"You should have stayed out," she said.

"Never." He clipped himself into the seat beside her. "You don't want me to ask it of you. Don't ask it of me."

She hesitated a moment, then gave a tight nod.

She suddenly threw the controls right, and the night lit up around them, rain dancing in the light of a laz strike from a warship.

Beside them, the forest exploded.

The blast rattled the runner, and Tally seemed to fight the runner as she lifted them up, into the low-slung cloud and higher still.

It was the only choice. If they were hit too close to the planet, it would burn.

The higher they got, the safer. For everyone but them.

He looked over at her profile, set and steady.

"The little helpers happy about this? Putting yourself in danger?"

She gave a low, cynical laugh. Glanced at him. "No. But after you were captured, we came to an arrangement."

He went still. "What sort of arrangement?"

But he knew there was only one answer. And it involved her risking herself for him.

She shook her head, lips tight. "It doesn't matter. It needed doing." Her expression softened as she glanced at him again. "It was a good thing."

He tore his gaze from hers, suddenly cold at the thought that they didn't know where the warship was.

But it was gone.

He checked again.

"Where could it be?"

Tally shook her head, her focus on sending them higher still.

They were close to the top of the atmosphere now, the clouds far behind them.

"That you, Guthrie?" The comms unit sprang to life.

Ben grinned at the temper in the voice. "Commander Reskit. What's happening?"

"We were in a tight spot with two warships, but then one raced off and came after you, and that left us with one, which evened the odds." He paused. "I gather we can thank that little Raxian for the information Garner transmitted up to us, information from the Caruson on why they were on Veltos, and the basics on what they use that mineral for."

Ben stopped smiling. "Her name is Tally Riva."

Reskit grunted. "I know her name. She stole a runner right from under my damn nose."

"She's flying this one now."

"I guessed." Reskit sounded touchy. "We're waiting for more of the fleet to arrive but the warship that ran off to deal with you is back, and it probably has something to do with the small fleet that arrived from Situ, towing a new satellite."

Ben went still. "What are they doing here?"

"We obviously couldn't signal them once we got into this system to let them know about the warships, and someone very efficient at Situ decided to come right away and replace the one that was lost." He sounded bemused. "We managed to put ourselves between them and the warships, and get them to come right in beside us, but now we're protecting them, and we can't maneuver like we could before."

"You need us to be a diversion." Ben stated it baldly.

"I don't know if you can be, but anything will be better than nothing. We've got support coming in at any time. I'm surprised they aren't here already. Captain Harris called for help before we even entered the Veltos solar system."

Ben looked over at Tally, and she gave a nod. "We'll do what we can," he said, and cut the commander off.

They were in near-space now but even so, when he looked down, far below, he saw the bloom of light.

"What do you think--?"

"One of those, maybe?" Tally gestured to the bombs in the back. "Dropped on the mine."

Ben stood right up against the window to get a better look. "That would have been Enn and Va-Laya down there. If you hadn't gotten them."

She nodded. "Do you think it will burn out? Can it really never stop?"

"I don't know." Urgency gripped him, because the Caruson could not get away with this. Could not be allowed to go back down and burn more.

"How do they drop them?" Tally asked. "They wouldn't put them on the ground in person, surely?"

No, they wouldn't. Not if they were this dangerous. He moved to the back, noticed the hatch on one side for dropping supplies.

"Question is, do they explode on impact, or do you have to set them?"

Tally came out the bridge and crouched beside him.

"Auto-pilot?" he asked, and she nodded, her hands moving over one of the bombs, as if learning the shape of it by feel.

Her face was set, her eyes closed. Like she was communing with it. Her whole body seemed to shudder in disgust.

"Here." She opened her eyes, and turned the cylinder around a little, and brushed her finger over an area that lit up. It was flashing a word. "I can't read that." Her voice was thick.

Ben shook his head. "Neither can I."

She swiped her finger over it, and it changed, changed again, and then it was back to the original word.

He stood, put out his hand to pull her up, to get her away from the cylinders, because her reaction to them was extreme.

They seemed to make her sick.

He drew her back to the bridge, tapped the comms unit. "Commander, I need to know what a few Caruson words mean."

He could hear Reskit's annoyance at having been cut off earlier in his commander's voice, but then the translator took over.

She gave him the terms as he read them out. Inert, Timer, Detonate on Impact.

He carefully set them all to inert, and moved back to the bridge.

"Got any ideas?"

She nodded. "The *Galaha* want a diversion, we can give them one."

"There they are." He pointed up ahead, and looming beside the moon were two warships. One was bigger than the other, and Ben guessed the smaller one had come after them earlier. The bigger one didn't look like it could easily dip into near-space and get back out again.

Tally opened up the engines, so the runner raced toward the big ships, and when they had almost reached them, he saw a runner just like theirs drop out of the launch bay of the smaller one, and head toward them.

Too slow, he hoped. The Caruson had noticed them too late.

Tally angled the runner toward the bigger warship and they were dwarfed by it, a tiny nothing beside its immense presence.

Tally moved around the back of the ship and then up the side, until eventually they hovered over the warship's roof.

The comms unit squeaked at them, and then poured out a torrent of Caruson. The warship began to move.

"I don't speak your language." Tally waited for the ship to move under them until their runner was in the middle and then landed, engaging the magnetic clips. "But I've got six of those incendiary bombs onboard, so if that runner you launched fires on me, this warship will burn."

Ben could see the runner out of the window, and didn't need the scanner to know it went into reverse.

"You will die, too." The Caruson who spoke sounded cautious.

"I expected to die a number of times today already," Tally said. "I'd rather not risk it again now, but if I do, I'll enjoy the irony of taking you with me with your own weapons."

"You cannot work the bombs," the Caruson said, his tone confident.

"Inert, Impact, Timer." Ben spoke each word carefully. "Easy enough to figure out."

There was silence. "So what is the plan? Why are you clamped to our ship?"

"I want you to douse the fire you started at your mine. Save whoever is not yet dead, and stop the burning."

"We cannot do that."

"You mean you won't do that. I don't believe you don't have something to douse the flames when you want to."

The comms unit cut off.

"They're talking among themselves." Ben leaned over and kissed her.

She sat, eyes huge in her face, circles under her eyes, her cheeks paler than they should be, quietly making demands like the head of an army.

She got up, stiff and jerky, as if every muscle hurt, and settled back down on his lap, leaning back to rest her head on his shoulder, and put her mouth against his neck.

He rested his cheek on the top of her head. Held her close.

She felt so delicate in his arms. He knew it was an illusion, she was the strongest person he knew, and yet he would do whatever he had to to protect her. Even while she was out-bluffing the captain of a Caruson warship.

He kissed her hair and felt her smile against his skin.

He hadn't seen her smile since before he'd been shot and captured by Vrk.

"What will you do when we've doused the flame?" The voice was back.

"I'll leave, and drop the bombs on the moon, rather than on your roof."

"You could leave the bombs on the roof, inert."

"Or I could leave the bombs on the roof, with the timer set." Her voice was sharp.

"We're not leaving you with these bombs." Ben added his voice to hers.

"We have more," the voice was almost amused.

"Still." Tally had become tense in his arms, and Ben started to really hate the Caruson on the other end of the comms unit. "You're not getting these ones back."

"We could shoot you as you move away." The suggestion sounded mild.

"I'm guessing six of these bombs are enough that if I'm close to your ship, you won't do that."

"And if we don't douse?"

He could feel Tally force herself to relax in an act of will.

"Then, I do leave the bombs behind on a timer."

"You won't get far, we'll shoot you."

"Maybe," Tally said. "Or maybe you'll use every available runner to try and deactivate the bombs."

A sigh. "A runner is leaving now to douse the fire."

Ben glanced at the scanner, saw a runner was flying down.

"How do we know if they're telling the truth?" Tally suddenly sat up on his lap. "We can't see down to the mine from here. I don't think the *Galaha* would be able to, either?" She looked at him, and he shook his head.

"I don't think so."

"So we have to trust them." She forced herself to lean back against him.

He didn't like it any more than she did.

"Or simply insist on proof, until the *Galaha's* backup arrives."

She nodded, but he could still feel the tension in her.

Then suddenly the runner's warning light began to flash.

They both leaned forward.

All around them, ships were appearing.

VSC ships.

"We would like to open a new negotiation." The smarmy had been completely wiped from the Caruson's voice.

"We're listening." Ben could guess what it was.

"We'll douse the flame, and allow you to unclip and move away, if both our ships can leave without harm. No shots have been fired here, after all."

Not at the *Galaha*, Ben thought. But that wasn't true on the planet below. He didn't say it though.

They knew well enough.

"We'll need proof you've put the fire out completely." Tally climbed off his lap, went to look out the window. There were eight new VSC warships all around them.

One looked Raxian, and Ben thought he saw Tally do a double take at the sight of it.

"You can ask one of your ships to check that we've done what we've promised."

"One moment." Ben flipped through to the channel Reskit had contacted him on before. "They want a deal."

"What deal?" Reskit sounded reluctant.

"They put out the incendiary fire they started on Veltos, which we don't think we can easily do, and they don't fire on Tally and me when we lift off their roof and fly to the *Galaha*, and they get to run away."

"They want us to let them go?" Reskit didn't sound as if he was going to go for it.

"What are you going to do with them anyway? Take them prisoner?" Tally asked him. "We've got prisoners down below already, as well as some Caruson who've turned themselves over to us. We've got information on what they were mining, how they use the mineral they were stealing, and their promise to stop the fire." She paused. "Can you send a runner to check they are doing that?"

"Riva makes a good point." Ben recognized the voice of Captain Harris. "We'll also have footage of them taking off as fast as they can go. Which is the kind of image I'm happy to spread around the galaxy."

"We need to talk to VSC headquarters." Reskit sounded grudging.

They waited, the minutes ticking by, until Harris came back on. "It's agreed. And the fire at the mine site is out. Their runner is coming back now."

Ben found the Caruson channel again. "It's a deal."

"As soon as our runner is back, we'll let you know, and you can disengage." There was not even pretend congeniality in the Caruson's voice anymore.

The wait wasn't long. Tally settled back in the pilot's chair and unclamped from the warship's roof.

As soon as they were clear, the warship moved away from the moon and then seemed to disappear, it moved so fast.

Tally steered the runner toward the moon. Leaned over the comms unit. "Is there anything on the moon, or is it dead?"

"It's dead." Harris sounded surprised. "Why do you ask?"

"Just wanted to make sure."

They were already over the small, barren rock, and she walked to the back.

He didn't tell her she didn't need to do it. That the VSC

wouldn't use something like this. There was something driving her. A compulsion.

"Do you think the little helpers come from a place where something like this was used?" he asked as he crouched beside her in the back.

She lifted her gaze from setting the timers. "I think . . . yes." She heaved a sigh. "Don't ask me not to do this."

He shook his head. "I won't."

She gave a single nod, held his gaze.

"Will you drop them out for me. I need to get us higher, just in case they explode on impact."

"Yes." He took out the first one, set it into the drop hatch compartment.

"Thank you." She looked like she wanted to say more, but then she gave another nod and stepped onto the bridge.

He felt them lift higher, heard the squeak of the comms unit which Tally ignored.

"Ready," she called.

He dropped them, one by one.

They didn't explode, and he came through to join her when they were all gone.

She turned the runner around and headed for the *Galaha*, not looking back, and then a bright light illuminated everything around them.

She smiled, and there was a world of satisfaction on her face. "It's done."

CHAPTER 44

A SMALL, sleek VSC runner entered the *Galaha's* launch bay ahead of them.

Tally landed away from it, still bad enough at it to worry she'd hit something.

When they rocked to a stop, she saw Soo and Lenny walk out the back of the runner that had preceded them, and she unclipped from her chair and was out the door as fast as the little helpers could take her.

Ben followed at a slower pace, but he wasn't far behind her.

"Soo!"

They turned, and she slowed down, worried by the look on their faces.

"Frangi?" She almost couldn't say the word, her throat was so tight.

Soo rubbed at her eyes, and then hooked an arm around Tally and pulled her close. "They don't know. They think they got her in time. Linn Fraser is with her. He sent down a high speed mobile medbay as soon as the rest of the fleet arrived."

She nodded, then gave a gurgling laugh as Lenny put his massive arms around the both of them.

"I'm so glad you're all right."

"So how was the Trail?" Lenny straightened, and Tally saw he was looking over her shoulder.

"Eventful." Ben slid an arm around her shoulder, and she thought of the soldiers he'd had to kill to keep Soo and Lenny safe.

She put an arm around his waist and squeezed.

Lenny was watching them, and he gave an imperceptible nod. "No one came after us."

Soo disentangled herself. "Which is hard to believe."

"They were stopped," Ben said. "That's all that's important."

They all stood in silence for a moment.

"Captain Guthrie." The call came from the doors into the launch bay.

Reskit and Veniur stood waiting. Ben sighed.

"I have to be debriefed. I'll find you." He nuzzled her temple and then made his way across to his commander.

"What now?" Tally asked them.

"By the looks of you, food, shower, sleep."

Tally nodded. She felt lightheaded now they were safe, now that she could relax.

The last thing she'd eaten were those two bars after she'd rescued Ben. Since then, she'd been to Veltos's mine twice, the *Galaha* twice, and even the moon.

She felt the world tilt a little, and Lenny's arm come around one side, Soo's around the other, and she forced herself straight.

She'd managed to eat almost all of her meal when they came for her in the dining room.

Harris and her own commanding officer, Hopl.

He cleared his throat at the sight of her. "Seems like there was a little more excitement on the Trail for you than Dr. Vetna had planned."

She tried to smile at his attempt at humor. "Yes, Commander."

"We need to talk to you, Riva. Have you had enough to eat?"

She nodded, stood, and glanced across at Soo and Lenny, who looked worried for her.

She gave them what she hoped was a reassuring smile and followed Harris and Hopl out, feeling a new wave of exhaustion break over her.

Hopl stood to one side of a doorway of a small lounge so she could enter before him and he pursed his lips in concern.

"Not a lot of sleep, Riva?"

"No, Commander. Very little, unfortunately." Her voice cracked as she spoke.

"We'll try to make it quick."

Harris flicked a glance at him, but he didn't acknowledge her.

Tally took a few steps into the room, and then lowered herself into a deep armchair before being given permission to sit, realized her error, and then decided she was too tired to care.

"You stole a runner from my launch bay." Harris stood behind the armchair opposite her, hands gripping the back.

"I took back the runner I'd brought to you. You didn't own it, as far as I'm aware." Tally closed her eyes, took a deep breath, and then opened them again, trying to keep sharp.

Harris said nothing for a beat, her gaze on Hopl, but her commanding officer shrugged. "Don't look at me like that, Captain. Is Riva correct?"

"That runner surrendered to my ship. So no, she is not. And she also failed to mention that she could fly it. I'd like to know how that came about."

Tally lifted her hands. "I'm Raxian Expeditionary Force, Captain Harris."

Harris barked out a laugh, looked at Hopl again in disbelief.

"She *is* Raxian Expeditionary Force," Hopl agreed.

"And you're saying you train your people to fly Caruson runners?" Harris turned on Hopl, expression fierce.

Tally felt a lurch of fear at what he would say in response.

"Captain, what my training did or did not entail is surely not the reason for this debrief. I'll make it easy. I was told, directly to my face, by you, that I was neither trusted, nor considered an asset in any way.

"Shortly thereafter, I saw an opportunity that was extremely time sensitive, which involved taking the runner. Knowing that my suggestion would be met with rejection, I acted independently, as a member of an allied, but separate, military force.

"As it happened, by doing so, I saved two of Captain Guthrie's team from being burned alive by the incendiary bomb at the mine, and was able to keep the Caruson warships distracted for long enough for your backup to arrive. So I would say that my decision more than paid off.

"As I said at the time, I do not answer to you, I answer to Commander Hopl, and as a member of the Raxian Expeditionary Force, I have been trained to use my own initiative when unable to contact my commanding officer." She ruined her dignified, reasoned answer by ending on a huge yawn.

"You find this an acceptable answer?" Harris lifted a brow at Hopl.

"Did you tell her you didn't trust her, and didn't think she would be needed?" Hopl countered.

Tally thought he looked even grimmer than usual, and realized it was probably more to do with the disrespect shown to Raxia than to her personally.

"She was unknown to me, and she had just negotiated aid for the Caruson."

"They were injured," Tally protested. "That is core to the Military Alliance Accord, isn't it?"

Harris waved that away. "Why did the Caruson really put you on that runner?"

She frowned. Why were they back to this?

"As I've already said, I was told by Irwin that they wanted to question me about the ghost ship."

Hopl looked at her sharply. "Did you tell them anything?"

She shook her head. "The warship where I assumed I was to be questioned was more concerned with getting away from their own people before they were ordered to kill them, than speaking to me. I never even made it onboard."

Hopl relaxed a little, and Harris seemed to get a little more tense.

"What's on that ghost ship you're so worried she'll talk about?" Harris asked.

Hopl turned to face her. "Is this about Riva taking the runner, and saving your people, or is it about Arkhor being worried that we aren't giving them everything we know about the ghost ship?" There was steel in Hopl's voice.

"It seems the Caruson were pretty desperate to get hold of her, and we can't understand why, given what you told us you found in there."

Hopl's eyes narrowed and he turned to Tally. "You're dismissed, Officer. Get some sleep." He turned back to Harris as if daring her to try to override him, but she did nothing but watch Tally leave, lips in a tight line.

Tally tried to pretend it was just exhaustion making her hold onto the wall as she walked to her assigned quarters, rather than relief.

They didn't care about her piloting the runner. It somehow hadn't been given much weight.

This was about the Arkhorans being put out they hadn't found the ghost ship themselves, and being sure something big was being kept from them. She hadn't realized telling them the Caruso wanted to question her about it would be what stood out to them, but it suited her just fine.

Hopl would be happy to play 'who's got more power' with Harris.

And good luck to them both.

SHE WOKE to a tapping on the door, and simply stared at it for a while from the bed.

She thought she was sharing with Soo, but it looked like no one had slept on the second bed.

"Tally, are you all right?"

Ben.

She *did* feel all right, she realized as she swung her legs over the side of the bed, walked to the door and opened it.

Ben slumped against the doorjamb. "You're alive."

She grinned. Better than all right. "I am." She stepped back, covering her mouth as she yawned, and then threw herself back down on her bed, patted the place next to her.

He carefully fitted himself beside her, booted feet hanging off the end, and drew her in close.

"What's happening? Are we declaring war with the Caruso?" She had gone to bed wondering about it, and she couldn't see another option.

"I think so." Ben worked his arm under her, to pull her close. "I don't think it's official yet, but at the least, they'll be considered a hostile force."

She remembered the incendiaries, and gave a nod. "At least."

They lay quietly for a moment, and then she turned in his arms to face him on her side. "Your commanders think Raxia is keeping big secrets about the ghost ship from them."

"I gather." He turned solemn eyes to her. "They wanted me to tell them what I'd learned from you."

She went still, but she didn't believe he would betray her. "What did you tell them?"

"I told them what you told all of us that night around the fire." He brushed a lock of her hair off her face.

"I'm assuming those facts weren't new to them?"

He shook his head. "They did seem disappointed. And your commander and Captain Harris seem to have a very chilly relationship."

"Yes, I think I might have helped that along." She didn't even feel guilty about it.

He smiled for the first time. "And there are very solid rumors going around the ship that Arkhoran Special Forces might just be shown up if we ever have to face the Raxian Expeditionary Force in a training exercise."

She felt a tug of unease. "Except, you wouldn't be."

He shook his head. "It's good for us to worry that maybe we aren't the best. Keeps everyone on their toes."

"Do you think someone will set up a contest or something?" Because while she was a proud Raxian, she'd seen Ben's team in action, and the Expeditionary Force were mainly scientists and technicians, not warriors.

Ben shrugged. "My guess is no. My side won't want to take the risk, and your side probably doesn't even understand where their amazing reputation is coming from."

A laugh escaped and she put a hand over her mouth.

"And what now?" He drew her closer, so her head was on his shoulder.

She sighed. "I don't know. I don't know that I can go back to doing what I was before. Who I was before. Not yet."

She couldn't see herself anywhere. And she would never be who she was before. She needed to accept that.

The military had been her life, but maybe it was time to get out. Nothing felt right anymore.

"What about coming over to Arkhoran Special Forces with the Verdant String Cooperation Initiative?"

She tipped her head up. "As what?"

"As a valuable member of the SF teams."

She scoffed. "Doing what?"

"Doing what you do." He lifted up on an elbow. "Pulling yourself up through a small gap into a handstand on someone's shoulders. Flying a runner. Working out how to activate Caruson weapons." He paused. "Running up walls."

"All that will get me is questions I can't answer."

"It will get you less questions than anywhere else." He lifted her palm, rubbed the center of it. "It will let you live more authentically as your new self than anything else you could do."

Was that true?

He lifted her palm to his lips and kissed it. "I'm not just saying this because it means I'll see you every day we aren't on assignment. Although that is a huge factor. I'm saying it because you shouldn't hide away out of fear, Tally. You deserve more than that."

"Is this even possible?" She didn't see any reason for either the Arkhorans or the Raxians to suggest it.

"I've already requested it." He lifted his shoulders. "You could say no, but I wanted to know if the idea would fly."

"And?"

"And it seems having the ghost ship girl is very appealing to the Arkhoran Special Forces command." He quirked a smile. "It's your side that seems reluctant to lose you. Something I can't fault them for."

His comm unit buzzed, and he swung to his feet.

"You and I are both due for another debrief in half an hour. I have to do some things first, so get ready, and I'll come fetch you."

She nodded and sat up, elbows on knees.

"Tally." He stopped at the door. "Think about coming over to the SF teams. And if you really don't want to do it, think about what the two of us could do together."

She stared at him, shocked, and then gave a nod as he closed the door.

CHAPTER 45

HARRIS AND HOPL both seemed surprised that Ben and Tally arrived together to the meeting. Reskit, though, didn't so much as twitch.

Tally was sure he would have seen Ben kiss her before he left her in the launch bay the night before and it wouldn't surprise her if he hadn't also questioned Ben's teammates about their relationship.

"I hope you'll excuse Officer Riva and I for a short meeting with the Raxian Fleet Commander, Captain Harris. We'll be back shortly." Commander Hopl had obviously been saving this announcement for Tally's arrival, because Harris was taken by surprise.

"Where will this meeting take place?" Harris managed to broadcast her offense with a sneer.

"On my runner in the launch bay. Just easier to set it up there, as our systems are already secure." Hopl gave an insincere smile, and Tally kept her head down as she followed him out.

They were close to the launch bay, anyway, but she wondered if it was wise to antagonize the Arkhorans to this extent.

She said nothing, though, and left it to the commander to close up the runner, and initiate the contact with the head of fleet.

"Admiral Min." Hopl gave a formal bow.

"Commander."

Tally had never spoken to the admiral before, not even on a comms link, but she recognized her well enough. "Admiral." She inclined her head and lifted a closed fist over her heart in the formal Raxian salute.

"What do you know of the request to join the Arkhoran Special Forces teams, Science Officer Riva?" The admiral's tone was no-nonsense.

"I only heard about it earlier this morning," Tally answered, noting Hopl's shock.

It looked like it was news to him.

"It's their way to get information out of her. Information they think we're hiding from them." Hopl sounded outraged.

"But we're not actually hiding any information from them," Tally pointed out. "Or are we?"

Min and Hopl exchanged a look.

"We are?" Tally's mouth fell open. "Oh."

"Not really." Min brushed it away. "We have some hypotheses that we are looking into first, is all."

"Like the ghost ship belonged to the original travelers that settled the Verdant String?" Tally asked. "Or might be from another Verdant String planet that we don't yet know about?"

There was shocked silence from both her superior officers.

"And what made you conclude that?" Min asked.

"I was on that ship for two weeks." Tally lifted her shoulders. "It wasn't Verdant String tech, but it was familiar, somehow. And everything was built to my size and physiology. It was a natural thing to wonder." Even the little helpers meshed with her only too well. And had been so eager to settle in, like they had been lonely and waiting a long time for a new host.

There was silence, and then Hopl cleared his throat. "Well, keep that speculation to yourself."

She nodded.

"Not only I, but the rest of my command team, agrees we should accept the offer of a placement for Officer Riva to join the Special Forces team. It's a good political move. It will also put a lot of their suspicions to rest." Min took a step closer to the camera. "Does that suit you, Officer Riva?"

Tally had been turning it over and over in her mind since she'd stepped in the shower after Ben had left her room.

"It suits me." She had wondered how much of her motivation to reveal as she'd dressed in the uniform Commander Hopl had had delivered for her.

"Why?" Hopl was looking at her directly, ignoring the annoyed frown of the admiral.

"Mainly because I have developed a romantic relationship with Captain Guthrie, Commander. And I understand it was he who put in the request for my transfer."

It was Hopl's turn to look stunned. "A . . . romantic relationship?"

"Yes, Commander." She looked straight ahead, refusing to meet his eyes.

"Well, then that works out rather nicely." Min looked like she was trying not to laugh. "And when you get tired of him, Science Officer Riva, you can come back, and we'll still have all the credit of having given you up."

That statement seemed to relax Hopl as well.

Tally merely nodded, but she had no intention of tiring of Ben Guthrie.

"Do you think they'll let her come over to us?" Reskit asked, his gaze on Ben.

"No." Harris cut in, shaking her head. "They're working out how to decline the request without looking like they have something to hide."

"I hope they will allow her to come. I hope she wants to." Ben's response earned a quick look from Harris, but Reskit nodded.

"And if not?"

Ben shrugged. "We'll see what they say, first."

"And what's this I'm hearing that she's with some top secret team?" Harris sounded aggrieved.

"We can't think we're the only ones with special forces," Ben said, trying not to smile. "Why wouldn't they send a high-level team in to the ghost ship? It's what we'd do."

Harris frowned as she considered it. "That's not on her file."

Ben lifted his shoulders. "Maybe they don't want anyone to know what they can do."

Reskit started frowning, as well. He turned to Harris. "What have you heard?"

"Enough that half the things don't sound possible. Running up walls, handstands from impossible angles."

Ben said nothing.

"They true?" Reskit asked him.

Ben met his commander's gaze. "People do amazing things when they have no choice."

He grunted. "True enough."

Someone knocked on the door, and then Tally and her commander stepped through.

Neither looked particularly unhappy, and Ben suddenly didn't know what choice she could have made.

He hadn't been lying earlier. If she didn't join the SF teams, he would have to find something else to do. As long as it was with her.

Because he wasn't going to lose her.

"Admiral Min and I are happy to accept your kind offer of including Science Officer Riva in the Arkhoran Special Forces as part of the VSCI. We hope it means an even deeper alliance and cooperation between our forces." Hopl sent Harris a knife-edged smile.

Ben had been watching Tally, though, not Hopl, and she lifted her gaze, and gave him a smile that seemed to light up every corner of him.

Reskit put out a hand in an Arkhoran greeting to Hopl. "We are extremely honored to have someone with Officer Riva's talent and bravery on the SF teams, Commander." He shifted his gaze to Harris, who was putting her neutral face on.

"Perhaps I can show Tally around the ship while you sort out the details," Ben said. He put out a hand, and Tally looked at it as if wondering if he really wanted to do this now, but when he continued to hold it out, she grabbed it.

Harris' eyes narrowed. "Guthrie?"

"Officer Riva and I will need to be assigned to different teams. Although it's a shame, because we work very well together."

"So noted." Reskit was watching them with a cool, considering eye.

Ben wondered what he was planning.

He pulled Tally out of the room, and quick marched her back to her quarters.

"I already know this part of the ship," she said, and when he looked down at her, her eyes were dancing with laughter.

"Maybe you do," he said as he locked her door behind them. "But I have some new territory I want to explore."

EXCERPT: SKY RAIDERS

BOOK ONE IN THE SKY RAIDERS SERIES

CHAPTER 1

HE'D ASKED her to wait for him, and then he'd disappeared for two years.

As he reached the top of the pass and started down the steep path to the valley below, Garek wondered just how angry Taya would be.

That she would be angry enough to have taken someone else sat like week-old loaf in his stomach, heavy and sickening.

He'd had no choice, had come as soon as he could . . . he tried to shake off the chill that touched him, despite the bright day. He'd take her anger, her fury--he'd take it all if it meant he didn't find her with someone else.

He forced himself to pay attention as the path became steeper still, and frowned at how badly maintained the way had become, as if no one had repaired the damage a winter in the mountains could do to a narrow track. The spring thaw had come and gone, replaced by a golden summer, and the snow had retreated to the tops of the mountains.

Kas should have done something about the erosion by now, even though this path was a shortcut few besides the villagers knew of, cutting across the Crag and shaving hours off the journey through the foothills.

The familiar landscape tugged at something inside him. He hadn't thought himself sentimental, and though he'd missed Taya with an ache that hurt worse than a knife to flesh, he hadn't thought the sight of the rolling hills and high peaks would affect him. The crowds and enclosing stone walls of Garamundo had been something to bear stoically, but he was surprised how easy it was to breathe here, and it wasn't just because the air was sweet with the scent of summer grass.

When he'd left two years ago, the only thing he'd regretted was leaving Taya behind him, and he'd come back only to fetch her.

Fetch her and run, as fast as possible.

As far away from West Lathor as they could get.

The shadow cast by Garamundo had a long reach, certainly long enough to reach out and try to grab him again if he stayed here, and he'd sworn when they'd finally released him that he would never go back.

He wouldn't give them a chance to conscript him again.

He was halfway down the mountain when he noticed there were no leviks on the slopes.

He stopped a moment, shading his eyes against the bright midday light of the Star to search for any sign of their golden, curly coats.

He could find none.

A breeze rose up, swirling about him, and he was struck by the silence.

His hearing was exceptional, and there was no sound of life. No ring of a hammer on anvil, no murmur of voices from the street.

Impossible.

His home town was small, but not that small. Pan Nuk had at least a hundred inhabitants when he'd left. And it was directly below him. Hidden by the thick line of trees it would take him only ten minutes to reach, but there nonetheless.

He started to run.

At first he ran under his own steam, and then, as the silence seemed to deepen, become more sinister, he opened himself up to the Change and felt the curious, slow, honey-thick flow of the air around him, the inbetween, and he was suddenly at the village gates.

He drew back to himself, stumbled a little at the feeling of disorientation such a quick Change generated.

He stood still, looking around him carefully. Took it all in.

The ripped doors. The shutters hanging by a single hinge. The smashed pots and baskets lying in the street.

The emptiness.

While the city of Garamundo had held him, forced him to help them protect themselves from the sky raiders, the sky raiders had been helping themselves elsewhere.

Helping themselves to Taya.

CHAPTER 2

THERE WOULD BE BLOOD.

Taya moved her gaze from Jerilia, weeping in soft, keening sobs, to the big Kardanx who gripped her arm, to the way Kas and the other men and women of the Illy began to gather to one side of the open area in front of the mine where they waited to be collected for the camp.

The Kardanx shifted his grip and Taya could see there were already dark smudges ringing Jerilia's upper arm where he held her.

The spike of anger that ripped through her made her gasp, made her force in a breath of dusty, cold air.

If she couldn't keep a cool head, she couldn't expect Kas and the others to do the same.

Behind the Kardanx, some of his fellow countrymen began to gather as well, their expressions more muted, more severe.

They didn't want trouble with the Illy. It seemed the big man who had grabbed Jerilia wasn't so worried.

Kas had already told him to let Jerilia go. Jerilia herself had demanded it. Taya looked into his eyes and knew he would not do it.

Perhaps if Jerilia hadn't screamed so loudly, made such a fuss. Perhaps if Kas's bellow of outrage hadn't made every head turn.

Or perhaps not.

Whatever the reason, to let her go now would be a loss of face the Kardanx would not be prepared to accept.

Taya could see it in the way his eyes narrowed, the way his mouth tightened. She had always had the gift of reading people's intentions from the way they moved their bodies, and the Kardanx was screaming pent up rage and defiance with every pore.

A small movement caught her eye. Kas, drawing something from the back of his pants, gripping it tightly in his fisted hand.

Was that a *knife*?

No.

She wouldn't let another she loved be hurt. Not because of the lust of a stupid Kardanx. The Kardanx were supposed to worship the Mother, but either this one wasn't an adherent to the belief, or he was simply one of the majority who twisted the meanings of their oaths so they could treat women with less respect. She saw the evidence before her now, in the way the Kardanx thought he could have Jerilia, even against her will.

Taya had heard another, even uglier whisper. That the reason there were only six women amongst all the Kardanx the sky raiders had taken was because the men had killed them, rather than have them taken by the enemy.

Taya had heard Kardanx men swore an oath to protect the Mother, and her avatars, all women, with their lives. But if they had killed their women to protect them, they were not honoring the Mother as an equal. They had killed them like they would kill their livestock so the invading army cannot use it. As they would burn their house, to give the enemy nothing to shield himself from the weather.

As one treats a possession, not a person, with their own will and choices.

The Kardanx took a step toward his own group, dragging Jerilia with him, and Kas and three others took a step forward.

The other Kardanx shouted something to their countryman, and he turned to look at them over his shoulder. He shouted back, and though Kardanx was close enough to Illian, it was said so fast Taya couldn't understand it. But the meaning was clear enough.

The Kardanx would not back down.

She wished, not for the first time, for Garek. Felt a need for him as strong as for her next breath. Then she shrugged off the paralysis of wanting something she could not have, and her gaze came to rest on their guard. When they'd first been brought here the metal skin of the two-legged, squat vehicle that enclosed him had been gleaming and new. Now she could see flakes of it falling off, and it was dull, corroded.

He was the only one on watch and his guns hung at his sides, mounted sleek and black on the stiff arms of his protective cover, above the pincers he could use as hands.

Kas took the first step out from the shouting group of the Illy, and without another moment's hesitation, Taya ran toward the sky raider.

He noticed her before she got to him, the head of the machine tipping down to look at her.

"Stop them." She looked straight up into the glass, and the dark tint faded to clear. For the first time, she found herself face to face with one of her captors.

Pale yellow eyes watched her with an interest that made her want to stumble back a step or two, turn tail and run.

She forced some saliva down her throat, worked her tongue off the roof of her mouth. "You need to stop it."

The robotic suit stayed still, but inside it, the sky raider tipped his head. "Why?"

The sibilant tones which made everything they said more frightening hissed over her. But now she'd been given a window into the helmet, she saw there was a disconnect between when the sky raider had spoken and when she'd heard the question.

It came to her in a flash that that wasn't how they sounded. They were using some device, some method of translating their language into Illian. It made her less afraid to know she wasn't dealing with something that sounded like she would expect a slither to sound like, if slithers could speak instead of hiss.

"We are different groups, we come from different parts of Barit. We are the Illy, they are the Kardanx. The Kardanx have different beliefs, different ways to us."

"We do not care." Again, his mouth moved and only after a beat did the hiss of his answer wash over her.

She shivered.

"Then you are stupid." She banged his leg with her fist in frustration, felt the gritty crunch of rusting metal. "If you want less work done in the mines, then you'll let that Kardanx take Jerilia. Because we're all mixed up in there. Kardanx and Illy together. And if he takes her, it will be against her will, and that will make us all feel like we have even less control than we already do. The Illy will fight the Kardanx. Fight them down in the shafts. Where you do not go."

She saw the pale yellow eyes blink in their narrow, sharp face that was otherwise not that different from her own, if you discounted the long, sharp incisors she caught the briefest glimpse of and the pale yellow fur that covered his face. He spoke again, although this time there was no hiss of reply to her.

She had the feeling he was talking to someone else. Getting advice. How he could do that, she didn't know. But then, most of what the sky raiders could do was new and magical to her.

He gave a sharp nod within his metallic cocoon, as if receiving an order, and then lifted both arms.

She heard something in the metallic suit whine. And the sky raider shifted, lifting up his arms. The barrel of one of his guns came level with her face.

But before she could think anything, feel any terror, the guard swung away from her and in two long steps was beside the Kardanx, gun leveled at his head.

"Let the woman go back to her kind." The hiss of the order fell into the silence that had descended, licking the air like a hungry tongue.

Without a word, the Kardanx released Jerilia, and she ran toward Kas and the others, stumbling in her haste.

They opened ranks for her, and then stepped back in to fill the gap, closing the line again.

"All who are the Illy, go this side. All who are Kardanx, go this side." He pointed with the guns, and Taya moved over to her group.

Some had been standing a little way away, watching without getting involved, and they began to move, pushing and weaving through each other to reach their people.

In the confusion, Taya saw one of the few Kardanx women in the camp slip amongst the Illy. The woman caught her eye and stumbled, and Taya realized her horror, and her anger, must have shown on her face.

If they sheltered one of the only Kardanx women left, if they took her to their side, that would be reason enough for another scene like the one today.

But hadn't she just seen how some of the Kardanx treated women? And hadn't she in these last few minutes come to the realization that the ugly whispers about men killing wives, sisters, mothers, and daughters was true?

Could she send a woman back to that against her will?

"Please." The woman was at her side faster than it seemed possible. Her hands came out to touch Taya's arm, and then drew back, fists clenched. "They don't want me anyway. They think me a witch. It's why I'm one of the few women in the group. I was living outside the village, and there was no man to kill me when the sky raiders came."

There was truth and desperation in her words. Her accent was thick, the vowels round and plump as a ripe plum, but she spoke Illian fluently.

Taya studied her, looking for some trick, some hidden motive. She was a few years older than Taya and her eyes were a pale, almost glacial green. Her skin was honey-gold, close to Taya's own skin tone. Her dark hair hung down her back with a glint of auburn in it.

With a grimace, knowing only trouble could come of it, Taya gave a quick nod and pushed the woman deeper into the crowd. She felt a brief, light touch of thanks on her shoulder, and the woman was gone, burrowing deep into the mass.

Silence fell as the last of the prisoners sorted themselves into Illy and Kardanx.

The Illy, with their equal mix of men and women, were the bigger group, because most of the Kardanx volunteered for night shift.

If it were true that for nearly every man standing here, at least one woman had died, the sky raiders must have had to attack many towns and villages in Kardai to get this many of them. And the blood must stain the ground in Kardai dark red.

Looking at the Kardanx, thinking of that many bodies, Taya felt the burn of nausea in her throat.

She should be thankful to Garamundo. Thankful for the protection they offered. Keeping the sky raiders away so that only a few places in West Lathor were hit.

But giving even a drop of thanks to Garamundo was beyond her because of Garek.

She felt something on her cheek, and lifted a hand to brush it away. Her finger came away with a single tear, and she rubbed it into the filthy tunic she wore.

The guard swiveled the head of his suit to her, one gun held steady on each group, then walked slowly back, so that he could see them all without having to turn. The glass of the dome that covered his head was opaque again. "We understand now. Your ways are different. It is decided. You do not mix. You do not fight. You work together peacefully. There must be no break in production." The sinister voice that came from the sky raider's suit drifted on the fading light of the evening as the Star sank down in the west. The threat in the words, the very sound of them, made her shiver.

In the distance, the transporter skimmed over the open ground toward them, bringing the night shift.

There must be no break in production.

She shivered again.

There had been a few demonstrations of what would happen if production should slow or even stop, right at the start.

She watched the Star as it lit the sky a deep violet, low on the horizon. She liked to think of it slipping away from them here on Shadow to rise in the east on Barit. Taking a part of her with it.

Kas came up next to her and put a hand on her arm, and when she looked across at him, she couldn't tell what he was thinking. He looked tired. Tired and worn.

She'd run to the enemy. Made a decision without consulting him first.

"I don't regret it."

Kas gave a slow nod. "This was the culmination of two weeks of antagonism." He blew out a breath, looked across at the Kardanx. "It was only a matter of time."

"Tell me." Taya's voice came out on a croak. "Are the rumors true? What they did to their women, that there are so few here?"

Kas looked away. "So I hear."

"Then I'm doubly glad I did it. That some man who has no woman in his bed because he slit her throat like a goat tried to take a woman from the Illy, rape her . . ." She couldn't finish the sentence, her throat too tight. She took a breath. "I'll deal with the sky raiders before I deal with them."

Her gaze was drawn to the big Kardanx, to his hands. She imagined him holding a woman against his chest, running a knife across her throat.

She could hear a singing in her ears, like the sound the massive sky raider ship had made when it hovered over Pan Nuk, and taken them all. A singing, soaring sound of rage.

"Taya."

She turned to Kas, and he took a half-step back.

"What?" The word came out slowly, and she frowned at him. "*What?*"

"You were . . ." Kas wet his lips, set his feet apart. "Taya, you were starting to call the Change."

ALSO BY MICHELLE DIENER

SCIENCE FICTION NOVELS

Verdant String series:

Interference & Insurgency Box Set

Breakaway

Breakeven

Sky Raiders series:

Intended (Exclusive to New Notification List subscribers)

Sky Raiders

Calling the Change

Shadow Warrior

Class 5 series:

Dark Horse

Dark Deeds

Dark Minds

HISTORICAL FICTION NOVELS

Susanna Horenbout and John Parker series:

In a Treacherous Court

Keeper of the King's Secrets

In Defense of the Queen

Regency London series:

The Emperor's Conspiracy

Banquet of Lies

A Dangerous Madness

Other historical novels:

Daughter of the Sky

FANTASY NOVELS BY MICHELLE DIENER

Mistress of the Wind

The Dark Forest series:

The Golden Apple

The Silver Pear

SHORT PARANORMAL FICTION

Breaking Out: Part I (Short story)

Breaking Out: Part II (Novella)

To receive notification when Michelle Diener's next book is released, you can sign up to her new release notification list.

ABOUT THE AUTHOR

Michelle Diener is an award winning author of historical fiction, science fiction and fantasy.

Michelle was born in London, grew up in South Africa and currently lives in Australia with her husband and children.

You can contact Michelle through her website or sign up to receive notification when she has a new book out on her New Release Notification page.

Connect with Michelle
www.michellediener.com

facebook.com/michelle.diener.author

twitter.com/michellediener

bookbub.com/authors/michelle-diener

amazon.com/author/michellediener

pinterest.com/michelle_diener

goodreads.com/michellediener

ACKNOWLEDGMENTS

Thank you so much to Edie, Diane, Deborah, Justin and Jo for your eagle eyes and great suggestions as always, as well as to my awesome reader team! Thanks as always to EJR Digital Art for the truly beautiful cover!

www.ingramcontent.com/pod-product-compliance
Lightning Source LLC
Chambersburg PA
CBHW021406110726
47901CB00008B/2083